EMILY

CASE 23: A LT. KATE GAZZARA NOVEL

THE LT. KATE GAZZARA MURDER FILES
BOOK 23

BLAIR HOWARD

Paperback ISBN: 979-8-9988024-8-5
Blair Howard Books
BlairHoward@BlairHowardBooks.com

With love to my new granddaughter, Ryder.

PROLOGUE

THE ALDRIDGE MANSION LIBRARY
September 19, 1925
12:47 AM

EMILY CALDWELL PACED the length of the library, her footsteps muffled by the Persian rug that stretched beneath the massive oak desk. Moonlight streamed through the tall windows, casting long shadows across the leather-bound volumes and polished mahogany. The grandfather clock in the corner ticked steadily toward one o'clock in the morning.

She checked her small wristwatch again—a birthday gift from her mother just three months ago, back when everything was still simple. Back when she was still just Emily Caldwell, the twenty-two year old, daughter of one of Nashville's most prominent families, with her whole life spread before her like an unwritten page.

That life was gone now. Replaced by this impossible situation that consumed her every waking thought.

Her hand moved unconsciously to her stomach, still flat beneath the emerald silk dress she'd worn to the party. Three months. The secret wouldn't keep much longer. Already her mother was asking pointed questions, making vague references to "visiting relatives in Atlanta" for the spring social season. Emily knew what that meant—disappear, have the baby in secret, give it away, return home as if nothing had happened.

But Emily refused to disappear. Refused to be hidden away like some shameful mistake, some problem to be managed and erased.

She had rights. Her baby had rights.

"I'm keeping the baby," she whispered to the empty room, rehearsing the words she'd practiced a thousand times. "With or without you, I'm keeping our child."

It sounded braver spoken aloud, though her voice trembled despite her determination.

The party had ended hours ago. The last guests departing around eleven-thirty, their laughter and chatter fading as automobiles rumbled down the long drive away from the Aldridge mansion. Emily had stayed behind, as arranged. A private conversation, she'd been promised. A resolution to the impossible situation.

She'd waited in this library while the household settled down for the night. Servants extinguishing lamps, closing up the first floor, retreating to their quarters. The great house falling silent around her.

Where was he? He'd promised to meet her here at midnight. Promised they would talk, would find a solution together.

Emily walked to the tall windows and looked out at the

moonlit gardens. September in Chattanooga. The heat of summer finally breaking, the first whisper of autumn in the night air. She could see the shadow of Lookout Mountain in the distance, dark against the starlit sky.

She'd been so happy just six months ago. The parties, the dances, the attention of eligible young men from good families. Her parents had such hopes for her: a proper marriage, a position in society, grandchildren they could dote on with pride.

Instead, she'd fallen in love with the wrong person. Or perhaps not love; she wasn't even certain anymore. Passion, certainly. Recklessness. The thrill of secret meetings, stolen kisses, the intoxicating feeling of being wanted so intensely.

She hadn't meant for it to happen. But here she was, three months pregnant and unmarried, waiting in a darkened library for a conversation that would determine the rest of her life.

The library door opened.

Emily turned from the window, relief flooding through her. Finally. They could talk now, could work this out like reasonable people. There had to be a solution, some way forward that wouldn't destroy both their families.

But as the figure entered and the door closed softly behind them, Emily's relief transformed to confusion, then fear.

"What is it? What's wrong?" she asked, her voice sharp with surprise.

"This situation is impossible," the voice said quietly. "Don't you see that?"

"It's not impossible," Emily insisted, hearing the desperation creep into her voice. "We can work something out. I'm not asking for much—just acknowledgment, just some security for the child. I'll go away if that's what everyone wants, but the baby deserves—"

"The baby," the voice interrupted, and Emily heard something dark in the tone that made her pulse quicken with the first whisper of real fear. "The baby is the problem. Don't you understand? This can't be allowed to happen."

"I'm not giving up my child." Emily backed toward the desk, her hands gripping the edge for support. "I've made my decision. I'm keeping the baby, and if no one will help me, I'll manage on my own. My aunt in Atlanta will take me in. I don't need—"

"You'll ruin everything. Both families. The scandal would destroy us all."

"Then help me!" Emily's voice rose, tears streaming down her face now. "Don't you understand? I'm terrified. I'm alone. I need help, not threats. Please. I'm begging you. Help me."

The figure moved closer, and in the moonlight Emily could see the expression on the face before her; not anger, exactly, but something colder. Determination. Resolve. The look of someone who had made a terrible decision and would see it through regardless of cost.

"I'm sorry, Emily," the voice said. "I truly am. But this can't be allowed to continue."

Emily didn't see the drapery cord until it was already around her throat.

She tried to scream, but the cord tightened, cutting off air and sound. Her hands flew to her neck, fingers scrabbling uselessly at the thick braided silk. She was strong—young and healthy and fighting for her life, for her baby's life—and she managed to twist partially away, her nails raking across her attacker's face and hands, drawing blood.

But it wasn't enough.

The cord tightened further, crushing her windpipe. Emily's vision began to darken at the edges. She thought of her mother, of her baby, of all the years of life she would never live. She tried to fight, but her strength was fading, the room spinning around her.

The last thing Emily Caldwell saw was the moonlight streaming through the tall windows, casting shadows across the leather-bound books that lined the walls of the Aldridge mansion library.

Then darkness.

The library fell silent except for the ragged breathing of Emily's killer and the steady ticking of the grandfather clock.

The figure stood over Emily's body for a long moment, looking down at what had been done. Then, with shaking hands, began to arrange the scene: straightening the drapery cord, positioning the body, making certain calculations about discovery and explanation.

The clock struck two.

There would be questions, of course. An investigation. But both families were powerful, socially prominent. The truth could be managed. The scandal contained.

It had to be.

The figure slipped quietly out of the library, leaving Emily Caldwell alone in the darkness.

SIX HOURS **later**

Dawn light crept through the tall windows of the library, pale and gray in the early morning. The grandfather clock had just chimed eight when Brigadier General Augustus Aldridge entered his library for his customary morning coffee and newspaper.

He stopped three steps into the room.

The young woman lay on the floor near his desk, the drapery cord still around her neck, her emerald dress spread around her like water. Her face was frozen in an expression of terror and disbelief, her eyes open and staring at nothing.

The general was seventy-nine years old, his uniform long retired to a trunk in the attic, his military service decades in the past. But his mind remained sharp, trained by years of command to assess situations with clarity and make decisions quickly.

He assessed this situation now with the same military precision he'd once used to evaluate battlefields. The positioning of the body. The evidence of a struggle: the overturned chair, scattered papers, scratches visible on the young woman's hands where she'd fought her attacker. The drapery cord, torn from the window and used as a murder weapon.

The implications for his family.

The general knew Emily Caldwell. Knew her family in Nashville, knew she'd been a frequent guest at social gatherings over the summer months. Knew she'd stayed late after the party ended, though he'd retired to bed before midnight and hadn't seen who else might have remained.

The general stood there for a long moment, staring at Emily Caldwell's lifeless form. A young woman, dead in his library. Someone in this house—family, guest, servant—had done this terrible thing.

Whatever had happened in his library that night, he knew from long experience, would destroy the families involved.

Emily Caldwell's prominent Nashville family. His own position in Chattanooga society, carefully built over decades.

A proper murder investigation would destroy them all: scandal, social ruin, endless speculation and gossip that would taint both families for generations.

The Aldridge name had to be protected. Whatever had happened here, whoever was responsible, the family legacy must survive.

The general walked to his desk, stepping carefully around Emily's body, and reached for the telephone. His hand hovered over the receiver for a long moment as he made his calculation.

Then he set the receiver back in its cradle without placing the call.

First, he needed to understand what had happened. Who had been in the library with Emily Caldwell. What the full truth was before the authorities were summoned and the situation became uncontrollable.

The general took one last look at Emily Caldwell, lying dead on his library floor, and made a decision that would echo down through a century.

He stood over the body, looking down upon it. Then he shook his head, took two steps back, turned on his heel and left the library, closing the door softly behind him.

By the time he returned to make that telephone call to the authorities, the general would have his story prepared, certain facts established, and the first pieces of a cover-up already in motion.

Emily Caldwell would be found dead in the Aldridge mansion library, strangled by an unknown assailant. The investigation would be cursory, the case quietly closed after a few months of perfunctory inquiry.

Both families would survive the scandal with their reputations mostly intact.

And Emily Caldwell's murder would remain unsolved, buried in old case files and fading memories, a mystery that would haunt the Aldridge mansion for ninety-nine years until, on a Monday morning in 2024, another body would be found in that very same library.

And the secrets buried in 1925 would finally demand a reckoning.

1

The Discovery

THE CALL CAME at eight forty-two on a Monday morning in October, just as I was pouring my second cup of coffee. I'd been at my desk since seven-thirty, working through the weekend reports and trying to catch up on the mountain of paperwork that seems to breed overnight in the Major Crimes Unit.

"Gazzara," I answered, cradling the phone between my shoulder and ear while I continued typing.

"Kate, it's Chief Johnston. I need you at the Aldridge mansion on Missionary Ridge. We have a suspicious death."

I stopped typing. Chief Wesley Johnston didn't personally call me about deaths unless they were politically sensitive. "What's the situation?" I asked.

"Augustus Aldridge the Third. Found dead in his library

this morning. Could be natural causes, could be something else. But given who he is—"

"You want it handled carefully," I finished.

"Very carefully. Augustus's widow Victoria is a personal friend. So is Judge Strange. The mayor's already called me."

Of course he had. The Aldridge family was Chattanooga royalty: old money, old name, the kind of people who had buildings and streets named after them. The kind of case that could make or break careers depending on how it was handled.

"I'm on my way," I said with an inward sigh, already closing the files and reaching for my jacket.

Samson raised his head from his bed in the corner of my office. My hundred-fifteen-pound German Shepherd had been with me long enough that he could read my moods better than most people.

"Come on, Sammy. We've got work to do."

He was on his feet immediately, tail wagging. Samson wore his official K9 harness and badge: honorary credentials that had become official after he'd helped solve three murders and saved my life twice. The department had finally acknowledged what I'd known from the beginning: Samson was more than a pet. He was my partner and constant companion.

The drive to Missionary Ridge took a little more than twenty minutes through morning traffic. The Aldridge mansion sat on ten acres of pristine property with a view of Lookout Mountain and the Tennessee River valley that probably cost more than I'd make in ten lifetimes. The estate was surrounded by a low stone wall that looked original to the property, with massive iron gates standing open for the emergency vehicles already assembled in the circular drive. Three patrol cars, a fire truck, an ambulance, and the medical examiner's big black SUV.

Doc Sheddon had beaten me to it, which meant he'd been called early. And he'd be expecting coffee, which I hadn't brought with me. *Oh well, he'll just have to suffer and bear it,* I thought as I pulled up behind his SUV and stepped out. Samson, who'd been riding in the passenger seat, followed me, leaping over the console onto the driver's seat and then down onto the ground at my side. The air had a chill to it, and I couldn't help but wonder if it might be a portent of things to come. It was barely nine-thirty, the sun was up, but it was just a watery orange globe in the eastern sky, and there were what looked like storm clouds gathering over the mountain.

The mansion itself was breathtaking: a Greek Revival structure that had to date back to before the Civil War. White columns, black shutters, a wraparound porch that spoke of mint juleps and antebellum elegance. I'd seen pictures of the place in historical society publications, but seeing it in person was something else entirely.

A uniformed officer met me at the front door. Officer Whitham, young and nervous, and this was probably his first death call at a prominent residence.

"Captain Gazzara," he said and introduced himself.

"You were first on the scene?" I asked him.

"Yes, ma'am. I was just, well, you know."

I smiled at him. "Well, tell me about it."

"The deceased is in the library. First floor, east wing. Doc Sheddon's with him now."

"Who found the body?"

"The housekeeper, Claudia Rivera. She's in the kitchen with the family."

"The family's all here?"

"Yes, ma'am, the widow, son and daughter-in-law, daughter and her husband. They all either live on the property or arrived shortly after the body was discovered."

That was interesting. I filed it away for future reference. "Has anyone touched anything in the library?"

"No, ma'am. The housekeeper entered, saw the deceased, backed out and called 911. She didn't touch him. Nobody's been in except for Doc Sheddon and the CSI team."

"Good. Let's keep it that way. I'll need statements from everyone, but nobody leaves until I clear them. And log everyone in and out. How many officers do we have?"

"Including me, five." He looked nervously down at Samson. "Does he bite?" he asked.

"Only when I tell him to," I replied with a smile. "I want two officers on the gate. Two patrolling the perimeter of the house, and you can handle the main entrance."

Whitham nodded. He looked relieved. Clear orders always helped young officers manage stressful situations.

I entered the mansion with Samson, and looked around. The interior was as impressive as the exterior. Marble floors, crystal chandeliers, paintings that looked like they belonged in museums. The entry hall alone was larger than my entire house.

Mike Willis met me in the hallway outside the library. The CSI supervisor looked more disheveled than usual: graying hair standing up where he'd run his hands through it, his untidy appearance somehow reassuring in its familiarity.

"Kate," he said. "Doc's inside with the body. I've been processing the scene, but we need to determine if this is a crime scene or just a death scene before I go full protocol."

"What's your initial assessment?"

Willis adjusted his thick-framed glasses and screwed up his mouth. "The victim is seated at the desk. He appears to have died while working. There are no obvious signs of trauma, no defensive wounds, no evidence of a struggle. Could be natural causes: heart attack, stroke. But there's something off about it."

"Off how?" I asked.

"I can't put my finger on it yet. It's just a feeling. Doc might know more."

I trusted Mike Willis's instincts. He'd been processing crime scenes since before I joined the force, and his "feelings" were usually based on subtle observations most people missed.

The library doors were massive; twelve feet tall, heavy wood with brass handles. Willis pushed one open and I stepped inside, Samson stayed close by my side.

The room took my breath away.

Two stories tall with a gallery level accessed by a wrought-iron spiral staircase. Floor-to-ceiling mahogany bookshelves lined three walls, filled with what looked like thousands of leather-bound volumes. A rolling ladder on brass rails. Massive windows along the fourth wall overlooking the gardens. An enormous marble fireplace that could have accommodated a small car.

And in the center of it all, behind a desk the size of my first apartment, sat Augustus Aldridge III.

He was slumped slightly to the right in a leather chair, his head tilted back, eyes half-open in that unmistakable way of death. He wore reading glasses pushed up on his forehead, and papers were scattered across the desk's surface. A laptop sat open, its screen dark.

Doc Sheddon looked up as I approached. His round face was serious behind his half-glasses, the jovial expression he usually wore completely absent.

"Kate. Hmm, no coffee, I see. Oh well, I'm glad you're here. This one's going to be complicated."

"Natural causes or...?" I asked, taking a closer look at the body.

"That's the question, isn't it?" he said as he stood upright, stretched, and said, "Ooof, I'm getting too old for this." He turned and looked at me, then continued, "My initial examination shows no obvious trauma. No wounds, no bruising, no petechial hemorrhaging. But look at this."

He gestured at Augustus's face. The skin had a slightly bluish tint, and there was foam dried at the corners of his mouth. What that meant, I didn't know, but I could guess: poison.

"Time of death?" I asked, and immediately regretted it. It's not a question Doc likes.

He gave a grim look, then smiled and said, "Based on rigor mortis and liver temp, I'd estimate it to be between nine PM and midnight last night. He's been dead approximately ten to twelve hours."

I glanced at my watch. Nine-thirty-four. The timeline fit.

"And cause?" I asked.

Doc shook his head. "Again, that's the question. The foam at the mouth, the slight cyanosis—"

"That's not typical for a simple heart attack," I observed.

"No, it's not. Could be cardiac arrhythmia, could be respiratory distress. I won't know until I get him on the table. But my gut is telling me this isn't a natural death."

"Poisoning?"

"Possible. I'll run a full tox screen, but, as you know, that takes time."

I studied the scene carefully, taking in every detail. An empty brandy glass sat on the desk near Augustus's right hand. A decanter of expensive-looking brandy on a sidebar. Two coffee cups: one on the desk, one on a small table by the leather reading chair.

"The brandy glass," I said, "has it been tested?"

Mike, who'd been photographing the desk, spoke up and said, "I did a preliminary field test. It shows residue consistent with brandy, but there's something else in there. I've bagged it for lab analysis."

"Something else like what?" I asked.

"Can't say for certain, not without lab confirmation, but it just doesn't look right. The residue has an unusual crystalline structure."

I looked at Doc Sheddon. "Could he have been poisoned through the brandy?"

"Possible. I'll test for common toxins—arsenic, cyanide, strychnine. But there are hundreds of plant-based poisons that could cause cardiac or respiratory failure. It'll take time to identify."

I walked around the desk, careful not to touch anything, examining the scene from different angles. Samson sat near the fireplace, watching everything. He wasn't agitated, but he was definitely interested in something near the mantel.

"Hey, Mike, what's Samson alerting on?" I said.

Willis followed my gaze and moved to the fireplace. He

photographed the area carefully, then pointed to some small white particles on the hearth.

"Looks like ash or powder of some kind. Could be from the fireplace, but it's been warm. Nobody's burning fires; not yet, anyway." He collected a sample. "I'll get it analyzed."

I turned my attention back to the desk. Among the scattered papers, I noticed a book left open on a reading stand, *Tennessee Families: A Genealogical History.* The page it was open to showed family trees and histories for Nashville families.

"D'you think he was researching something specific?" I asked Mike.

"Looks like he was into genealogy. There are printouts of birth records, death certificates, old newspaper articles. He was deep into something, that's for sure."

"Hmm, interesting," I muttered, "but it might not be relevant. Rich people often become obsessed with their family histories, tracing lineages back to European nobility or high ranking officers. There's one in the family, I believe." Where that came from, I don't know. It just popped into my head.

The French doors on the far side of the library led to a garden terrace. I checked them. They were unlocked.

"These doors were unlocked when you arrived?"

"Yes," Mike confirmed. "The housekeeper said Augustus often stepped outside for a cigar in the evening, then reentered through these doors rather than walking all the way around to the main entrance."

So anyone could have entered through the garden without being seen by the household, I thought. *That complicates things.*

"I want this treated as a potential crime scene until we rule out homicide," I said. "Full processing: prints, trace evidence, photographs, the works. Pull the Wi-Fi router logs, and smart home logs—terrace door sensors, motion lights, the lot. Doc, please see if you can expedite that tox screen."

"I'll make it a priority," Doc agreed. "But Kate, even expedited, I'm looking at forty-eight to seventy-two hours for comprehensive results."

I nodded. That was the reality of toxicology. It took time. Which meant I'd be investigating a suspicious death without knowing for certain if it was murder.

"Where's the family?"

"Kitchen and parlor areas," Willis said. "The housekeeper, Claudia Rivera, is pretty shaken up. The widow, Victoria Aldridge, is... composed. Very composed. Almost eerily so."

I'd seen both reactions to sudden death; people who fell apart completely, and people who shut down emotionally, presenting a calm facade that seemed inappropriate but was really just shock manifesting differently.

Or sometimes it was guilt.

"I'll talk to them now. Mike, I want your preliminary report by this afternoon. Doc, call me as soon as you have anything from the autopsy."

"Will do," they both said.

I took one last look at Augustus Aldridge III, slumped in his chair behind the massive desk, dead in his own library. If this was murder, someone had killed him in his home, in a room that spoke of power and privilege and security. Someone he'd probably known and trusted.

That made it personal. And personal murders were always the most complicated.

Samson and I left the library, ready to meet the Aldridge family and figure out who might have wanted Augustus dead.

By then my team had arrived, including my partner, Sergeant Corbin Russell.

I met them in the grand entry hall and quickly gave them their immediate assignments.

"Corbin, you're with me interviewing the family. Hawk, you work the crime scene with Mike Willis. I want your eyes on everything, and you know what to look for. Cooper, start background checks on everyone in this house, family and staff. Focus on financials: debts, assets, recent transactions, anything unusual. Tracy, you start interviewing the household staff separately from the family. Get their statements, their observations, anything that seemed unusual about last night or this morning. I want to know what the staff saw and heard."

Everyone nodded, understanding the assignments and the stakes. They knew how high-profile this case was.

"One more thing," Corbin added. "There was a murder in this house in 1925. A woman named Emily Caldwell, was killed in the same library where Augustus Aldridge died."

I looked at him in surprise. "How did you know that?" I asked.

"It's old history," he replied with a shrug.

I gave him a look, then continued, "The victim was researching the Caldwell family genealogy before his death. I don't know if it's connected, but I don't believe in coincidences. Cooper, add that 1925 case to your research—pull everything you can find."

"On it," Cooper said quietly.

Hawkins headed back toward the library. Cooper and Ramirez moved off to begin their assignments. Corbin fell into step beside me as we headed toward the parlor where the family was waiting.

The parlor was everything I expected from a house like this: antique furniture that probably cost more than my annual salary, oil paintings of stern-faced ancestors in gilded frames, fresh flowers in crystal vases, Persian rugs that whispered money with every fiber.

The Aldridge family was assembled like actors waiting for their cue.

Victoria Aldridge sat in a high-backed chair near the fireplace, her posture perfect, legs crossed at the ankles, hands together in her lap, her silver hair styled immaculately despite the early hour and traumatic circumstances. She wore a simple but clearly expensive navy blue dress, pearl earrings, and an expression of composed grief that struck me as either admirable control or suspicious detachment.

Seated on the sofa to her left was a man in his early forties who I just knew had to be Augustus Aldridge IV. He was sweating despite the cool air in the room, his face flushed, his hands fidgeting with his phone. Next to him, a blonde woman about his age, perfectly coiffed and made up, her expression carefully neutral. That would be Allison, the daughter-in-law.

In chairs near the windows sat a younger woman: late thirties, dark hair, red eyes from crying, and a tall man standing protectively behind her with his hand on her shoulder. The daughter Melissa and her husband, Dr. Graham Crawford.

Five people. Five potential suspects if this turned out to be murder.

Samson entered the room with me and immediately sat at attention, his eyes sweeping the assembled family. He wasn't growling or showing any signs of aggression, but he was alert, watchful. Reading the room the way he always did.

"Mrs. Aldridge," I began, addressing the matriarch. "I'm Captain Catherine Gazzara, Chattanooga Police Department, Major Crimes Unit. This is Sergeant Corbin Russell. I'm very sorry for your loss."

Victoria's eyes met mine; sharp, assessing, taking my measure in an instant. "Thank you, Captain. I appreciate your promptness. Chief Johnston called to let me know you'd be handling the investigation personally."

Of course he had. Making sure I understood the political dimension of this case.

"I understand this is difficult, but I need to ask some questions. The sooner we can establish what happened here, the better."

"Of course." Victoria's voice was steady, controlled. "Whatever you need, Captain."

I looked at each family member in turn. Augustus IV avoided my eyes. Allison stared at me with cool assessment. Melissa dabbed at her eyes with a tissue. Graham Crawford met my gaze directly, his expression professionally sympathetic: the calm demeanor of someone used to dealing with death and crisis.

A doctor. That was potentially relevant, especially if this turned out to be poisoning. Medical knowledge could be useful for murder.

"I'll need to speak with each of you individually," I said. "But first, I need to understand the timeline from last night. Who was here at the house? What time you all went to bed? When was Mr. Aldridge last seen alive?"

Augustus IV shifted uncomfortably. Melissa's crying intensified slightly. Graham's hand tightened on his wife's shoulder.

And Victoria Aldridge sat perfectly still, watching me with those sharp eyes, her composure never wavering.

Someone in this room might have killed Augustus Aldridge. Or maybe they were all innocent, and this was just a tragic natural death that happened to look suspicious.

But my instincts, honed by twenty-four years on the force and too many murder investigations to count, told me otherwise.

Something was very wrong in the Aldridge family. And before this day was over, I was going to find out what it was.

2

The Family

THE MANSION EXHALED AROUND US LIKE AN OLD CREATURE settling into discomfort. Every creak of floorboard and distant whisper seemed amplified in the silence that followed the removal of Augustus Aldridge III's body. I've stood in plenty of houses after death—trailers, brownstones, penthouses—but old money homes carry their grief differently. Here, sorrow wore perfume and pearls.

Corbin hovered at my shoulder, notebook in hand, his pen already poised. Samson lay beside the parlor door, the great shepherd's ears twitching to every sound. His tail didn't move; he was alert, all business.

"Let's start with the matriarch," I said quietly.

Corbin nodded. "She's waiting in the front parlor."

I nodded and asked the others to wait in adjacent rooms while we conducted individual interviews, and although Augustus IV looked like he wanted to object, one sharp look from his mother silenced him.

Victoria Aldridge sat in an armchair near the marble fireplace, posture perfect, one elegant hand resting on a porcelain teacup she hadn't touched. Her silver hair caught the light from the chandelier, every strand in place. If grief had come for her, it had knocked politely and been told to wait in the hall.

Samson lay down near the fireplace, his head on his paws, but his eyes never left Victoria. He was still in working mode, still watching.

"Mrs. Aldridge," I began, sitting across from her while Corbin remained standing, notebook ready. "I need to understand what happened last night. Can you walk me through the evening, starting with dinner?"

"Of course," she said in a controlled, almost melodic voice. "Augustus and I had dinner separately. He preferred to work through the evening. I ate in the small dining room at six-thirty; he took a tray into the library."

"Do you know what he was working on?" I asked.

Her fingers flexed around the cup. "Family research. Genealogies, correspondence—he'd been chasing some old story about the Caldwell girl. He told me once the past had a long reach. I told him to leave it alone.

"Not specifically. Augustus was always researching something—family history, business matters, investments. He was a meticulous man, Captain. He liked to understand things thoroughly."

"When did you last see him alive?" I asked.

Victoria paused, and for the first time, a crack appeared in her composure. Her eyes flickered away from mine, just for a moment, before returning. "I went to bed around nine o'clock. Augustus was still in the library. I assumed he'd come to bed later, as he often does. We have separate bedrooms, we have done for years. It's not uncommon for him to work late and go to bed after I'm asleep."

"So you went to your room at nine and didn't see him again?"

"That's correct."

"Did you call him? Check on him during the evening?"

Another pause. "I called the library around nine forty-five. Just to ask when he planned to retire for the night. We spoke briefly—maybe a minute or two. He said he had more work to do and would be up when he'd finished. That was the last time I spoke with my husband."

I made a mental note of that call. We'd verify it with phone records.

"Did he sound all right?" I asked.

Her eyes flicked toward the mantel clock before returning to mine. "Tired. Perhaps annoyed. But that wasn't unusual."

"What time did you fall asleep?"

"I'm not certain. I read for a while, perhaps until ten-thirty or eleven. I take a sleep medication when I'm stressed, which I did last night. After that, I slept soundly until Claudia knocked on my door this morning."

"Were you stressed about something specific last night?" I asked.

Victoria's expression tightened almost imperceptibly. "Augustus and I had been having some discussions about... some family matters. Nothing unusual for a marriage of forty years, but yes, there was some tension."

"What kind of family matters?"

"That's private, Captain. I don't see how it's relevant to Augustus's death."

I let that sit for a moment. People always thought they could decide what was relevant to a murder investigation. They were always wrong.

"Mrs. Aldridge, we don't yet know how your husband died. Until we rule out foul play, everything about his life, his relationships, and his recent activities is potentially relevant. So I'll ask again—what family matters were you discussing that caused tension?"

Victoria met my gaze, and I saw steel beneath the Southern belle exterior. "Augustus was considering making changes to his will. He felt some adjustments were necessary. I disagreed with his reasoning. We'd been discussing it for several weeks."

"What kind of changes?"

"That's between Augustus and our attorney. I'm not comfortable discussing the details without legal counsel present."

Fair enough. I'd get that information from the attorney directly. "Did anyone else in the household know about these will changes?"

"I don't believe so. Augustus was private about financial matters."

Corbin spoke up for the first time. "Mrs. Aldridge, did your husband have any enemies? Anyone who might want to harm him?"

"Augustus was a businessman and a prominent member of this community. I'm sure he made decisions over the years that some people might have disagreed with. But enemies? No, I don't believe so. He was respected, admired even."

"No disputes with neighbors, business associates, family members?"

"Nothing that would lead to—" Victoria stopped, seeming to realize what we were implying. "Captain, are you suggesting someone killed my husband?"

"We're not suggesting anything yet, ma'am. We're gathering information. Did your husband have any health conditions? Heart problems, high blood pressure, anything that might cause sudden death?"

"No. Augustus was in excellent health for his age. He had annual physicals, took no medications except vitamins. His doctor can confirm that."

I filed that away. If Augustus was healthy and Doc Sheddon's instincts about poisoning were correct, we were definitely looking at murder.

"One more question for now. Did your husband seem worried or upset about anything in recent days? Any unusual behavior, phone calls, visitors?"

Victoria considered this for a few seconds, then said, "He'd been preoccupied with his genealogy research. That book you probably saw in the library—he'd been working on tracing some family connections. But upset? No, I wouldn't say upset. Focused, perhaps. Determined to understand something."

"Do you know what he was trying to understand?" Corbin asked.

"He mentioned something about Emily Caldwell. The young woman who was murdered here in 1925. Augustus had found some old family documents and became interested in solving that mystery. He could be rather obsessive when something caught his attention."

So Augustus had been actively investigating Emily Caldwell's murder. That was more than casual genealogy. That was a man looking for answers to a ninety-nine-year-old crime.

"Thank you, Mrs. Aldridge. We'll need to speak with you again, I'm sure. For now, please don't leave the property without notifying us."

Victoria's eyes flashed briefly. She wasn't used to being given instructions. But she nodded gracefully. "Of course, Captain. Whatever helps you find out what happened to Augustus."

As she stood to leave, I added, "One more thing. We'll need fingerprints from everyone in the household—family and staff. For elimination purposes."

"Elimination from what?"

"From the crime scene, ma'am. Standard procedure in any suspicious death."

Victoria's composure wavered again, just slightly. "I see. Of course. Whatever you need."

After she left, Corbin looked at me. "She's hiding something."

"Agreed. Did you catch the hesitation when I asked about last night? And that phone call at nine forty-five—that's significant. We need those phone records."

"You think she's a suspect?"

"Everyone's a suspect until we rule them out. But yes, she had opportunity; she was in the house. And something about those changes to his will is important. People kill for money all the time."

"What about motive beyond money?" Corbin asked. "She said there was tension over family matters."

"Which she wouldn't discuss. That's interesting. Very interesting." I stood. "Let's talk to the son next. Augustus the Fourth."

AUGUSTUS IV WAS AN ENTIRELY different creature from his mother. Where Victoria was composed, Augustus IV was nervous, energy barely contained. He sat on the edge of the sofa in the small study where we'd asked him to wait, his leg bouncing, his hands fidgeting with his phone.

His wife Allison sat beside him, perfectly still, her expression giving away nothing. She reminded me of Victoria in that way: controlled, calculating, watching everything.

"Mr. Aldridge," I began, and Augustus IV flinched slightly at his name. "I know this is difficult, but I need to ask you about last night."

"I wasn't here," he said immediately, the words tumbling out. "I mean, I was here, I live here, but I wasn't here when Dad—when it happened. Allison and I were at a charity event at the Read House downtown. We didn't get home until after eleven."

"What time did you leave for the event?" I asked.

"Around seven. Maybe seven-fifteen. We got to the hotel by seven-thirty when the cocktail hour started."

"And you were there the entire evening?"

Augustus IV glanced at his wife. "Yes. Until eleven. Then we came home."

Allison spoke for the first time, her voice smooth and cultured. "The event was a fundraiser for the Children's Hospital. We stayed through the entire program; cocktails, dinner, auction, the speeches. We can provide you with a list of people who saw us there if you need verification."

"We'll need that list, yes," I replied, then turned again to

Augustus. "Mr. Aldridge, when did you last see your father alive?"

"Yesterday afternoon. Maybe around three o'clock? I stopped by his office—his study, I mean—to discuss something. We talked for maybe fifteen minutes, then I left."

"What did you discuss?"

Augustus IV's face flushed. "Business matters. A loan I was hoping to secure. Dad was... he wasn't interested in helping."

"You asked your father for money?" Corbin asked.

"A business loan. I have an opportunity, a real estate development project that needs capital. Dad refused. He said he wasn't going to throw good money after bad." The bitterness in his voice was unmistakable.

"Bad money?" I said. "What did he mean by that?"

Augustus shifted uncomfortably. "I've had some business setbacks. A development deal that went south a few years ago. Dad held that against me. He wouldn't help me with new ventures even though this one was solid."

"How much money did you ask for?"

"Five hundred thousand. It wasn't charity—I was offering him a stake in the project, an equity position. You know, a proper return on investment. But he said no. He also said I needed to figure out my own finances."

Corbin made notes. "That must have been frustrating," he said.

"Of course it was frustrating. I'm his son. He had millions, and he wouldn't help me when I needed it. But I didn't—" Augustus IV stopped, realizing how bad that sounded. "I mean, I was angry, but I didn't hurt him. I loved my father. I just wished he had more faith in me."

"Did your father know about your other debts?" I asked.

Augustus IV's face went pale. "What debts?"

"We'll be conducting a financial investigation as part of this case, Mr. Aldridge. If there are debts we should know about, now would be the time to mention them."

He looked at Allison, who gave him a barely perceptible nod.

"I owe some money. Business loans, credit cards, some personal loans. Maybe three-quarters of a million total. I've been trying to consolidate, but without Dad's help..." He trailed off.

Three-quarters of a million dollars. That was a powerful motive for murder if Augustus IV thought he'd inherit money from his father's death.

"Who inherits your father's estate?"

"I assume my mother, then eventually my sister and me. But I don't know the details of Dad's will. He didn't discuss that with us."

But Victoria had said Augustus was making changes to his will. Had Augustus IV known about that? If he stood to lose his inheritance, that changed the equation entirely.

"Mr. Aldridge, did your father mention anything about changing his will?"

"No. Why? Was he going to cut me out?" The alarm in Augustus IV's voice sounded genuine.

"I'm asking if you had knowledge of any such plans," I said.

"No. I knew Dad was disappointed in me, but cut me out of the will? That would be extreme, even for him."

I couldn't tell if he was lying or not. His nervous energy made him difficult to read—everything looked suspicious when someone was already anxious.

"Where did you go after you returned home from the charity event?" I asked.

"Straight to our wing of the house. We have our own entrance, our own suite of rooms. We didn't see Dad or anyone else. We went straight to bed."

"Did you hear anything unusual during the night?"

"No. Nothing."

Allison added, "Our rooms are on the opposite side of the house from the library. We wouldn't hear anything happening there."

Convenient. I thought. *Or true. It was hard to say.*

"Mrs. Aldridge—" I addressed Allison directly. "How would you describe your relationship with your father-in-law?"

"Cordial. Augustus was always polite to me, and I to him. We weren't close, not by any means, but we got along."

"Did you know about your husband's financial difficulties?" Corbin asked.

"Of course," she snapped. "We're married. We share finances."

"And you agreed with his request for a loan from his father?"

Allison's expression remained neutral. "I supported my husband's business plans. Augustus could have helped if he chose to. He had the means."

There was something cold in the way she said it. This was a woman who'd married into money and expected to live accordingly. Augustus's refusal to fund her husband's projects must have rankled.

"Do either of you know why your father was researching Emily Caldwell's murder?"

Augustus IV looked blank. "Who?"

"The woman who was killed in this house in 1925. Your father had been researching her family history."

"I have no idea. Dad was always researching something—family trees, historical records, that kind of thing. He never mentioned Emily Caldwell to me."

Allison shook her head. "Nor to me."

Either they genuinely didn't know, or they were both good liars.

"All right. That's it for now. Thank you for your time. We'll need those fingerprints before you leave, and please don't go anywhere without informing us. Oh, and Mr. Aldridge, I'd like to talk to you again tomorrow morning. Shall we say around ten?"

"Well... um, yes, I suppose."

After they left, Corbin and I spent a few minutes comparing notes.

"The son has motive," Corbin said. "Desperate for money, father refuses to help, three-quarters of a million in debt. If he inherits, his problems are solved."

"If he inherits. The mother said Augustus was changing his will. If Augustus IV knew about that, it makes him more suspicious. If he didn't know, it weakens his motive."

"The wife's a cold one, isn't she?" he muttered.

"Agreed. She married into money and wants to live like it. Probably pushing Augustus IV to get money from his father."

"You think they could have done it together?"

"Anything's possible. We need to verify their alibi at the charity event. And we need to know what was in Augustus' will and what changes he was planning."

"What about the mother? Victoria?"

"She's hiding something. That tension over the changes to

the will, the phone call at nine forty-five, her weak alibi. She's definitely a person of interest."

Corbin nodded. "Who's next?"

"The daughter and her husband. Let's see what they have to say."

MELISSA ALDRIDGE-CRAWFORD WAS STILL CRYING when we brought her into the study. She wasn't hysterical, but tears streamed down her face continuously, and she clutched a tissue like a lifeline. Her husband Graham stood behind her chair, his hand on her shoulder, the picture of a supportive spouse.

"I'm so sorry for your loss, Mrs. Crawford," I said gently. "I know this is difficult, but I need to ask you some questions."

Melissa nodded, unable to speak for a moment.

Graham spoke for her. "We understand, Captain. We want to help however we can. Melissa's just—this is a great shock. Augustus was her father."

"Of course. Mrs. Crawford, when did you last see your father?"

Melissa took a shaky breath. "Yesterday. Sunday afternoon. I came by around two to drop off some fabric samples—I'm an interior designer, and Mother had asked me to help her with redecorating one of the guest rooms. I saw Daddy briefly. We talked for maybe ten minutes."

"How did he seem?"

"Normal. Maybe a little distracted. He was working on something in the library. He said he had some research to finish. But he was fine. He was healthy, he was happy—how could this happen?"

"That's what we're trying to determine," I replied. "Did your father mention what he was researching?"

"Something about family history. He'd been doing genealogy work for weeks, tracing the family tree. He loved that kind of thing—history, connections, understanding where we came from."

"Did he mention Emily Caldwell?"

Melissa looked confused. "Who?"

"The woman who was murdered in this house in 1925."

"Oh, that old story. I'd heard about it, but Daddy never talked about it specifically to me. Why?"

"He was researching her family when he died. We're trying to understand why."

Graham interjected smoothly. "Augustus was a thorough man. If he became interested in a historical mystery, he'd pursue it completely. It might not mean anything beyond intellectual curiosity."

I looked at Graham Crawford. Tall, fit, probably early forties. He had the calm, professional demeanor of someone used to managing crises. A cardiovascular surgeon, according to the preliminary information. Smart, educated, with extensive medical knowledge. Medical knowledge that could include poisons.

"Dr. Crawford, where were you last night?"

"I was on call. We had an early dinner at home, then I got an emergency call around six-thirty. A patient came in with a heart attack. I was at the hospital in surgery from about seven until after midnight. Melissa was home alone."

"Can anyone verify that?"

"Of course. At least a dozen people at the hospital—I'm a surgeon at Erlanger—they can verify my schedule."

"What was your relationship with your father-in-law like?"

"Good. Cordial. Augustus was always polite to me, supportive of Melissa's career and our marriage. We weren't close friends, but we got along well enough."

That was the second time I'd heard "cordial" used to describe Augustus's relationships with his in-laws. Polite distance seemed to be the family dynamic.

"Mrs. Crawford, your mother mentioned that your father was planning to make changes to his will. Do you know anything about that?"

Melissa's face crumpled further. "What? No. What kind of changes?"

"That's what we're trying to determine," I said. "He didn't discuss it with you?"

"No. Why would he change his will? Did he—was he cutting me out?"

I watched her reaction carefully. The distress seemed genuine, but people could fake emotion.

"Your mother mentioned he was concerned about spending. Do you know what he meant by that?"

Melissa flushed. "Daddy thought I spent too much on my business. I've been expanding my design firm, taking on bigger projects, hiring more staff. It requires capital investment. Daddy didn't understand that. He thought I was being irresponsible."

"Were you in financial trouble?"

"No! My business is successful. I just need to invest in growth right now. Daddy was being old-fashioned, thinking I should stay small and cautious. He was planning to reduce my inheritance because of that?" Her voice rose with a mix of grief and anger.

Graham's hand tightened on her shoulder. "Melissa, we don't know what Augustus was planning. Let's not jump to conclusions."

But I could see it in Melissa's face: hurt, betrayal, anger at her father for judging her business decisions. Strong emotions. Motive, potentially.

"Mrs. Crawford, did you enter the mansion at any time last night after you left in the afternoon?"

"No. I went home after dropping off the fabric samples. I didn't come back until Mother called this morning."

"Dr. Crawford, have you ever been in Augustus's library?"

"Many times. Family gatherings, holidays, occasional visits. Augustus liked to show people his book collection. He was proud of it."

"So your fingerprints would be in that room?"

Graham's eyes narrowed slightly. "Probably. I haven't been in there recently—maybe a month or two ago—but yes, my prints would likely be there. Why? Do you think Augustus was murdered?"

"We don't know yet. We're investigating all possibilities. Dr. Crawford, given your medical background, could you speculate on what might have caused Augustus's death?"

Graham considered this carefully. "Without seeing the body or knowing the symptoms, I couldn't say. But Doc Sheddon is an excellent medical examiner. He'll determine the cause. If you want my opinion after he completes the autopsy, I'm happy to consult. I've worked with law enforcement before on medical questions."

That was interesting. Either Graham was being genuinely

helpful, or he was positioning himself to monitor the investigation.

"We may take you up on that. One more question—do you know anyone who might have wanted to harm Augustus?"

Melissa and Graham looked at each other.

"No," Melissa said. "Daddy could be difficult, he had strong opinions, but I can't imagine anyone wanting to kill him."

Graham added, "Augustus was a pillar of this community. Respected and admired. I've never heard anyone speak ill of him."

That matched what Victoria had said. But someone might have killed Augustus Aldridge, and if so, they had a reason. I just needed to find it.

"Thank you both. We'll need fingerprints from both of you, and please stay available for further questions."

They left, and I looked at Corbin questioningly. "So, what d'you think?"

"The daughter has motive if the changes to the will were reducing her inheritance," Corbin said.

"And she has the emotional temperament for it," I said, thoughtfully. "That anger about being judged by her father. But the husband..."

"The doctor. You're thinking poison?" Corbin said.

"He'd have the knowledge. And his helpfulness bothers me. It's either genuine or calculated."

"He has what appears to be an airtight alibi," Corbin said. "His wife, though; she was alone at home."

"Agreed. We need to verify his hospital schedule. And we need to find out more about Graham Crawford. Background, financials, relationship with Augustus."

Corbin made notes. "So far we have multiple family

members with motive, weak alibis, and access to the victim. Classic family murder scenario."

"If it's murder. We still don't know that for sure."

But I was becoming more certain by the minute. Augustus Aldridge had been killed, probably poisoned, by someone he knew. Someone in his family or household. Someone who wanted him dead badly enough to plan it carefully.

I just needed to figure out who, and why, and how to prove it despite the political pressure that was only going to get worse as this investigation continued.

No pressure at all.

3

Augustus Aldridge IV

MORNING CREPT OVER MISSIONARY RIDGE IN PALE STREAKS OF gold and gray. A second storm had rolled through overnight, leaving behind a bruised sky and the scent of wet earth. Mist clung to the gardens like ghostly breath, curling around the stone fountains and wrought-iron gates of the Aldridge estate. The house, tall and solemn, looked older than it had the day before, like grief had aged it overnight.

I arrived just before ten with Corbin and Samson. The front steps were slick with rain, and the brass door knocker felt cold under my hand. Inside, the air smelled faintly of lemon polish and old paper. The mansion had been cleaned since yesterday, but nothing could wash away the echo of death. Some houses never stop remembering.

Samson sniffed the air, alert but calm. His ears flicked once toward the library before he followed me into the hallway. I trusted his instincts. They were rarely wrong.

We found Augustus Aldridge IV waiting in what had once

been the music room. The piano was gone, replaced by a replica mahogany desk and a pair of leather chairs that looked more expensive than comfortable. The walls were lined with books arranged by color rather than content. A designer's trick to suggest intellect. The whole room felt curated, not lived in.

"Captain Gazzara," he said, rising from behind the desk as Corbin and I entered. "I appreciate you giving me some time to collect myself before we spoke. Yesterday was, as you can imagine, quite overwhelming. Please sit down."

I studied him. Dark circles under his eyes. Fresh shave. Same suit, different tie. The kind of man who thinks presentation can disguise truth.

"Thank you for meeting us again," I said, taking a seat. Corbin stayed near the door, notebook ready. Samson settled beside my chair, watchful.

I hadn't given Augustus IV time to collect himself. I'd deliberately made him wait until this morning, letting him spend the night in this house with his father's body being processed by the medical examiner's office, knowing that waiting and worrying often loosened tongues more effectively than any interrogation technique.

"I understand this is difficult," I said. "We appreciate your cooperation."

Augustus IV returned to his desk chair. He was forty-two but looked older, his face showing the wear of someone who has lived harder than his circumstances should have required. His suit was well-tailored, his watch expensive, his shoes Italian leather. But there was something hollow about him, like he was wearing a costume rather than clothes.

"How can I help?" he asked.

"Tell me about your relationship with your father."

He paused, and I saw him calculating what to say, how much truth to reveal, what image to project. That hesitation told me more than whatever words would follow.

"My father was a difficult man," he finally said. "Demanding. Exacting. He had very specific ideas about how things should be done, how the family should conduct itself. He didn't tolerate deviation from his expectations."

"Were you able to meet those expectations?"

Another pause. "Not always. No one could. My father's standards were impossible."

"Tell me about your business in Atlanta."

His jaw tightened. "That's not relevant to his death."

"Please," I said as I looked him in the eye. "Tell me about Atlanta."

Corbin shifted slightly near the door, a subtle reminder that this was not a casual conversation.

Augustus IV sighed. "I moved to Atlanta five years ago to establish a real estate development company. Commercial properties, primarily. Shopping centers, office complexes. It was going well initially, but the market shifted. Interest rates, financing issues, several deals fell through. The business failed eighteen months ago."

"How much did you lose?"

"That's personal," he snapped.

"Your father was murdered in this house yesterday morning," I said, easily. "Nothing is personal anymore. How much, Augustus?"

"Everything," he said quietly. "My investment capital, borrowed funds, money from investors. Approximately four point two million dollars."

I let that number settle in the air between us. Four point two million. That was serious desperation money.

"Did you ask your father for help?"

"Of course I did. He's my father... He was my father."

"What did he say?"

Augustus IV stood and walked to the window overlooking the estate grounds. His hands were shaking slightly.

"He said no. He said I had made irresponsible choices, that I needed to face the consequences of my failures, that bailing me out would only enable further poor decisions. He said I could come back to Chattanooga if I wanted, live in the carriage house on the property, but he would not give me money to throw away on another failed business venture."

"How did you respond to that?"

"How do you think I responded? I was angry. Hurt. This is my father, my family. I had nowhere else to turn. My creditors are demanding payment, investors threatening lawsuits. And he just... said no. Like it was nothing. Like I was nothing."

"When was this conversation?"

"Six months ago. I moved back here in August. I have been living in the carriage house, working for my father as an assistant estate manager, making seventeen dollars an hour like some college kid with a summer job."

The bitterness in his voice was acid, eating through his careful control.

"That must have been humiliating," I said.

"You have no idea," he muttered, staring out of the window.

"Did your father's refusal to help you cause problems with other family members?"

He turned from the window. "What do you mean?"

"Did your wife blame him for your financial situation? Did it create tension between them?"

"Allison does not... she did not have much interaction with my father. They were polite to each other. That's all."

That was a lie. I could hear it in his voice, see it in the way he wouldn't meet my eyes.

"Where were you between nine p.m. Sunday night and seven o'clock Monday morning?"

"We've already done this, Captain. I told you; I was at a charity event until eleven. Then we came home to my apartment. The carriage house. I went to bed around eleven thirty, woke up at six fifteen when Allison called me about Father."

"Can anyone verify that?" I asked.

"No. Allison and I don't share a bedroom. She was in the main house, I was in the carriage house."

"You don't share a bedroom with your wife?" I asked, frowning.

He returned to his desk chair, suddenly interested in straightening papers that didn't need to be straightened.

"Allison prefers her own space," he muttered. "We have... separate arrangements."

"How long has that been the case?"

"Oh, honestly!" he snapped. "What the hell does my marriage have to do with my father's murder?"

"Please answer the question," I said quietly.

"Two years. Maybe three. We have grown apart. It happens."

I let the silence stretch, watching him fidget with the papers, adjust his cufflinks, check his watch. Guilty people cannot sit still. They need to fill silence with words, movement, anything to avoid the weight of unspoken accusations.

"Tell me about the will," I said.

His head snapped up. "What about it?"

"Your father was planning to change it. What were the proposed changes?"

"I don't know the details. I didn't even know he was planning to change it. He mentioned he was meeting with his attorney to review his estate plans. But he didn't share specifics with me."

"Did you ask?" Corbin said.

"Of course I asked," he snapped. "He said it was none of my business until after he was dead."

The irony of that statement seemed to occur to him a moment after he said it.

"Did you believe you would inherit the estate?"

"I am the only son. This house, the property, the family legacy; it should pass to me. That's how these things work."

"Should? But you weren't certain about it, were you?" I said.

He stood again, pacing now. "My father was unpredictable. Vindictive, sometimes. He enjoyed keeping people off-balance, uncertain. It gave him power over us. So no, I wasn't certain. But I hoped. I had expectations."

"Expectations based on what?"

"Based on tradition. Family. The fact that I am his son, that I have put up with his controlling behavior my entire life, that I have tried to live up to impossible standards even when I failed. Surely that counts for something."

"Does it?" I asked.

He stopped pacing and looked at me directly for the first time since the interview began.

"I don't know anymore, Captain. I honestly don't know if anything I did in my entire life meant anything to him at all."

There was real pain in that statement. Whatever else Augustus IV might be—failed businessman, bitter son, potential suspect—his relationship with his father had damaged him in ways that money couldn't fix.

"Do you gamble, Mr. Aldridge?" I asked.

The question clearly surprised him. His eyes widened slightly, and he took a small step backward.

"Occasionally," he replied, quietly. "Nothing serious."

"Define occasionally," I said.

"Social gambling. Poker games with friends. Maybe a casino trip once or twice a year."

"Do you owe anyone money?"

"I told you, I have creditors from the business. That's public record."

"I am not asking about business creditors. I am asking about gambling debts. Do you owe money to individuals who might be less understanding about repayment schedules than the banks?"

His face went pale. "I want my attorney present."

"You are not under arrest, Mr. Aldridge. You are free to request an attorney anytime, but that will end this conversation immediately, and you will have to come to the station for any future interviews. Is that really what you want?"

He stood frozen, caught between self-preservation and the knowledge that requesting counsel would make him look guilty.

"I had some bad luck in Atlanta," he finally said. "Cards, sports betting, some online gambling. It got out of hand. I owe approximately forty thousand dollars to some people who are not particularly patient about collection."

"Are these people threatening you?"

"They are encouraging prompt repayment. Let us leave it at that."

"Have they contacted you since you moved back to Chattanooga?" I asked.

"They know where I am. And they make sure I know they know."

I made a note. Forty thousand in gambling debt to dangerous people, plus four point two million in failed business ventures. Augustus IV had approximately four million reasons to want his father dead.

"Did your father know about the gambling debts?"

"No. Absolutely not. If he had known, he would have cut me off completely, used it as more evidence of my failures, my poor judgment, my inability to manage my life properly."

"Tell me about yesterday morning. When did you learn about your father's death?"

"Allison called me at six fifteen. She was hysterical, barely making sense. She said Father was dead in the library, and that I needed to come immediately. I threw on clothes and ran to the main house. Mother was there, standing in the doorway of the library. Marcus was trying to keep everyone out. Melissa arrived a few minutes later."

"What did you do between arriving at the house and my team taking over the scene?"

"Nothing. I just stood there. I could see Father through the doorway, slumped at his desk. I couldn't quite process it. He has always been this immovable force in my life, always there, always judging, always controlling. And suddenly he was just... gone."

"Did you enter the library?"

"No. Marcus told me not to touch anything, that the police were coming."

"Did you see anyone else in or near the library?"

"No. Just Mother in the doorway, looking like a ghost."

I studied Augustus IV for a long moment. He was nervous, defensive, clearly hiding things. But was he hiding murder, or just the general shame and resentment that comes from being the disappointing son?

"Is there anything else you think I should know?" I asked.

He considered the question carefully. "My father was not a kind man, Captain. He was successful, intelligent, respected in the community. But he was not kind. He used money and status and family legacy as weapons against the people who should have mattered most to him. If you're looking for someone who wanted him dead, you will find a long list of people he hurt, disappointed, or destroyed over the years."

"Are you on that list?" I asked, watching him carefully.

"I suppose I am. But I didn't kill him. For all my failures, for all my anger and resentment, he was still my father. I wanted his approval more than I wanted his death."

That might have been the most honest thing he had said during the entire interview.

"Thank you for your time," I said, standing. "We'll need to speak with you again. Don't leave town without informing me first."

"Am I a suspect?" he asked.

"Everyone is a suspect until the evidence proves otherwise," I replied. "That is how murder investigations work."

The thunder rolled again outside, and for the first time since stepping into the Aldridge mansion, I felt the faint chill of something deeper than murder, something old, inherited, waiting to be uncovered.

"Come on, buddy," I said to Samson. "Let's go find Allison Aldridge. I want to hear her side of the story before the storm breaks again."

The dog rose, tail low, muscles tense. As we crossed the marble hall, I caught sight of a portrait of Brigadier General Augustus Aldridge—the original patriarch—staring down from the wall. His painted eyes seemed to follow me, unblinking, as if he already knew the truth I was about to uncover.

"He's hiding something," Corbin said quietly.

"He's hiding several things," I replied. "The question is whether one of those things is murder."

Corbin nodded. "Four million in business losses plus forty thousand in gambling debts. That is serious motive."

"It is. But motive is not evidence. We need to verify his timeline, check his alibi, see if anyone saw or heard him Sunday night into Monday morning."

"The carriage house is two hundred yards from the main house," Corbin said. "He could have easily walked here, killed his father, and returned without anyone noticing."

"Easily," I agreed. "Which is why we are going to have Hawk check his shoes, his clothes, anything that might show he was in the library during the relevant timeframe. And we need to check his alibi."

"What about the wife? Allison?"

"She's next on my list. Let's see if her version matches his, particularly about their separate sleeping arrangements and their relationship with the victim."

We walked back toward the main staircase, Samson padding quietly along beside me. He'd sat patiently through the interview, but now he was alert, ears forward, eyes everywhere.

The Aldridge mansion felt different today than it had yesterday. The shock had worn off, replaced by tension and suspicion. People moved through the hallways carefully, watching each other, wondering who among them was a killer. Because someone in this house had murdered Augustus Aldridge III. Someone had entered his library while the household slept, administered poison that Doc Sheddon would identify, and left him to die alone at his desk.

And that someone was still here, living under this roof, pretending to grieve while calculating their next move.

My phone buzzed. I took it from my jacket pocket and glanced at the screen. It was a text from Doc Sheddon: "Preliminary findings ready. Can you come by this afternoon?"

I texted back confirmation. The autopsy results would give us crucial information about time of death, exact cause, and possibly evidence about who had access to the murder weapon.

"Captain," Hawk appeared at the top of the stairs. "There's something in the library you need to see. Evidence of the antique book being moved recently, and what looks like a hidden compartment in the desk."

A hidden compartment. In a mansion full of secrets, that was almost too perfectly on brand.

"Show me," I said.

As we headed toward the library, I thought about Augustus IV and his desperate need for approval from a father who would never give it. About Allison and her separate bedroom.

About forty thousand in gambling debt and four point two million in failed dreams.

But mostly I thought about what Doc Sheddon had said yesterday: poisoning is personal, intimate, and it requires planning and access.

Augustus IV had access to his father's study, his food, his entire life. He had motive measured in millions of dollars and debts measured in threats, but did he have opportunity and... the weapon, whatever it was? More to the point, did he have the cold calculation required to poison his own father and watch him die?

That was the question that would define this case. And somewhere in this mansion, among the antique furniture and hidden compartments and century-old secrets, the answer was waiting to be found.

We just had to look in the right places. And keep everyone alive long enough to find the truth.

4

———

The Staff

THE HIDDEN COMPARTMENT IN AUGUSTUS ALDRIDGE'S DESK was exactly the kind of detail that made old mansions like this both fascinating and infuriating. The scent of polish still clung to the wood, mixed with the faint musk of age and dust. Hawk had discovered it while processing the library crime scene — a small drawer concealed behind a decorative panel in the desk's lower right corner, accessible only if you knew precisely where to press.

"It's craftsman work," Hawk said, demonstrating the release mechanism. "See how this rosette pattern has a slightly different grain? Press here and here simultaneously, and..."

The panel clicked open with a sound like a breath releasing, revealing a space about eight inches deep and twelve inches wide. Inside lay a leather journal, several manila folders, and a small wooden box that smelled faintly of cedar.

I pulled on latex gloves and carefully removed the journal first. The leather was old but supple, the pages filled with Augustus III's precise, slanted handwriting. I flipped through quickly — financial notations, investment records, personal observations. Nothing immediately screamed relevance to murder, but I'd have Jack North go through it line by line.

The folders held correspondence — letters yellowed at the edges, business and personal alike. One was labeled "Emily Caldwell — 1925" in faded ink. I opened it carefully.

Inside were newspaper clippings about Emily's murder, police reports that looked like photocopies of originals, and several handwritten letters. One was dated September 1925, written in elegant script:

"My dearest Augustus, I must speak with you. The situation has become untenable. I can no longer keep this secret. Please meet me at the library Sunday evening. We must discuss our future and the child. Yours always, Emily."

"Well," Corbin said quietly, reading over my shoulder. "That's interesting."

"Very," I agreed. "Augustus knew Emily Caldwell was pregnant. And she wanted to meet him in the library."

"The same library where she died," Corbin finished.

I photographed the letter with my phone, then carefully placed everything in the evidence bags Hawk provided. "Get this all to the lab. I want a complete inventory and analysis. And find out if there are any other hidden compartments in this house."

"Already on it," Hawk said. "I've got uniforms checking every room."

My phone buzzed—a text from Ramirez: "Staff interviews complete. Ready when you are."

"Good," I replied. "4 PM."

Chapter 4

I checked my watch. It was just past noon. Time to talk to Allison Aldridge before the day got away from me.

ALLISON OCCUPIED a guest suite on the second floor — a bright, sterile contrast to the rest of the house. Everything was white and chrome and glass, gleaming under recessed lighting. It felt defiant, as if she were trying to erase the past one coat of lacquer at a time. The faint scent of gardenia perfume hovered in the air.

She answered the door in designer loungewear that probably cost more than my car payment. Her blonde hair was perfect, her lipstick unsmudged. If grief lived here, it wore diamonds.

"Captain Gazzara," she said, her drawl smooth as sweet tea. "I've been expecting you. Please, come in."

Corbin and I stepped inside. Samson padded over to the doorway, settling like a sentry. Allison's eyes flicked to him nervously before she perched on the edge of a white leather chair.

"I assume you want to talk about yesterday morning," she said.

"Among other things, yes," I replied, lowering myself onto the couch that looked more art piece than furniture. "You found the body. Tell me about it."

She took a deep breath, composing herself. "I woke up around six a.m. I couldn't sleep well—I never do in this house. Too many noises, too much history pressing down on everything. I decided to make coffee, maybe read for a while before anyone else was up."

"You were staying in the main house, not the carriage house with your husband?"

A flicker of something—annoyance? embarrassment?—crossed her face. "Augustus and I have separate sleeping arrangements. It works better for both of us."

"How long has that been the case?"

"Two, maybe three years. We're still married, still committed to each other, but we both value our personal space."

That wasn't quite how Augustus IV had described it, but I let it pass for now.

"Continue," I said.

"I came downstairs to the kitchen. The house was quiet, just that old-house silence that feels heavy. I made coffee, then thought I should check if Augustus Senior wanted breakfast. He was always an early riser, usually in his library by six thirty."

"Did you often check on him?"

"Sometimes. Victoria's getting older, and I thought it was a kind gesture. Plus, it gave me something to do. This house can feel very empty even when it's full of people."

"What time did you go to the library?"

"Around six-thirty, I think. Claudia was already there, and she was sitting on a chair outside in the hall, crying. The door was open and... and..."

Her voice wavered slightly, the first crack in her composed facade.

"And?" I prompted.

"He was sitting at his desk, slumped forward. At first I thought he'd fallen asleep while working—he did that sometimes. But I could see... his face was gray. His eyes were open but not seeing anything. I knew he was dead."

"What did you do?"

"I screamed and called Augustus—my husband. Then I called Victoria. I didn't touch anything. I just stood in the hallway trying not to panic until Marcus arrived and took control of the situation."

"Did you notice anything unusual in the library? Anything out of place?"

She thought about it. "Not really. I didn't. Go in. It looked like he'd been working. There were papers on his desk, his reading glasses, a coffee cup. Everything looked normal except for him being dead."

"Tell me about your relationship with Augustus Senior."

"It was cordial. Polite. He was my father-in-law, I respected him."

"But you didn't like him."

It wasn't a question, and she knew it.

"He was difficult," she said carefully. "He had very high standards and very specific ideas about how things should be done. He didn't approve of me, didn't think I was good enough for his son. He made that clear in subtle ways—never outright rude, just... cold. Distant."

"Why didn't he think you were good enough?"

Her jaw tightened. "Because I came from a middle-class family in Dalton, Georgia. Because my father worked in carpet manufacturing, not investment banking. Because I was a pageant girl who didn't go to Vanderbilt or Sewanee or any of the 'right' schools. In Augustus's world, that made me unsuitable."

"That must have created tension."

"It did. Especially when Junior's business failed and we had to move back here. Augustus Senior made it very clear that we were living on his property by his sufferance, that we should be grateful for his charity."

"Were you grateful?"

"I was furious," she said bluntly. "My husband lost everything trying to build something independent from this family. And instead of helping, his father used it as an opportunity to humiliate him, to force him into a minimum-wage job managing the estate like some kind of hired hand."

"Did that make you angry enough to want Augustus Senior dead?"

She met my eyes directly. "I wanted him to suffer the way he made us suffer. I wanted him to understand what it felt like to lose everything and be at someone else's mercy. But kill him? No. That wouldn't solve anything. Dead, he's still controlling us through whatever he put in that will."

"Do you know what's in the will?"

"No. He kept it secret, used it as leverage to keep everyone in line. That's how he operated—information was power, and he hoarded both."

"Where were you Sunday night between nine p.m. and midnight?"

"In my room. Reading, watching television, trying to relax."

"Can anyone verify that?"

"No. Like I said, Augustus and I have separate rooms. I was alone."

"Did you hear anything unusual? See anyone moving through the house?"

She shook her head. "This house is huge, and the walls are

thick. I could have a party in my room and no one would hear it from the other end of the hallway."

I paused, watching her carefully. The nervousness beneath her polished exterior was evident now—the way her fingers twisted together in her lap, the slight tension in her shoulders. She was holding something back, but whether it was guilt or simply fear of judgment, I couldn't yet tell.

"Tell me about your husband's gambling," I said, shifting topics abruptly.

Her composure cracked completely. "How do you know about that?"

"He told me. Approximately forty thousand dollars in debt to people who aren't patient about repayment. Did you know?"

"Yes," she whispered. "I found out about six months ago. He promised he'd stop, that he'd get help. But I don't think he has."

"Did Augustus Senior know?"

"God, no. If he'd found out, he would have cut us off completely. Used it as more proof that Junior was irresponsible, unworthy of the family name."

"Forty thousand is a lot of money. Money that would become available if Augustus Senior died and left the estate to his son."

"You think we killed him for the inheritance?" She laughed bitterly. "We don't even know if there is an inheritance. For all we know, Augustus left everything to charity out of spite."

"But you must have hoped."

"Of course we hoped. What else did we have? Junior's business is gone, his reputation is destroyed, we're living on charity in a house where we're not wanted. Yes, we hoped that when Augustus finally died, we'd at least get enough to start over somewhere else."

"Start over without the gambling debts?"

"Start over period," she said firmly. "Build a life that isn't controlled by this family and this house and all these secrets."

"What secrets?"

"I don't know specifically. But you can feel them in this place. In the way people don't talk about certain things, the way rooms are kept locked, the way Victoria looks at that portrait in the library like it's haunting her. This family has secrets buried so deep they've become part of the foundation."

Samson shifted near the door, drawing my attention. He was watching Allison with his head cocked slightly—not aggressive, just intensely interested. Dogs often pick up on things humans miss.

"Is there anything else you think I should know?" I asked.

Allison hesitated, then shook her head. "Just that Augustus Senior wasn't a good man. He was successful and respected, but he wasn't kind. And kindness matters more than people in this family seem to understand."

"Thank you for your time," I said, standing. "We'll need to speak with you again."

"I'm not going anywhere," she said. "Where would I go?"

———————————

By four o'clock, the squad was back in my office. Outside, thunder was grumbling again over Missionary Ridge. The room smelled of wet coats, coffee, and paper. Corbin, Hawk, Cooper, Ramirez, and Jack North filled the available chairs and leaned against filing cabinets.

"All right," I said. "Let's consolidate what we know. Ramirez, you interviewed the staff. What did you find?"

Ramirez flipped open her notebook. "We started with Claudia Rivera, the housekeeper. She's been with the family for twenty-five years, worked her way up from maid to head of houschold staff. She's fiercely loyal to Victoria Aldridge specifically, not the family as a whole."

"How fiercely?" I asked.

"Would-take-a-bullet-for-her fiercely," Ramirez replied. "Her words, not mine. She said Victoria saved her from an abusive situation years ago, helped her get documented, treated her like family when no one else would."

"What's her story about Monday morning?" Cooper asked.

"She arrived at six a.m., started her normal routine in the kitchen. Heard Allison screaming around six twenty. She was the first to reach the library. She saw Augustus dead at his desk, immediately called 911, then Marcus Webb to secure the scene, then stayed with Victoria while we were notified."

"Did she notice anything unusual?"

"Only that Augustus's coffee cup was empty. She'd brought him fresh coffee Sunday evening around nine thirty—he'd asked for it specifically. But when she saw the body Monday morning, the cup was drained."

I made a note. "What about Marcus Webb?"

Cooper took over. "Marcus Webb, estate manager, eight years with the family. Former Army Ranger, twenty years military service. He's got keys to everything, knows every inch of this property. He arrived at five forty-five Monday to supervise the grounds crew."

"Five forty-five?" I said. "That's early."

"He says it's normal for landscaping days. The crew starts

at seven thirty, he likes to walk the property first, plan the work."

"What's his relationship with Augustus?"

Cooper's expression turned grim. "That's where it gets interesting. Webb admits he was in the library Saturday afternoon, going over estate finances with Augustus. The conversation got heated."

"How heated?"

"Augustus questioned some expenditure irregularities. Nothing huge—a few thousand dollars over six months—but Augustus was meticulous about money. Webb says he explained the expenses were legitimate, maintenance issues and equipment repairs, but Augustus wasn't satisfied."

"Did Augustus threaten to fire him?"

"Webb claims no, but he got very defensive when I pressed about the financial details. Started talking about how he's dedicated his life to this property, how he's improved security and maintenance, how he doesn't deserve to be questioned like a criminal."

"So he's got motive," Corbin said. "Access, opportunity, and financial pressure."

"He also has military training," Hawk added. "Rangers know about poisons, covert operations. If anyone on this estate could plan and execute a murder, it's Marcus Webb."

I nodded. "Keep digging into those financial irregularities. I want to know exactly where that money went. What about Helen Park?"

RAMIREZ CONSULTED HER NOTES. "Helen Park, the cook, sixty-two years old, fifteen years with the family. She's got culinary training, prepares all meals. And here's the thing—Augustus was forcing her into retirement."

"Forcing her how?"

"He told her that at the end of October, her services would no longer be needed. He offered a severance package, but she'd have to vacate the cottage she's been living in on the property, and that cottage is her home."

"So she's about to lose her job and her home," I said. "That's motive."

"It gets better," Ramirez continued. "Helen prepared Augustus's Sunday dinner—roast chicken, vegetables, apple pie. He ate it alone in the library while working. She brought the tray at six p.m., collected it at eight-thirty when he was done."

"Did she notice anything unusual about him?"

"She says he seemed fine. Focused on his work, barely acknowledged her. But she had access to his food for at least two hours before he ate it, and access to the library when she collected the tray."

"Did she seem nervous during the interview?"

"Defensive," Cooper said. "Very defensive about her background, her skills, her dedication to the family. She's terrified of losing everything she's built here."

"Terrified enough to commit murder?"

"Maybe," Ramirez said. "She's got the means—access to all food and drink in this house. She's got motive—desperation about forced retirement. And she's got opportunity—she was in the library Sunday evening."

"What about Rosa Martinez?" I asked.

"Rosa Martinez, head gardener, fifty-two years old," Cooper said. "She's been with the estate for twenty-seven years. Horticulture degree, worked briefly at Rockefeller estate before returning to Chattanooga."

"What did she tell you?"

"She saw lights in the library Sunday evening around ten p.m. She was checking irrigation systems—apparently there's a sensor issue in one zone, and she wanted to verify it was working properly before the grounds crew came Monday morning."

"Ten p.m.," Corbin said. "That's within our time-of-death window."

"Did she see anyone enter or leave the library?" I asked.

"No. Just noticed the lights were on, which wasn't unusual. Augustus often worked late."

"Did she mention anything else unusual?"

Cooper hesitated. "She was nervous about something. Every time I asked about the estate's history or old buildings, she'd tense up. Like there's something she knows but doesn't want to talk about."

"Press her on that," I said. "What about her father?"

"Miguel Martinez," Ramirez said softly. "Eighty-three years old, retired head gardener. Worked here for forty years before retiring twelve years ago. Now lives in a cottage on the property. He's got early-stage dementia."

"How bad?"

"Bad enough that his memories are fragmented, mixing past and present. We tried to interview him, but he kept talking about 'the old place' and 'secrets buried' and something about 'the girl in the library.' His daughter Rosa had to translate some of it—his English comes and goes."

"The girl in the library," I repeated. "Emily Caldwell?"

"That's what we figured," Cooper said. "But getting clear information from him is nearly impossible. One minute he's talking about gardens, the next he's back in 1925 or somewhere else entirely."

"But he was here in 1925?" I asked.

"No. He wasn't born until sixteen years later. But his father might have been on staff then. Rosa says her grandfather worked at the mansion in the twenties, grounds maintenance."

I sat back, processing everything. Staff members with access, opportunity, and motive. Financial irregularities. Forced retirement. Knowledge of toxic plants. And an old man whose confused memories might hold crucial information about a ninety-nine-year-old murder that somehow connected to this one.

"Jack," I said, turning to our computer crimes specialist. "I need you to dig into Marcus Webb's finances. Find out where that money went. Also check Helen Park's background—immigration records, previous employment, anything that might explain her defensiveness."

"On it," Jack said.

"Corbin, you and I are going to have a conversation with Rosa Martinez. If she knows something about this property's history, we need to find out what."

"What about Miguel?" Ramirez asked. "Should we try interviewing him again?"

"Not yet. But I want someone watching him. His confusion might clear up occasionally, and when it does, he might say something important."

I stood, gathering my notes. "Everyone document everything. This case is getting complicated fast, and I want clear records of every interview, every observation, every piece of evidence. Chief Johnston is already getting pressure from the city council about this, and I need our work to be airtight."

"One more thing," Cooper said. "I went through Augustus's calendar and recent communications. He had a standing appointment every Sunday evening at eight p.m."

"With whom?"

"His attorney, Dr. Nathaniel Ross. Phone calls, not in person. They'd been discussing changes to the will for the past three weeks."

"Changes," I said. "Do we know what kind of changes?"

"Ross is claiming attorney-client privilege. But whatever Augustus was planning, he was doing it methodically and keeping it secret from the family."

That was the pattern emerging from this investigation— secrets layered upon secrets, a family that communicated through silence and subtle manipulations rather than honest conversation.

"Get me a meeting with Ross," I said. "Tomorrow if possible. And prepare a warrant request if he won't cooperate voluntarily. We need to know what Augustus was planning to change in that will."

The team dispersed to their various tasks. Corbin lingered behind, waiting until we were alone.

"What are you thinking?" he asked.

"I'm thinking this family has been keeping secrets for so long they don't know how to tell the truth anymore. And I'm thinking that Sunday evening, between nine p.m. and midnight, someone walked into that library and decided those secrets were worth killing for."

"Multiple suspects with means, motive, and opportunity."

"Exactly. Which means we're missing something. Some piece that connects everything together."

"The Emily Caldwell connection?"

"Maybe. Augustus had files about her murder hidden in his desk. Rosa saw lights in the library at ten p.m. Miguel keeps talking about 'the girl in the library' and secrets buried. There's a link there, I just can't see it yet."

My phone buzzed—a text from Doc Sheddon: "Autopsy complete. Results are interesting. Come by tomorrow morning?"

I showed Corbin the message.

"Interesting is never good in our line of work," he said.

"No," I agreed. "It's not."

Outside, the rain had picked up again, drumming steadily against the windows. The old station house settled with familiar creaks and groans, sounds I'd heard a thousand times but tonight felt different somehow. Ominous. Like the building itself was warning me about what we were uncovering.

Someone in that house was a murderer. Someone who'd carefully planned Augustus Aldridge's death, administered poison, and watched him die. Someone who was still there, living among the family and staff, pretending to grieve while hoping we wouldn't find the truth.

But we would find it. We always did.

Even if it was buried under a century of secrets.

Even if uncovering it destroyed what was left of the Aldridge family.

As the team packed up, the office lights hummed softly, the storm easing into a fine drizzle outside. Samson stirred from his spot under the window, ears twitching toward the thunder's retreat. He padded over to me, his dark eyes meeting mine with that uncanny intelligence that sometimes made me wonder just how much he understood.

I scratched behind his ears. "Someone in that house killed Augustus Aldridge," I said quietly. "And the house knows who."

Samson's tail wagged once, a slow deliberate movement, as if acknowledging the truth in my words. Houses like the Aldridge mansion held memories in their walls, secrets in their hidden compartments, ghosts in their libraries. And one of those secrets had finally turned deadly.

5

The Autopsy

THE HAMILTON COUNTY MEDICAL EXAMINER'S OFFICE ALWAYS smelled the same—antiseptic, industrial cleaner, and something else I could never quite identify. Death, maybe.

Doc Sheddon was waiting in his office when Corbin and I arrived.

"Kate, Corbin," he said, gesturing to the chairs across from his desk. "Thanks for coming."

"Your text said the results were interesting," I replied, settling into the chair. Corbin took the seat beside me, notebook already open. "In our line of work, that's never good."

"No," Doc agreed. "It's not."

He opened the file on his desk, adjusting his reading glasses. Behind him, the morning light filtered through windows that overlooked the parking lot. Professional certificates lined the walls—medical degree from Vanderbilt, forensic pathology certification, twenty years of service commendations.

"Augustus Aldridge III died from acute digitalis poisoning," Doc said. "Specifically, digitalis toxicity causing fatal cardiac arrhythmia. The toxicology results show levels far exceeding any therapeutic dose."

"Digitalis," Corbin said, writing quickly. "That's a heart medication, right?"

"It is. Derived from the foxglove plant. In controlled doses, it's used to treat certain cardiac conditions—strengthens the heart's contractions, regulates rhythm. But in high doses, it's extremely toxic. Causes irregular heartbeat, nausea, visual disturbances, and eventually cardiac arrest."

"Augustus had no history of heart problems?" I asked.

"None. I reviewed his medical records thoroughly. No cardiac issues, no prescriptions for digitalis or any related medications. This wasn't an accidental overdose or medication error. This was intentional poisoning."

I leaned forward. "Time of death?"

"Based on body temperature, rigor mortis, and stomach contents, I'm putting it between nine p.m. and midnight Sunday. The digitalis was likely administered one to two hours before death, so somewhere between seven and ten p.m."

That narrowed our window considerably. Helen Park had collected Augustus's dinner tray at eight-thirty. Rosa Martinez saw library lights at ten. Someone had poisoned him during that timeframe.

"How was it administered?" Corbin asked.

"No injection sites, no evidence of forced ingestion. This was oral administration, almost certainly in food or drink. The problem is, digitalis is extremely bitter. It would be very difficult to mask in solid food."

"But not in drinks?" I said.

"Correct. Strong coffee or alcohol could potentially hide the taste, especially if the victim wasn't expecting it. I understand there was both brandy and coffee in the library?"

"Yes. Willis's team is testing both."

Doc nodded. "I'd focus on those. The bitterness would still be noticeable, but someone who's drinking expensive brandy or strong coffee might attribute any odd taste to that rather than poison."

"How much digitalis would it take to kill someone Augustus's size?"

"Not as much as you'd think. A few grams of crushed foxglove leaves, properly prepared, would be more than sufficient. It's a remarkably effective poison if you know what you're doing."

"Know what you're doing," I repeated. "So this requires specialized knowledge?"

"You'd need to know which parts of the plant to use, how to extract or prepare the digitalis, what dosage would be fatal. Google could teach you the basics, but practical application takes some understanding of botany or pharmacology."

I thought about the bitter taste of digitalis, how difficult it would be to mask in food. Helen Park would know how to hide flavors, what spices and seasonings would work. She had the knowledge and the access.

A knock on the door interrupted us. Doc called out, "Come in."

Dr. Graham Crawford entered, carrying a leather messenger bag. He was dressed in surgical scrubs under a white coat—apparently he'd come straight from the hospital.

"Sorry I'm late," he said. "I had an emergency arise at the

hospital and the surgery ran longer than expected. Has Doc filled you in on the findings?"

"Just getting to the details," Doc Sheddon said. "Graham, thanks for coming. Your expertise on cardiac toxicology is exactly what we need here."

Graham settled into the third chair, pulling out a tablet from his bag. He looked tired but focused, the kind of professional competence you'd want in a surgeon. Despite the circumstances—his father-in-law's murder—he seemed determined to help.

"Digitalis poisoning," Graham said, scrolling through something on his tablet. "Nasty way to die. The therapeutic window is incredibly narrow—the difference between a helpful dose and a fatal one is minimal."

"You've treated digitalis toxicity before?" Corbin asked.

"A few cases over the years. Usually accidental—elderly patients taking too much medication, or someone confusing their pills. Intentional poisoning is rare, though."

"Walk me through what happened to Augustus," I said.

Graham set his tablet aside. "Digitalis affects the heart's electrical system. In therapeutic doses, it strengthens contractions and regulates rhythm. In toxic doses, it causes the heart to beat irregularly, eventually leading to ventricular fibrillation and cardiac arrest."

"How long would it take?"

"Depends on the dose. With the levels Doc found, I'd estimate Augustus started experiencing symptoms within thirty to sixty minutes. Nausea first, maybe visual disturbances—he might have seen halos around lights. Confusion, weakness. Then the cardiac symptoms would escalate."

"Would he have known he was dying?"

Graham considered the question. "Probably not at first. He might have thought it was a heart attack or severe indigestion. By the time he realized something was seriously wrong, he would've been too weak to call for help."

"So he suffered," Corbin said quietly.

"Yes. I'm sorry to say it, but this isn't a peaceful death."

Doc Sheddon spread several photographs across the desk. "I found no defensive wounds, no signs of struggle. Augustus was sitting at his desk when he died. The position suggests he was working, felt ill, but didn't have time or strength to stand up or call for help."

"What about the coffee and brandy?" I asked.

"Both tested positive for digitalis," Doc replied. "The brandy had a significantly higher concentration—whoever did this wanted to guarantee success."

"So the killer poisoned both drinks?"

"Looks that way. Insurance, maybe. Or they weren't sure which one Augustus would consume."

Graham frowned. "That suggests planning. They had to extract the digitalis, prepare it, get access to the library, and poison both drinks without being seen. This took time and knowledge."

"Who would have that knowledge?" I asked.

"Medical professionals," Graham said. "Gardeners, horticulturists, anyone familiar with plant toxins. Maybe someone with a chemistry background or pharmaceutical training."

"That's helpful," I said. "Dr. Crawford, I appreciate you taking time from your practice to assist with this."

"Of course. Augustus and I had our differences, but he was family. I want to see justice done."

After Graham left, Doc walked us to the door. "One more

thing, Kate," he said. "The amount of digitalis in those drinks suggests the killer had access to multiple foxglove plants. This wasn't a matter of picking a few leaves. They harvested enough to extract a concentrated dose."

"How many plants are we talking about?"

"Hard to say exactly, but probably at least a dozen mature plants. And they'd need to know which parts to harvest—the leaves are most toxic in the second year of growth."

"So our killer knows plants," I said.

"Or they had help from someone who does."

WE WRAPPED up the meeting and headed back to the station. The rain had started again, a steady drizzle that made the city look gray and tired. Traffic on Market Street moved sluggishly, and I found myself thinking about the foxglove growing in the Aldridge gardens—beautiful, ornamental, deadly.

Back at headquarters, my team had assembled in the conference room. I briefed them on Doc Sheddon's findings—digitalis poisoning, administered between seven and ten p.m. Sunday.

"So we're looking at a three-hour window," Hawk said.

"Correct. And the poison was in both the coffee and brandy, which means the killer had access to the library, knew Augustus's habits, and had time to prepare without being interrupted."

"Let's run through our main suspects," I said. "Helen Park, the cook. She prepared Augustus's dinner, collected the tray at eight-thirty. She has access to all food and drink in the house.

And she's being forced into retirement, losing both her job and her home."

"Does she have the knowledge to extract digitalis from foxglove?" Corbin asked.

"That's what we need to find out," I said. "Jack, dig into Helen's background. Education, previous employment, any connection to herbal medicine or traditional remedies."

"On it," Jack said.

"Rosa Martinez," I continued. "Head gardener with a horticulture degree. She knows every plant on this estate, including the foxglove varieties. She saw library lights at ten p.m., putting her on the property during our timeframe."

"But would she have accessed the library?" Hawk asked.

"We need to verify that. Ramirez, interview Rosa again. Find out exactly where she was Sunday evening and whether she entered the main house."

"Will do."

"What about Victoria?" Cooper asked. "She lives in the house, has access to everything."

"Victoria's in her eighties," I said. "The physical act of harvesting plants, extracting poison, moving through the house without detection—I'm not ruling her out, but she's lower on my list."

"Unless she had help," Hawk suggested.

"Which brings us back to the staff," I said. "Everyone in that house is connected somehow. Claudia Rivera is fiercely loyal to Victoria. Rosa Martinez has been there for decades. Even Marcus Webb—eight years as estate manager means he knows everyone's routines, everyone's secrets."

"Marcus Webb," Cooper said. "Estate manager with military background. He had that heated argument with Augustus about financial irregularities Saturday afternoon."

"How much money are we talking about?" I asked.

"About eight thousand over six months," Jack said. "Could be embezzlement, could be sloppy bookkeeping. I'm still tracing where it went."

"Not a huge amount, but enough to ruin his reputation if Augustus reported it," Corbin said. "And Rangers know about field medicine, possibly plant toxins."

"His military training concerns me," I said. "Someone who's been trained in covert operations, survival skills, knows how to plan and execute without leaving evidence. That fits the profile of what we're seeing here."

We spent another hour building timelines, comparing access and opportunity. The pattern was clear—multiple suspects with means, motive, and opportunity. No smoking gun, no obvious culprit. Just a web of relationships, resentments, and secrets.

"This was premeditated," I said finally. "This isn't a crime of passion. This is calculated murder."

"Which suggests someone with a strong, sustained motive," Corbin said. "Not just anger or resentment, but something deeper."

"Like what?" Cooper asked.

"Financial desperation. Fear of exposure. Protection of someone they love. Or revenge for something that happened long ago." I thought about the Emily Caldwell files hidden in Augustus's desk. "There's history here we don't fully understand yet."

"The 1925 connection," Ramirez said. "Emily Caldwell's

murder. Miguel Martinez talking about 'the girl in the library.' You think that's relevant?"

"Augustus kept files about Emily's murder in a hidden compartment," I said. "That's not casual interest. He was investigating something, or protecting someone, or covering something up. And now he's dead in the same library where she died."

"You think the murders are connected?" Hawk looked skeptical.

"I think the past matters to this family more than we realize. And I think whatever secret Augustus was keeping got him killed."

"That's what we need to figure out," I said. "Jack, I need deep background on everyone's history. Financial records, personal histories, relationships with Augustus. There's a reason someone wanted him dead badly enough to plan and execute a sophisticated poisoning. We just have to find it."

My phone rang—Chief Johnston.

"Captain," he said without preamble. "I need an update. The mayor's office is asking questions, the Aldridge family attorney is making noise about harassment, and the city council wants to know when we'll have someone in custody."

"We have cause of death—digitalis poisoning, definitely murder. We're building the case methodically. I'd rather take the time to get it right than rush and lose it in court."

"Understood. But don't take too long. The pressure's mounting, and this is a prominent family. We need results."

He hung up, and I looked at my team. The weight of expectation was visible in their tired faces—Cooper's bloodshot eyes, Ramirez's third cup of coffee, Hawk's military-straight posture that betrayed stress in the set of his shoulders. They were good people doing hard work, and they deserved better than political pressure.

"All right, people," I said. "We've got cause of death and method. Now we need to find out who had both the knowledge and the motive to poison Augustus Aldridge. Cooper, you take Marcus Webb's background—military service, any disciplinary issues, financial situation. Ramirez, focus on Helen Park and Rosa Martinez—look for connections, shared history, anything that might explain coordination between them. Hawk, I want a complete survey of the foxglove plants on the property by end of day. Jack, keep digging into those financial irregularities."

"What about you?" Corbin asked.

"I'm going to have another conversation with Victoria Aldridge. She's been in that house for sixty years. If anyone knows the real history, the buried secrets, it's her. And I think she's been waiting for someone to finally ask the right questions."

The team dispersed, each to their assigned tasks. Outside my office window, the rain continued its steady drumbeat against the glass. Somewhere in this city, a murderer was going about their day, believing they'd gotten away with it. Believing that Augustus Aldridge's secrets had died with him.

They were wrong.

Secrets don't die. They just wait to be discovered.

And I was very good at discovering things people wanted to keep hidden.

6

_____

Financial Motives

IT'S BEEN MY EXPERIENCE THAT MONEY HAS A WAY OF revealing people's true character. Give someone enough of it, and they'll show you who they really are. Take it away, and they'll show you what they're capable of.

The conference room smelled faintly of burnt coffee and old paper—an odor that always reminded me of long cases, sleepless nights, and truths dragged reluctantly into daylight. Rain tapped softly against the window, a gray Tennessee afternoon settling over the city like a wet shroud. I'd been staring at the same family tree for so long that the Aldridge name felt like a brand burned into my retinas.

Cooper and Jack North had spent the morning buried in financial records, bank statements, credit reports, and estate documents. By early afternoon, they had assembled a picture of the Aldridge family finances that looked nothing like the wealthy facade the family presented to Chattanooga society.

Samson lay curled under the table, snoring softly, a

comforting presence amid numbers and deceit. It struck me again how the calmest souls in any investigation were usually the ones without a stake in human ambition. Dogs didn't understand greed. Maybe that's what made them trustworthy.

I sat across from them in the conference room, Corbin beside me, as Cooper laid out the findings.

"Augustus Aldridge III's estate is worth approximately twelve million dollars," Cooper began, spreading documents across the table. "Eight million in the mansion and property, four million in investments and cash. Sounds impressive until you look at the costs."

"What costs?" I asked.

"Maintaining that estate runs about four hundred thousand a year. Property taxes, insurance, staff salaries, utilities, grounds maintenance, repairs on a house that's over a hundred and seventy years old. It's a money pit."

"But Augustus had four million liquid to cover it," Corbin said.

"He did. But that money was carefully managed. Augustus tracked every dollar, questioned every expense. He wasn't wealthy because he spent freely. He was wealthy because he was meticulous about not spending at all."

Jack pulled up a spreadsheet on his laptop. "Let's talk about the family members. Augustus IV is in serious financial trouble. He owes approximately four million four hundred and fifty thousand dollars to various creditors."

I whistled low. "That's more than the business losses he mentioned."

"Much more. The business failure accounts for about four million. The rest is personal debt accumulated over the past five years. Credit cards, personal loans, and—" Jack paused, highlighting a section of the spreadsheet. "—approximately two hundred thousand to what we'd call questionable creditors."

"Loan sharks?" Corbin asked.

"Private lenders who don't report to credit agencies and charge interest rates that would make a credit card company blush. The kind of people who get very creative about collection methods."

"He's been pressing his father for money," Cooper continued. "We found email exchanges going back six months. Augustus IV asking for help, Augustus III refusing. The tone gets increasingly desperate on the son's end, increasingly cold on the father's."

I thought about Augustus IV in his reproduction study, surrounded by false sophistication and real desperation. Four million four hundred and fifty thousand in debt. That was serious motive.

"What about Allison?" I asked.

Cooper took out another file. "Allison Aldridge has her own credit card debt. Approximately two hundred thousand dollars across eight cards. Luxury purchases, mostly. Designer clothes, jewelry, spa treatments, country club fees. She's been maintaining a lifestyle she can't afford, apparently hoping Augustus Senior would eventually bail them out."

"So between them, they're more than four and a half million dollars in debt," Corbin said.

"And living in a carriage house on an estate worth eight million," I added. "That had to create resentment."

"It gets better," Jack said. "We pulled phone records. Augustus IV has been in contact with several of those questionable lenders in the past two weeks. The calls are getting more frequent. We can't prove what was said, but the pattern suggests they're pressuring him for payment."

Outside the window, the clouds thickened, pressing the afternoon into early twilight. The flicker of fluorescent light made the stacks of paper gleam like thin bones. Every column of figures was another confession, another quiet scream for help. Money didn't just talk—it whispered, pleaded, and sometimes killed.

I made notes. Augustus IV and Allison both had powerful financial motives. Millions of dollars in combined debt, creditors closing in, and a father who refused to help while sitting on a twelve-million-dollar estate.

"What about Melissa?" I asked.

"Melissa's interior design business is actually quite successful," Cooper said. "She's pulled in about three hundred thousand a year for the past three years. She's got steady clients, a good reputation, and solid financials."

"So she doesn't need her father's money?"

"Not for the business. But—" Cooper glanced at Jack, who pulled up another file.

"Dr. Graham Crawford," Jack said. "Cardiovascular surgeon at Erlanger, excellent reputation, income in the high six figures. On paper, they should be financially comfortable."

"But?" I prompted.

"But two years ago, Graham faced a malpractice lawsuit. A patient died post-surgery, family claimed negligence. The case went through extensive litigation before settling for five hundred thousand dollars."

Corbin leaned forward. "That's a lot of money."

"It is. Graham's malpractice insurance covered three hundred thousand, but he was personally responsible for the remaining two hundred thousand. Plus legal fees, which ran about a hundred thousand. So Graham took a three-hundred-thousand-dollar hit."

"That would strain anyone's finances," I said.

For a brief moment, the room was silent except for the rustle of paper. Corbin leaned back in his chair, eyes narrowing in thought. We'd seen greed before, plenty of it, but there was something different about this case. It wasn't raw desperation—it was entitlement polished into a family tradition. The Aldridges didn't see money as survival. They saw it as birthright.

"It did," Cooper confirmed. "They took out a second mortgage on their house, liquidated some investments. They're not broke, but they're not comfortable either. And Melissa's spending habits didn't change. She's still buying art, redecorating their house, maintaining an expensive lifestyle."

"So they could use an inheritance," Corbin said.

"Absolutely," Jack agreed.

I thought about Melissa at the breakfast table, elegant and controlled, showing no obvious grief for her father. About Graham being helpful during the autopsy consultation, professional and detached. They both had financial pressure, though not as desperate as Augustus IV.

"What about Victoria?" I asked.

Cooper smiled slightly. "Victoria Aldridge is the one family member who doesn't need Augustus's money. She has substantial personal wealth from her own family—old Tennessee money, trust funds established generations ago. We estimate she's worth about five million independent of Augustus's estate."

"So she's financially independent," Corbin said.

"Completely. Which weakens her motive significantly. She doesn't need the inheritance, and she already has lifetime residence rights at the estate as Augustus's widow."

That was interesting. Victoria had the least obvious financial motive, yet she'd been the most composed about her husband's death. Maybe because she genuinely didn't care about the money. Or maybe because she had other reasons for wanting him dead.

Victoria's calm face flashed in my mind—the careful control, the way she spoke like grief was a duty rather than a wound. Maybe that's what wealth did after enough generations: replaced emotion with etiquette, sorrow with poise. But poise could hide anything.

"Now here's where it gets really interesting," Jack said. "Augustus Senior met with his family attorney, Nathaniel Ross, three weeks ago about changing his will."

I sat up straighter. "What kind of changes?"

Jack pulled up a document on his laptop. "The current will, dated five years ago, splits the estate as follows: Augustus IV gets forty percent, Melissa gets forty percent, Victoria gets twenty percent with lifetime estate residence rights. Pretty standard distribution."

"And the proposed changes?"

"Augustus wanted to cut his son out altogether, and reduce Melissa's forty percent to twenty percent. That twenty percent along with his son's forty percent would go to various charities: the Chattanooga Land Conservancy, the Hunter Museum, the Red Cross."

"He was cutting Augustus out of his will altogether and his daughter's inheritance in half?" Corbin said.

"Yes. The documentation Ross provided includes Augustus's notes. He cited 'irresponsible spending' and 'lack of financial discipline' as reasons. He felt Melissa and Graham were wasting money, living beyond their means, and he didn't want to fund that lifestyle."

"How much money are we talking about?" I asked.

Cooper did quick math. "Augusts IV would get nothing and, based on the estate value, Melissa would lose about two point four million dollars. Her inheritance would drop from about four point eight million to two point four million."

I let that sink in. Two point four million dollars. That was serious money. Money that could pay off Graham's malpractice debt, rebuild their financial cushion, maintain Melissa's lifestyle indefinitely.

"Was the new will signed?" I asked.

"No," Jack said. "Augustus died before signing it. Ross says they were scheduled to finalize everything this week. Augustus wanted to think about it over the weekend, make sure he was certain about the changes."

"So if Melissa knew about the proposed changes—" Corbin began.

"She had a very strong motive to make sure that new will never got signed," I finished. "Does she know? Did Augustus tell her?"

"Ross won't say. Attorney-client privilege extends to conversations about the will. But it's possible Augustus confronted Melissa about the spending, warned her he was making changes."

"Or she might not have known at all," Cooper added. "Augustus was secretive about his finances. He might have planned to change the will without telling anyone until after it was done."

I thought about the timing. Augustus died Sunday night. He was scheduled to finalize the will changes this week. If Melissa knew about the proposed changes, she had less than a week to stop them. That kind of deadline could drive someone to desperate action.

A cold ripple worked its way down my spine. Deadlines had a way of pushing people over edges they didn't know existed. I'd seen it in soldiers, in addicts, in desperate husbands. Give them a ticking clock, and you'll find out how far they'll go to stop it from reaching zero.

"What about Marcus Webb?" I asked, shifting focus to the staff.

Cooper's expression turned grim. "Marcus Webb has been embezzling from the estate for the past three years. Small amounts, carefully hidden in the accounts, but it adds up. We're looking at approximately fifty thousand dollars total."

"Fifty thousand," Corbin said. "That's serious."

"It is. We tracked the money through various accounts. Marcus was taking it out as 'estate expenses:' equipment repairs, maintenance costs, landscaping supplies. Most of it went to covering gambling debts. Online poker, sports betting, casino trips to Cherokee and Tunica."

"So he's also got a gambling problem," I said.

"A significant one. And here's the thing; Augustus discovered it last week."

"How do you know?"

Jack pulled up email exchanges. "Augustus sent Marcus an email last Wednesday. Very direct, very cold. He'd done his own audit of the estate accounts, found the discrepancies, and confronted Marcus. The email gives Marcus thirty days to repay the full fifty thousand dollars, or Augustus would fire him and press criminal charges."

"Thirty days?" Corbin said. "That's impossible for someone who's already in debt."

"Exactly," Jack replied. "Marcus responded, admitted the embezzlement, said he'd made mistakes but would find a way to repay. But there's no way he could come up with fifty thousand dollars in a month. Not legitimately."

I leaned back in my chair and stared at the two as yet to be filled white boards, processing it. Marcus Webb had a powerful motive. He was facing not just unemployment but criminal charges, prison time, destruction of his reputation. He was a former Army Ranger. He had the skills to plan and execute a murder. He had keys to everything on the estate, access to the library, knowledge of the grounds including where foxglove grew.

I stared at the printout of Webb's service record and imagined the man standing in formation, spine straight, eyes forward, duty drilled into his bones. Discipline could turn to defiance when cornered. Pride could turn lethal.

"Do we know if anyone else knew about the embezzlement?" I asked.

"Not from what we can find," Cooper said. "Augustus's email to Marcus was very private, sent to Marcus's personal email address. There's no indication Augustus told Victoria or anyone else."

"So only Marcus knew he was about to lose everything," Corbin said.

"As far as we can tell, yes."

I stood and walked to one of the whiteboards, picking up a marker. I wrote out the financial motives:

AUGUSTUS IV: $4,450,000 debt, desperate, creditors pressuring

ALLISON: $200K personal debt, expensive lifestyle

MELISSA: Losing $2.4M inheritance if new will signed

GRAHAM: $300K malpractice debt, financial strain

MARCUS WEBB: $50K embezzlement discovered, 30-day ultimatum, facing prison

VICTORIA: $5M personal wealth, financially independent (weak motive)

I stood back, folded my arms and stared at the board. "These are all strong motives," I said, studying the board.

"Any one of them could've decided murder was the solution," Corbin said.

"Not just them," I said. "We also have to consider the cook and the head gardener."

"It could be a conspiracy," Cooper suggested. "Augustus IV and Allison working together. Or Melissa and Graham."

"Possible," I said thoughtfully. "But poisoning is usually a solo act. Too risky to involve someone else. One person plans it, executes it, keeps the secret."

It was at that moment I received a text from Tracy: "Rosa Martinez interview complete. Something you need to hear. Can you come to the estate?"

I showed Corbin the message.

"Let's go," he said.

I turned to Cooper and Jack. "Excellent work on the financials. Write up detailed reports on each family member and Marcus Webb. I want every transaction documented, every debt accounted for. We're building a case here, and I need it airtight."

"You got it," Cooper said.

As Corbin and I and Samson headed for the parking lot, I thought about the web of debt and desperation we'd uncovered. The Aldridge family wasn't old money living comfortably on inherited wealth. They were people drowning in debt, clinging to a lifestyle they couldn't afford, waiting for Augustus to die so they could finally access the money.

And one of them had decided not to wait any longer.

"Twelve million dollars," Corbin said as we got into my Taurus. "That's a lot of motive."

"It is. But here's what bothers me—why Sunday night? Why not months ago, if you're Augustus IV with creditors breathing down your neck?"

"The timing had to matter somehow," he muttered.

"Exactly. Something happened, some trigger that made Sunday night the moment to act. We just have to figure out what."

As Corbin and I stepped out into the fading daylight, the clouds finally broke open, rain striking the pavement in sharp, rhythmic bursts. I tightened my coat and looked toward the river, where the gray water curled like smoke. Somewhere in that mansion, among all those debts and secrets, someone had decided that murder was easier than confession. And I had a feeling the money was only the surface—the rot ran far deeper.

7

The Historical Echo

SOMETHING HAD BEEN NAGGING ME ALL MORNING: THAT SECRET drawer in Augustus' desk and its contents, but mostly the Emily Caldwell folder. *Why would Augustus keep nearly century-old newspaper clippings and police reports about a murder that happened decades before he was born?* I wondered. *And why hide them in a secret compartment?*

The thought stuck to me like smoke I couldn't wave away. The more I tried to focus on the financials, the more that thin folder crept back into my mind — like a whisper from the walls of that house. There was something cold about a secret kept alive for a hundred years. Secrets don't rot; they calcify. They wait.

I'd been staring at the crime scene photos on my whiteboards when the connection hit me. Emily Caldwell died in the Aldridge library. Augustus Aldridge III died in the same library ninety-nine years later. *That couldn't be coincidence, could it?* I frowned at the thought.

Rain streaked down the window behind my desk, the kind of steady drizzle that made everything outside look like it was being washed slowly away. Inside, the light buzzed faintly overhead, reflecting off the laminated photos — two deaths, nearly a century apart, each captured in a frozen frame of ruin. It was like the house itself had a memory.

"Come on, Jack," I said, grabbing my jacket. "We're going to records."

"Oh yeah, why?" he asked, falling into step beside me.

"The original Emily Caldwell murder file from 1925. Augustus had copies of some of the documents, but I want to see the complete case file. I'm thinking that maybe whatever he was researching got him killed, and I need to know why."

The Chattanooga Police Department's records room in the basement smelled like old paper, dust, and forgotten crimes. It was the kind of smell that clung to your clothes, the ghost of a thousand unsolved cases. Rows of boxes stretched away into the shadows, their labels fading, their contents waiting for someone to remember. Jack and I spent the next hour digging through archival boxes dating back to the 1920s, looking for the Emily Caldwell murder file. It was a dirty, nasty job, and I wished I'd bothered to wear a mask. Samson, bless him, decided to stay just outside the door.

"Got it," Jack said, finally, pulling a manila folder from a box labeled "1925 - Unsolved Cases." The folder was thin, barely a quarter-inch thick. For a murder investigation involving prominent families, it seemed suspiciously light, even for those days.

We spread the contents across a table in the records room. Crime scene photographs, yellowed with age. A brief police report. Witness statements. An autopsy report. And not much else.

Emily Caldwell had been twenty-two years old when she died. The photograph showed a beautiful young woman with dark hair, elegant features, and eyes that held intelligence and warmth. She came from a prominent Nashville family—old money, social connections, the kind of background that opened doors in 1920s Tennessee.

I studied her photograph longer than I should have. Time had turned the edges brittle, but her eyes still held light — that kind of open, reckless light that makes people dangerous to those with reputations to protect.

On Saturday, September 18, 1925, Emily attended a party at the Aldridge mansion. It was a lavish affair, celebrating Brigadier General Augustus Aldridge's birthday. The guest list included Chattanooga's social elite: businessmen, politicians, society families.

According to witness statements, Emily had been seen talking with the young Augustus Aldridge II throughout the evening. He was twenty-four, recently returned from university, heir to the Aldridge fortune. Several guests noted they seemed quite friendly, perhaps more than friendly.

The party ended around ten p.m. Most of the guests departed, but Emily stayed behind. Augustus II claimed in his statement that he and Emily talked in the library until approximately eleven p.m., discussing literature and family matters. He said she was alive and well when he left her to retire for the evening.

On Sunday morning at seven o'clock, the housekeeper found Emily's body in the library. She'd been strangled with a drapery cord, her body left on the floor near the desk. The medical examiner estimated time of death between eleven on Saturday evening and two on Sunday morning.

Augustus II was questioned extensively. His story never changed. He left Emily alive at eleven, went to his bedroom, heard nothing unusual during the night. His father, Brigadier General Augustus Aldridge, corroborated the timeline. Several servants provided alibis, though reading between the lines of their statements, I suspected those alibis were coached.

Jack exhaled softly beside me, the sound swallowed by the basement hum. I could almost see the scene playing out in sepia tones — the music fading, guests leaving, a young woman waiting in a room lined with books, unaware she was about to become a footnote. *History isn't written by the victors*, I thought grimly; *it's written by those with the power to erase the rest.*

No arrests were ever made. The investigation lasted about three months before quietly fading away. Both families were prominent, both had social influence, and both apparently wanted the scandal buried.

"This is a thin file for a murder investigation," I said, flipping through the sparse documentation.

"Very thin," Jack agreed. "In 1925, they didn't have our forensic capabilities, but even accounting for that, this feels incomplete. Like someone removed pages."

"Or never wrote them in the first place," I said. "This investigation was buried deliberately."

The file's thinness said more than any report ever could. Paper can lie, but absence never does.

I noticed the similarities immediately. Emily died in the Aldridge mansion library, the same room where Augustus III was murdered ninety-nine years later. Both victims were from wealthy families. Both deaths created potential scandal. Both cases involved the Aldridge family directly.

But there had to be more connecting them than just location and social standing.

I read the ME's report more carefully. Most of it was straightforward: cause of death, strangulation, time of death estimate. But there was a handwritten notation at the bottom of the page, almost an afterthought: "Subject approximately 12-14 weeks pregnant at time of death. Family requested this detail be omitted from public record."

I sat up straighter. "Jack, look at this."

He leaned over, reading the notation. "Emily Caldwell was pregnant."

"Three months pregnant. And both families wanted it kept secret."

A chill prickled the back of my neck. I'd read a hundred autopsy notes, but this one felt personal, like the voice of the dead had reached across time to demand attention.

"If Augustus II was the father—" Jack began.

"Then he had a powerful motive to silence her," I finished. "Especially in 1925. An unmarried pregnancy would've been catastrophic for both families. If Emily was threatening to go public, to demand marriage or financial support—"

"Augustus II or his father might've decided she was too dangerous to let live."

I thought about the general discovering Emily's body at dawn, his cold calculation to protect his son and the family name. About how quickly the investigation was shut down, how thin this file was, how deliberately the pregnancy was hidden.

"This was a cover-up that extended from the crime scene to the police investigation to the public record," I muttered as I continued to read. "Someone with power made sure Emily Caldwell's death was buried along with her secrets."

It made sense now why Augustus III might've been digging into it. Families like the Aldridges live off the illusion of legacy. But legacies built on lies always find ways to come apart. Sometimes they do it violently.

"And ninety-nine years later, Augustus III dies in the same room," Jack said. "Coincidence?"

"Maybe," I said. "Maybe not. Someone in the current case knows about Emily. Someone who cares enough about a century-old murder to kill again."

My thoughts were interrupted by a call from Hawk.

"Captain, you need to get back over here," he said. "Willis and I found something in the library evidence."

I looked at my watch. "Okay. Twenty minutes."

———

TWENTY MINUTES LATER, Corbin and I stood in the evidence processing room. Hawk and Mike Willis had spread crime scene materials across two of the six examination tables: photographs, evidence bags, lab reports.

"So, let's hear it. What've you got?" I asked.

Willis took out two evidence bags. "Augustus's brandy glass and his coffee cup. We tested both for digitalis."

"And?" I prompted.

"As I mentioned in my text," Willis said, "the brandy was heavily contaminated with enough digitalis to kill three people. The coffee, not so much. Which tells us something about timing and opportunity. The coffee was probably used as a backup, should he not drink the brandy. The brandy was obviously intended as the primary weapon."

For a moment, the room seemed to shrink around us. Murder by poison had its own language: patience, precision, detachment. Whoever did this hadn't acted in rage; they'd planned, waited, and poured a dose of death into a bottle like it was routine.

"So the poison was added to the brandy bottle, not the glass," I said.

"Exactly. We tested the bottle. It was also contaminated. When Augustus poured himself a drink Sunday night, he was pouring poison."

Hawk took out a fingerprint analysis reports. "We found Augustus's prints all over the glass and bottle. But there's also a partial print on the bottle that doesn't match Augustus or anyone in our database."

"A partial," I said. "How partial?"

"About forty percent of a thumbprint. Not enough for a CODIS identification, but enough to compare against a known suspect if we bring someone in."

"So if we take our suspects, we can potentially match the killer," Corbin said.

"If the partial is clear enough, yes," Hawk confirmed.

I thought about that. The killer had touched the brandy bottle, left a partial print. They'd been careful but not perfect. They'd made one small mistake that could identify them.

"Anything else?" I asked.

Hawk picked up an evidence bag containing a book— leather-bound, old but well-maintained. "We found this on

Augustus's desk. It was under some papers, but Mike noticed it because it was the only book not on the shelves."

I looked at the title embossed on the cover: "Tennessee Families: A Genealogical History."

"Genealogy," I said.

"Right. And it was left open to a specific page." Hawk carefully took the book from the evidence bag, opened it carefully, and showed me the marked page. "The Caldwell family of Nashville."

I leaned closer, reading the text. It was a detailed family tree dating back to the early 1800s, tracking the Caldwell family's marriages, children, business connections. And there, in a section covering the 1920s, was a brief entry:

Emily Caldwell (1904-1925), daughter of Harrison and Margaret Caldwell. Died tragically at age 22.

"Why was Augustus reading this?" I asked. "Why was he reading about Emily Caldwell the night he died?"

"Maybe he was researching something," Hawk suggested.

I shrugged, then said, "We already know she died ninety-nine years ago, and that she was murdered. What the book means, and the fact that he was reading about the Cadwell family the night he died, we'll probably never know. Is it significant? Perhaps. Let's set it aside for now and concentrate on what we know."

Jack, who'd followed us from the records room, picked up the book and studied the genealogy page. "The Caldwell family was prominent in Nashville. Lots of marriages into other wealthy families, business connections throughout Tennessee. Maybe Augustus was tracking some connection we haven't seen yet."

I shook my head as I thought about Emily's murder all

those years ago, pregnant with an Aldridge child. The crime buried, the pregnancy hidden, the truth erased from public record. And now Augustus III, great-grandson of the general who covered it up, was researching Emily's family the night he was poisoned in the same library where she died.

"Okay, so maybe there is a connection," I said. "Between Emily's murder and Augustus's murder. I just can't see it." And yet, I could feel it; the rhythm of repetition, the same pulse of secrecy running from 1925 to 2024. History wasn't echoing; it was repeating, and someone had decided to make sure it stayed that way.

"Could be coincidence," Willis suggested. "Two murders, same location. Maybe Augustus was just interested in family history. It happens."

"Maybe," I said. But I didn't believe in coincidences, not in murder investigations.

"We need to talk to Dr. Nathaniel Ross," I said. "The family attorney. He's represented the Aldridges for thirty years. If anyone knows the family's secrets, including what really happened in 1925, it's him."

"You think he'll talk?" Corbin asked.

"He'll talk or I'll get a court order compelling him to talk. This is a murder investigation, and attorney-client privilege doesn't protect information about crimes committed before his representation began."

I took out my phone and called Ross's office. His secretary answered, professional and guarded.

"This is Captain Kate Gazzara, Chattanooga Police Department, Major Crimes Unit. I need to speak with Dr. Ross regarding the Augustus Aldridge murder investigation."

"Dr. Ross is with a client, Captain. Can he return your call?"

"No. This is urgent. I need him here at the police department as soon as possible."

"I don't think—"

"No, don't think," I said, cutting her off. "This is not a request. I don't want to have to send officers to bring him in. His choice."

There was a pause. "I'll give him your message."

"Thank you. I appreciate that."

I hung up and looked at my team. "Hawk, Mike, continue processing the evidence. I want every fingerprint analyzed, every trace examined. If there's anything in that library that connects our killer to the crime, we need to find it."

Hawk nodded. Mike didn't answer.

"Jack, I need you to dig deeper into the genealogy records. We know Emily Caldwell's baby couldn't have survived, but maybe there's something else, a connection. Check the hospital records, birth certificates, adoption records, anything from late 1918 through 1927."

"That's going to take time," Jack warned. "Records from 1925 aren't always digitized."

"Then make calls. Visit archives. Do whatever it takes."

"Got it."

Corbin, Samson and I headed back to my office. Through the window, I could see the fire department lot; not the most inspiring sight, but better than a blank wall..

"What are you thinking?" Corbin asked.

"I'm thinking that Augustus III figured something out. He pulled that genealogy book for a reason. He was researching the Caldwell family Sunday night. And that might be what got him killed."

"Or maybe the genealogy book is a red herring," Corbin said, flopping down in a seat at the table. The Emily Caldwell connection might be historical curiosity, nothing more."

"You don't believe that, Corbin," I said. "And neither do I."

My desk phone rang. I almost ignored it, but I didn't, thinking it might be the chief. It wasn't. "Dr. Ross will be there in 30 minutes."

8

The Attorney's Secrets

DR. NATHANIEL ROSS ARRIVED AT THE POLICE DEPARTMENT exactly thirty minutes after his secretary's call, dressed in a charcoal suit that probably cost more than my monthly salary. He was seventy years old, with silver hair, a lawyer's measured bearing, and the kind of dignified presence that came from decades representing wealthy families.

He moved with the calm precision of a man who had spent his life managing other people's chaos. Even his footsteps seemed measured, deliberate; the kind of rhythm that made you think of courtroom clocks and closing statements. The faint scent of expensive cologne lingered as he passed, something understated but unmistakably expensive. People like Ross didn't just wear money; they exhaled it.

I met him in the lobby and escorted him to Interview Room Two. Corbin was already there, notebook ready. Samson settled in his usual corner, watching our visitor with mild interest.

"Dr. Ross," I said as we sat down. "Thank you for coming in."

"Captain Gazzara." His voice was cultured, careful. "I'm happy to help with your investigation, though I must tell you upfront that attorney-client privilege limits what I can discuss."

"I understand. But Augustus Aldridge is dead, and privilege doesn't protect information relevant to his murder."

"I'm aware of the legal boundaries, Captain. I've practiced law for forty-five years."

"Then we shouldn't have any problems," I said. "Tell me about your relationship with Augustus Aldridge III."

Ross settled back in his chair, composing his thoughts. "I've represented the Aldridge family for thirty years. Augustus was meticulous about his legal affairs: estate planning, property matters, business contracts. We spoke regularly, and met quarterly to review his holdings."

"And recently?" I asked.

"We'd been in more frequent contact over the past month. Augustus was reviewing his estate plans and considering changes to his will."

"What kind of changes?"

Ross hesitated. "That falls under attorney-client privilege."

"Not if those changes give someone motive to murder him," Corbin said.

"The changes were never finalized. Augustus died before signing the new will, so legally, it doesn't exist. The current will, dated five years ago, remains in effect."

"But people knew he was planning changes," I said. "Did he tell his family?"

"I can't speak to what Augustus discussed with his family."

I leaned forward. "Dr. Ross, we already know the proposed changes. Augustus wanted to reduce Melissa's inheritance from forty percent to twenty percent. That's two point four million dollars she stood to lose if he signed that new will. So let's not waste time with privilege arguments. Tell me why Augustus wanted to cut his daughter's inheritance in half."

Ross studied me for a long moment, clearly deciding how much to reveal. "Augustus cited spending concerns. He felt Melissa and her husband were living beyond their means, making poor financial decisions. He didn't want to fund what he called 'financial irresponsibility.'"

"What specifically concerned him?"

"Melissa's business expenses, her personal purchases, the second mortgage on their house. Augustus believed she was prioritizing lifestyle over financial security. He hoped reducing her inheritance would force her to develop better habits."

"So this was about teaching her a lesson?" Corbin asked.

"Augustus preferred the term 'financial discipline,'" Ross replied. "He grew up during harder times, built his wealth through careful management. He found it difficult to watch his children squander money."

His tone held no judgment, but there was something cold about the way he said it, as if compassion had long since been traded for habit. People like Ross didn't live in moral gray areas; they navigated them, charging by the hour.

"Did Melissa know about the proposed changes?"

"I don't know. Augustus discussed telling her but wasn't certain if he would. He wanted to finalize his decision first."

"When was he planning to sign the new will?"

Ross shifted slightly. "We were scheduled to meet this

Friday to review the final documents. If Augustus was satisfied, he would have signed then."

Five days after his death. If Melissa knew about the changes, she'd had a very narrow window to stop them.

I jotted a note but my mind drifted. The more I heard about Augustus's meticulous control, the clearer it became that this wasn't just about money. Power was the family's true inheritance, and it never passed hands easily.

"What about Augustus IV?" I asked. "His inheritance wasn't being reduced?"

"Correct. His remained at forty percent. Augustus felt his son needed the financial support, despite his business failures. He believed Augustus IV had learned from his mistakes."

That seemed inconsistent. Reducing Melissa's inheritance for poor financial decisions while maintaining Augustus IV's despite his four and a half million in debt. But families were rarely logical about money.

Corbin scribbled something in his notebook and gave me a look I recognized: that slow, skeptical raise of the brow that meant he was thinking the same thing I was: hypocrisy wrapped in privilege. Families like this didn't make sense unless you stopped trying to apply logic to them. They ran on ego, guilt, and appearances.

"Tell me about Augustus's recent activities," I said. "The past few weeks. Was he researching anything unusual? Asking questions about family history?"

Ross frowned slightly. "Why do you ask?"

"Because we found materials in his desk suggesting he was interested in old family matters. Specifically, events from 1925."

The change in Ross was subtle but unmistakable. His

shoulders tensed, his fingers tightened on the arms of his chair. He knew exactly what I was talking about.

The air in the room changed; a subtle shift, like the pressure drop before a storm. Even Samson lifted his head, sensing it.

"Dr. Ross," I said carefully, "tell me about Emily Caldwell."

He was quiet for several seconds. When he spoke, his voice was measured. "That's ancient history, Captain. It has no relevance to Augustus's death."

"I think that's up to me to decide," I said quietly. "You know the story?"

"I know of it. The Aldridge family has... historical complexities. Emily Caldwell was murdered at the mansion in 1925. It was a tragedy, but it happened nearly a century ago."

The word "tragedy" stuck with me. Tragedy implied accident, inevitability. This wasn't that. This was choice disguised as fate. My stomach turned slightly. Ninety-nine years and the same family still bleeding from the same wound. The sins of the fathers, written in ledgers and wills, never quite erased. He said it like reciting a line from a family prayer, practiced, stripped of emotion. But the pulse in his neck betrayed him, a faint beat of unease under all that polish.

"In the same library where Augustus was murdered," Corbin pointed out.

"A coincidence," he snapped.

"I don't believe in coincidences," I said. "Augustus had files about Emily's death hidden in his desk. He was researching her family the night he died. Why?"

"I don't know. Augustus didn't discuss it with me."

"But you know. Don't you? Tell me what happened."

Ross sighed, clearly uncomfortable. "Emily Caldwell

attended a party at the mansion in September 1925. She stayed late, was found dead the next morning. Strangled. The case was never solved."

"And she was pregnant," I said.

Ross went very still. "Where did you learn that?"

"The medical examiner's report from 1925. Emily was three months pregnant when she died. Both families wanted it kept secret. Why?"

"Captain, this is ancient family business that has nothing to do with—"

"Answer the question, please, Dr. Ross. Why hide the pregnancy?"

Ross's composure cracked slightly. "Because it would have destroyed both families' reputations. Emily was unmarried. Pregnant. In 1925, that was catastrophic. The scandal would have ruined her family and damaged the Aldridges by association."

"Who was the father?"

Ross looked at me directly. "Augustus Aldridge II. The current Augustus's grandfather."

"So Emily was carrying an Aldridge heir," Corbin said.

"She was carrying Augustus II's child, yes. But the baby died with Emily. There was no heir."

My stomach turned slightly. Ninety-nine years and the same family still bleeding from the same wound. The sins of the fathers, written in ledgers and wills, never quite erased.

"Did Augustus II kill her?" I asked.

"I don't know. The case was never solved. Both families wanted it buried, and it was."

"But you have suspicions, don't you?" I asked, leaning back in my chair.

Ross was quiet for a moment, then said, "I've heard stories, family whispers. Whether Augustus II killed Emily himself or his father covered it up, I can't say. But the pregnancy was the motive. Emily wanted Augustus II to marry her. He refused. She threatened to go public, ruin the family reputation. Someone decided she was too dangerous to let live."

"And the killer was never prosecuted," I said.

"No. The case went cold. Both families moved on. Emily was buried in Nashville, the pregnancy hidden, the truth erased."

"Until now," Corbin said. "Until Augustus III started researching what really happened."

Ross looked genuinely confused. "I don't know why Augustus was interested in Emily Caldwell. He never mentioned it to me. As far as I knew, it was old family history, nothing more."

"But Sunday night, hours before he died, Augustus took out a genealogy book and researched Emily's family. He was looking for something. What?"

"I honestly don't know."

I gave him a wry look, studied him carefully. He seemed genuinely puzzled, not defensive. Whatever Augustus had been researching, he hadn't shared it with his attorney.

"Did Augustus have any enemies?" I asked, shifting topics. "Anyone who might want him dead?"

"Augustus was demanding, controlling. He made people uncomfortable. But enemies? I can't think of anyone who'd commit murder."

"What about the staff? Marcus Webb, for instance?"

Ross's expression tightened. "What about Marcus?"

"You know about the embezzlement."

"I do. Augustus discovered financial irregularities three weeks ago. He consulted me about legal options."

"And you advised him to what? Press charges?"

"I advised him to document everything, give Marcus an opportunity to repay, and if Marcus couldn't, then consider criminal charges. Augustus gave Marcus thirty days."

"That's an impossible deadline for someone already in debt," Corbin said.

"Augustus believed in consequences. Marcus made choices, and those choices had repercussions."

"Repercussions that gave Marcus powerful motive for murder," I said.

Ross considered that. "I suppose so. But Marcus has worked for the family for eight years. He's been loyal, competent. Would he really kill over fifty thousand dollars?"

"People have killed for a lot less."

We spent another twenty minutes going through the details: Augustus's relationships with family members, his business dealings, his daily routines. Ross answered carefully, protecting what he could behind privilege, revealing what he couldn't avoid.

Finally, I stood. "Thank you for your cooperation, Dr. Ross. We'll need to speak with you again, I'm sure."

"Of course." He rose, adjusting his suit jacket. "Captain, I hope you understand. The Aldridge family has been through a great deal. Augustus's death is tragic enough without dragging up century-old scandals."

"I'm investigating a murder, Dr. Ross. If century-old scandals are relevant, I'll drag up whatever I need to find the truth."

He nodded stiffly and left.

After he was gone, Corbin closed his notebook. "He's hiding something."

"About Emily Caldwell?"

"About something. He got very uncomfortable when you mentioned her. And his explanation about why Augustus was researching her family didn't make sense. Why would Augustus suddenly care about a murder from 1925?"

"Unless he discovered something that connected past to present," I said. "Some link between Emily's death and current events."

"Like what?"

"I don't know. But Ross knows more than he's telling us. And whatever Augustus found out, it scared someone enough to poison him."

My phone buzzed with a text from Tracy: "The Rosa Martinez interview is done. She's nervous about something, won't say what. Suggested her father Miguel might remember old stories about 1925. Want me to try talking to him?"

I showed Corbin the message.

"Miguel's dementia makes him unreliable," he said. "But if he worked here in the twenties, he might know things the official records don't."

"Have Tracy try," I said. "Even confused memories might give us something."

We went back to my office and I stood before the whiteboard in my office, staring at the list of suspects and motives. Financial desperation, reduced inheritance, embezzlement, forced retirement. All strong motives. But now we had something else: a century-old murder, a hidden pregnancy, and a victim who'd been researching family secrets the night he died.

I turned and looked at the rain-streaked glass, and for a moment I saw my own reflection layered over the whiteboard behind me: suspects, motives, secrets. The lines blurred, past and present overlapping until it was impossible to tell one from the other.

"We're missing something," I muttered. "Some connection between Emily Caldwell and Augustus Aldridge's murder. It's there, I just can't see it yet."

"Maybe Jack will find something in the genealogy records," Corbin said.

"Maybe. Or maybe the answer is right in front of us, hidden in plain sight like that secret drawer in Augustus's desk."

I thought about Emily, strangled in the library while pregnant with an Aldridge child. About Augustus III, poisoned in the same library while researching Emily's family. About ninety-nine years of secrets and lies, of truth buried beneath wealth and social standing.

Someone knows, I thought. *Someone knows what connects those two murders. Someone who carefully planned Augustus's death, administered poison, and walked away believing their secret was safe.*

In the end, I gave it up, sighed, shook my head and said, "Let's go back to the estate. I want to talk to Miguel Martinez. Even if his memories are confused, he might remember something about 1925 that matters now." I looked at my watch. It was almost six and I was bushed, not to mention hungry. "It's late. We'll do it tomorrow morning. I'm going home. C'mon, Sammy."

Corbin grabbed his jacket. "You think he knows who killed Emily Caldwell?"

"I think he might know things that weren't in the official file. And right now, I'll take whatever information we can get."

We headed for the parking lot, Samson padding along beside us. The afternoon sun was starting to fade, the October light turning golden and cool. Somewhere in Chattanooga, a killer was going about their day, believing they'd gotten away with murder.

But the thing about secrets, they never stay buried forever. Sooner or later, the earth shifts, and what's been hidden rises to the surface. The Aldridge legacy wasn't just about wealth; it was about what people would do to protect it. And I had no intention of letting this one fade quietly into history.

think he might know things that weren't in the official
file. And right now I'd like whatever information we can get.

We headed for the parking lot, each spending our own
thoughts as the afternoon sun was starting to fade. The October
light felt like a folder, and soon enough here I was thinking... a
killer was going about their day, believing they'd gotten away
with murder.

But the thing about secrets: they never stay buried forever.
Sooner or later, [they] reach a tipping point, and when they do, it
comes to the surface. The thing is I knew what that meant: we didn't
care about what people would do to protect it, and I had no
intention of letting this one fade quietly into history.

9

The Gardener's Discovery

IT WAS SIX FORTY-FIVE IN THE MORNING, BARELY LIGHT outside, and I'd just poured my second cup of coffee when my phone rang. The caller ID showed an unknown number.

"Captain Gazzara," I answered.

"Captain, this is Rosa Martinez. I need to speak with you." Her voice was tight with tension. "I found something. Something you need to see."

"What kind of something?"

"I can't explain over the phone. Can you come to the estate? Now?"

I looked at my coffee, at Samson sitting hopefully by his food bowl, at the morning that had promised to be quiet. "Not now, Rosa. I'll be there at eight-thirty. Where d'you want to meet?"

"Thank you. I'll meet you at the old carriage house. The one behind the main stables."

She hung up before I could ask more questions.

The kitchen felt suddenly too still. Outside, the sky had that thin pre-dawn color like paper held to a window, and a jay scolded from the oak by the fence. Samson's ears pricked; he didn't know the words, but he knew the tone. Quiet mornings never stayed quiet in my line of work.

I sighed, stared down at my coffee and my half-eaten bagel, then picked up the phone and called Corbin.

———

CORBIN MET me at the estate gates. The morning was cold and gray, October asserting itself with damp air that smelled like coming rain.

A low fog clung to the lawn, blurring the edges of the statues and hedges. The mansion sat back on its rise like a patient thing, watching us arrive. Places like this kept their own weather, and their own memory.

Rosa was waiting by a weathered stone building set back from the main house. The old carriage house had probably been elegant once—now it was just functional, used for storage and equipment. Paint peeled from the wooden doors, and ivy had claimed much of the eastern wall.

"Captain, Sergeant," Rosa said as we approached. She looked like she hadn't slept. "Thank you for coming."

"Thank you for calling, Rosa," I said. "It must have been important. What did you find?"

"My father has been talking about the General's hiding place for years. Ever since his dementia got worse. He'd say the General hid things in the old carriage house, that there were secrets buried there. I thought it was just confused memories, stories mixed up with reality, you know?"

"But?" Corbin prompted.

"But yesterday, after your sergeant asked about the family history and the 1925 murder, I started wondering. What if Papa's stories weren't confused at all? What if he really did know something?"

"So you decided to investigate," I said.

"I followed what I could understand from his directions. He kept saying 'behind the General's horses,' which made no sense to me until I realized this building used to be the main stable. The horses would've been kept here before the current stables were built in the 1950s."

She led us inside. The carriage house was dim, smelling of old wood and dust. Equipment was stored along one wall: lawnmowers, tools, supplies. The other side held old furniture, boxes, things that belonged in an attic.

"There," Rosa pointed to the far corner, where wooden planks formed what looked like a solid wall. "I noticed the dust pattern was wrong. Like someone had disturbed it recently."

I moved closer, pulling out my flashlight. The planks were old but the disturbance was obvious once you looked for it: scratches in the dust, a gap where boards had been moved.

"Have you touched anything?" I asked.

"No. I found this yesterday afternoon. I looked inside just enough to see what was there, then locked it back up and called you first thing this morning."

"Show me, please."

Rosa pushed against a section of planking. It swung inward. It wasn't a wall; it was a door, cleverly disguised to look like the rest of the structure. Behind it was a small room, maybe eight by ten feet. A single window, now boarded over, would've provided light.

Cold air spilled out, carrying the stale breath of decades. My light caught motes turning lazily, as if even the dust hadn't expected company. The silence in that little room had weight; I felt it settle across my shoulders.

I stepped inside carefully, Samson close behind me. He immediately alerted, nose working the air, body tense.

"Someone's been here recently," Corbin said, examining the dust. "Look at the footprints."

He was right. The floor was dusty, but there were clear footprints; recent ones, not decades-old. And in the corner, on a small, rickety table, sat a battery-powered lantern, still working when I clicked it on.

"This has been used in the past week," I said.

The room contained an old wooden desk, a filing cabinet with a broken lock, and some storage boxes. But what caught my attention was the metal box sitting on the desk. It was old but well-maintained, the kind of strongbox people used to store important documents.

I pulled on latex gloves and carefully opened it.

Inside were papers, photographs, letters; all carefully preserved. I lifted out the first item: a leather-bound journal, small and elegant, with "Emily Caldwell" embossed on the cover in faded gold letters.

"Her diary," I said quietly.

Corbin looked over my shoulder as I carefully opened it. The pages were yellowed but readable, filled with elegant handwriting. I flipped through slowly, reading entries from 1925.

April 15, 1925: Augustus is everything I imagined love could be.

He's kind, intelligent, and when he looks at me, I feel like I'm the only person in the world.

June 3, 1925: I haven't told anyone yet, but I'm almost certain. Augustus will be thrilled. We'll have to marry quickly, of course, but his family will understand.

August 12, 1925: I was wrong. He doesn't want to marry me. His father forbids it. Says I'm not suitable, that my family isn't important enough. But I'm carrying his child. Surely that matters?

September 10, 1925: I've made my decision. I'll tell everyone at the birthday party. Augustus can't refuse me then, not in front of all of Chattanooga society. He'll have to do the right thing.

The last entry was dated September 17, 1925—the day before she died.

Tomorrow night at the party, I'll make my announcement. Augustus will be angry at first, but he'll see I'm right. We'll be married before the scandal can ruin either family. Our child deserves a name, a father, a future.

Her words were so alive they felt warm in my hands. Hope has a handwriting; you can see it in the pressure of the pen, in the loops of the letters. Hope also makes people brave, and bravery can be fatal.

I set the diary down carefully. Emily had gone to that party planning to force Augustus II's hand by publicly announcing her pregnancy. She'd believed she could shame him into marriage, save her reputation and their child's future.

Instead, someone had strangled her in the library.

The next documents were letters—correspondence between Augustus Aldridge II and his father, Brigadier General Augustus Aldridge. They were dated September and October 1925.

I read the first one, from Augustus II to his father:

Father, Emily Caldwell threatens to destroy our family. She plans to announce her condition at your birthday celebration, forcing me to acknowledge the child and marry her. I cannot allow this. She is unsuitable, her family inadequate. Please advise how to handle this situation.

The General's response was cold and direct:

Son, the situation will be resolved. Do not concern yourself further. I will ensure Miss Caldwell understands the consequences of her threats. Our family's reputation must be protected at all costs.

There were more letters, increasingly desperate from Augustus II, increasingly cold from the General. And then, dated October 1, 1925—two weeks after Emily's murder—a letter from Augustus II to someone unnamed:

I cannot live with what I've done. Father insists it was necessary, that Emily would have destroyed us all. But I see her face every night. I hear her begging me to stop, feel her struggling as I pulled the cord tight. Father says I saved the family, but I've damned my soul. She was carrying my child. Our child. I murdered them both.

I read it again, carefully. This was a confession. Augustus Aldridge II admitting to strangling Emily Caldwell.

"Holy hell," Corbin said quietly.

The lantern's light trembled, just enough to make the handwriting ripple. I'd taken confessions before, but on paper, it's different. It doesn't bargain, it doesn't cry. It just tells the truth and waits to be believed.

"The family covered it up for ninety-nine years," I said. "The General's son murdered a pregnant woman, and they buried the evidence, paid off investigators, erased the truth."

"But why keep this confession?" Rosa asked. "Why not destroy it?"

"Insurance," I said. "Or guilt. Maybe Augustus II couldn't

bring himself to destroy the evidence, even as he helped cover up the crime."

I continued sorting through the box. There were photographs—Emily and Augustus II together, smiling, clearly in love. Emily alone, beautiful and young, with her whole life ahead of her. The Aldridge family at various occasions, maintaining their wealthy facade while hiding murder.

And then, at the bottom of the box, I found recent documents. Photocopies of genealogy records, birth certificates, marriage licenses. Research notes in handwriting I recognized from Augustus III's desk—meticulous, organized, dated within the past month.

Augustus had been tracking Emily Caldwell's family tree. Not just her immediate family, but extended relatives, marriages into other families, descendants of her siblings. Pages and pages of family connections, branching out through decades, tracing bloodlines through Tennessee and beyond.

"He was searching for Emily's descendants," Corbin said, reading over my shoulder.

"But Emily died pregnant," I said. "Her baby died with her. There are no direct descendants."

"She had siblings though. The diary mentions her brother Harrison. If he had children, they'd be Emily's indirect descendants. Nieces, nephews, their children and grandchildren."

I flipped through the pages. Augustus had been thorough, tracking the Caldwell family through four generations. Birth records, marriage certificates, death records. A complete genealogical study spanning nearly a century.

But the most recent pages were missing. The research

stopped abruptly in the 1990s, as if Augustus had run out of time or deliberately removed the final conclusions.

"He found something," I said. "He traced Emily's family to the present day and found someone. But these pages—the ones that would show who he found—they're not here."

"Removed recently?" Corbin asked, examining the box.

"Maybe. Or Augustus kept them somewhere else. But he was researching Emily's descendants for a reason. He discovered something that connected the past to the present, and that discovery got him killed."

"By someone who didn't want that connection exposed," Corbin said.

"Exactly. Someone who knew about Emily's murder, who had a reason to keep it secret. Someone who had access to this room and removed the final pages of Augustus's research."

Rosa had been quiet during our discussion, but now she spoke. "My father knew about this room. He tried to tell us about the General's hiding place, but we thought it was just the dementia. He remembered. All these years, he remembered the family's secrets."

"Where is Miguel now?" I asked.

"At home in his cottage. He's having a bad day, very confused."

"We'll need to talk to him eventually. Even if his memories are fragmented, he might remember more about 1925 than the official records show."

I carefully photographed every document in the box with my phone, then called Hawk. "I need you and Mike at the Aldridge estate. The old carriage house behind the main stables. We've got a crime scene to process; not the murder scene, but evidence storage. Bring everything you need for a thorough examination."

"On our way," Hawk said.

While we waited for the team, I stood in that small hidden room and thought about secrets buried for almost a century. About Emily Caldwell writing in her diary, hoping to force the man she loved into marriage. About Augustus II strangling her in the library while his father covered up the crime. About Augustus III discovering the truth and researching Emily's descendants for reasons we didn't yet understand.

"Captain," Rosa said hesitantly. "Should I be worried? I found this room. If someone doesn't want these secrets exposed..."

It was a good question. Someone had murdered Augustus to keep something hidden. If that someone knew Rosa had found this evidence, she could be in danger.

"You're staying at the main house for now," I said. "We'll have officers watching the estate. And don't mention this discovery to anyone except the police. Not the family, not the other staff. No one."

"What about my father?"

"He's safe. His confused memories actually protect him— no one takes his stories seriously. But you need to be careful."

Hawk and Mike arrived with their equipment. I briefed them on what we'd found, and they began processing the hidden room. Every surface would be examined for fingerprints, every document photographed and catalogued. If anyone had been here recently—and those fresh footprints suggested someone had—we'd find evidence of it.

Corbin and I headed back to the police department, leaving the crime scene team to work. The morning was fully light now, gray sky promising rain. Chattanooga was waking up, people going about their normal Thursday, unaware that we'd just uncovered evidence of a century-old murder and its connection to our current case.

"We need to figure out who Augustus found," I said as we drove. "He traced Emily's family to someone in the present day. Someone who matters to this case."

"Could be anyone," Corbin said. "Emily's siblings had children, those children had children. We could be looking at dozens of descendants."

"But Augustus focused on someone specific. He removed those final pages from his research—or someone else did. Either way, the identity of Emily's descendant is crucial."

"What if it's not about descendants at all?" Corbin suggested. "What if Augustus was researching something else? Some other connection between Emily's murder and the present?"

"Like what?"

"I don't know. But we're assuming the research was about finding Emily's relatives. Maybe it was about something else entirely."

It was a good point. We were making assumptions based on incomplete evidence. Augustus had been researching Emily's family, but we didn't know why or what he'd discovered.

"We need to get Jack working on the genealogy," I said. "Have him trace Emily's family forward from 1925. See if any descendants connect to our current suspects."

"That could take days," Corbin said.

"Then we work the case from other angles while he's doing it. We've got financial motives, opportunity, access to poison.

The Emily Caldwell connection is important, but it's not the only avenue of investigation."

"What about the fingerprint on the brandy bottle?" Corbin asked.

"We need to get prints from all our suspects. Voluntarily if possible, court order if necessary. If we can match that partial to someone, we've got our killer."

"When do we bring people in for printing?"

"Today. Everyone who had access to the estate Sunday night. Family and staff. We'll tell them it's routine elimination prints for the investigation."

We drove in silence for a few minutes. I thought about Emily's diary, her hope that public announcement of her pregnancy would force Augustus II into marriage. Her miscalculation had cost her life and her unborn child's life. And now, ninety-nine years later, that old crime had somehow triggered a new murder.

"The confession letter proves Augustus II killed Emily," I said. "That's not in question anymore. What we don't know is why that matters now. Why did Augustus III's discovery of that confession lead to his murder?"

"Maybe someone in the current family didn't want it exposed," Corbin suggested. "Even though it happened a century ago, it could still damage the family reputation."

"Enough to commit murder?"

"The Aldridges have spent ninety-nine years maintaining their image. Maybe someone decided protecting that legacy was worth killing for."

It was possible. Victoria was fiercely protective of the family name. Augustus IV and Melissa both benefited from the family's social standing. Even the staff had reasons to protect the Aldridge reputation—their livelihoods depended on it.

But murder to protect a century-old secret seemed like an extreme response. There had to be more to it than simple reputation management.

As the wipers beat a slow rhythm across the windshield, the mansion's silhouette faded in the rearview. Somewhere ahead, the river cut its patient line through the city, indifferent to who lived, who died, and who lied. We weren't just chasing a killer anymore. We were unspooling a story the Aldridges had kept tied in a tight, elegant knot. And knots, I reminded myself, always come loose, especially if you take an ax to them.

10

The Second Victim

"I NEED EVERYONE'S COOPERATION, PLEASE," I SAID, STANDING before the assembled group in the Aldridge mansion's dining room. Augustus IV and Allison, Melissa and Graham Crawford, Victoria, Marcus Webb, Claudia Rivera, and Helen Park. The staff looked nervous. The family looked annoyed. "We're taking elimination fingerprints from everyone who had access to the estate Sunday night."

"Is that really necessary?" Graham asked. "We've already given statements."

"It's routine in a murder investigation," I replied. "We use them for elimination purposes."

"And if we refuse?" Augustus IV said.

"Then I get a court order and we do this the hard way," I replied.

No one refused. Over the next hour, Hawk and Mike Willis methodically fingerprinted each person. Digital scans, ink prints, the full process. Some cooperated without a complaint.

Others, like Marcus Webb, seemed uncomfortable but compliant. Victoria maintained her composed dignity throughout, as if being fingerprinted was just another social obligation.

The dining room's chandelier buzzed faintly, a high electric whine that threaded through the silence. Ink rolled on cards with a slow, sticky whisper; scanners chirped; cuffs of expensive shirts rode up over pale wrists. Nobody looked anyone else in the eye for long. The air smelled of lemon polish and nerves.

By noon, we had complete sets of prints from everyone. Now it was just a matter of comparing them to the partial print on the brandy bottle. If we got a match, we had our killer. If we didn't, it was back to square one.

———

SATURDAY MORNING, I was in my office drinking my second cup of coffee when my desk phone rang.

"Captain Gazzara? This is Officer Davis at the front desk. There's a very agitated gentleman here. He says his name is Miguel Martinez. He's asking for you. He says something happened to his daughter."

"Send him up."

Miguel appeared five minutes later, escorted by Davis. The old man looked terrified and confused, his eyes darting around my office. He was speaking rapidly in Spanish, occasionally switching to English.

"Mi hija, mi Rosa. She went back. She went back to the hiding place. Something's wrong. I can feel it."

I pulled out a chair for him. "Mr. Martinez, please sit

down. Tell me what you know."

"Rosa called me Wednesday night. She was excited, said she'd found something else in the General's hiding place. Something important. She was going to check it again Thursday evening after work."

"Did she say what she found?"

"No. Just that it was important. That someone needed to know." Miguel's hands shook. "She didn't come home Thursday night. I waited. I thought maybe she stayed with a friend. But Friday, still nothing. And I keep having this feeling, this terrible feeling."

"Mr. Martinez, did Rosa mention meeting anyone Thursday evening?"

"She said... she said someone was asking questions. About the old days. About the hiding place." His face crumpled. "I should have warned her. But my mind, it gets confused. I can't remember right."

"Who was asking questions?"

"I don't... I can't remember." He looked at me with desperate eyes. "Please find my Rosa."

His jacket smelled like fertilizer and rain. It made the room feel smaller. Samson rose to his feet and pressed a warm head to Miguel's knee; the old man's fingers found the dog's ruff and steadied.

I called Tracy and Hawk. "Get a team to the Aldridge estate. The old carriage house, the hidden room, and search the surrounding woods. Rosa Martinez went back there Thursday evening and never came home. Miguel thinks she found something."

Within an hour, we'd assembled a full search team. Miguel

insisted on coming despite his confusion, saying he could help find his daughter.

We started at the hidden room in the carriage house. It looked exactly as we'd left it—except the metal box was slightly ajar, as if someone had gone through it recently. I turned Samson loose and he immediately began to search the place.

"She came back here," I said. "Miguel was right."

Almost immediately, Samson picked up a scent, leading us out of the carriage house and into the woods beyond. The rain had stopped, but the ground was soft and muddy. We followed Samson through overgrown paths, deeper into the estate's wooded area.

The timbered ravine breathed out cool air. Wet leaves slicked underfoot, and somewhere a woodpecker hammered a slow, morbid beat. Samson's tail dropped to a level line—his working posture—and the team fell quiet in that collective way cops do when the world is about to change.

Two hundred yards from the carriage house, Samson stopped, whining, looking down into a ravine.

I saw her jacket first; bright orange, partially hidden by brush. Then I saw Rosa.

She was lying at the bottom of the ravine, twenty feet down, her body partially covered by leaves and branches. Even from above, I could see she wasn't moving.

"Call Doc Sheddon," I said quietly. "And get a recovery team."

It took forty minutes to safely retrieve Rosa's body. Miguel waited at the top of the ravine, held back by officers, weeping quietly. By the time Doc arrived, we'd secured the scene and documented everything.

Rosa Martinez was dead. The back of her skull showed obvious trauma: blunt force, significant. She'd been killed somewhere else and her body had been dragged to and dumped in the ravine, an attempt to hide her in the isolated woods.

"Time of death?" I asked Doc.

He gave me one of his looks, then examined her carefully. "Based on the liver temperature, rigor, and decomposition, approximately forty-eight hours. Thursday evening between six and eight p.m."

"Cause of death?"

"Blunt force trauma to the posterior skull. Single blow, possibly with a rock or heavy object. Death would've been relatively quick, but she was conscious when struck. There are defensive wounds on her hands that suggest she saw it coming and tried to protect herself."

Unlike Augustus's calculated poisoning with its careful planning and sophisticated method, this was violent and immediate. Someone had hit Rosa hard enough to kill her, dragged her body into the woods and threw her body into the ravine.

"This is different from the first murder," Corbin said.

"Very different," I agreed, thoughtfully.

"Or perhaps she arranged to meet someone here," Doc suggested. "The location is isolated. No one would see or hear anything."

We searched the immediate area. Hawk found Rosa's phone about fifteen feet from where her body lay; smashed deliberately, screen shattered, casing cracked.

"Someone didn't want us reading her messages," Hawk

said, carefully bagging the phone. "But Jack might be able to recover data from it."

Near the phone, Mike Willis found something else: a small jewelry box, old and tarnished, lying in the mud. It was open, and empty.

"This wasn't there when we processed the hidden room," Willis said. "Rosa must have taken it with her Thursday evening."

"Bag it," I said. "Maybe we'll get prints."

We expanded the search, looking for the murder weapon, any other evidence. But the rain had washed away much of what might have been there. No footprints, no blood trail, nothing that would tell us who'd killed Rosa Martinez.

From the ridge, the mansion's slate roof flashed dully between the trees, indifferent as a closed eye. Two murders in four days.

By late afternoon, we'd transported Rosa's body to the medical examiner's office and Miguel to his cottage, where Claudia Rivera promised to stay with him. The old man had collapsed after seeing his daughter's body, his already-fragile mind shattered by grief.

Back at the police department, Jack North was working on Rosa's damaged phone. The screen was destroyed, but the internal memory appeared to be still intact.

"How long?" I asked.

"Give me a few hours. If the chip survived, I can pull data. Messages, photos, call logs."

While Jack worked, I sat in my office with Corbin, staring at the whiteboards. We now had two victims: Augustus Aldridge III, carefully poisoned in his library, and Rosa Martinez, violently killed in the woods. And I was sure both murders connected to Emily Caldwell's century-old secret.

"Rosa found something," I said. "Something in that hidden room that we missed. Something important enough to kill for."

"The jewelry box," Corbin said. "It was empty when we found it, but Rosa took it Thursday evening. What was inside?"

"That could be what got her killed," I replied. "Whatever was in that box, someone didn't want it exposed."

It was at that moment Jack called. "Captain, I pulled data from Rosa's phone. You need to see this."

We went down to Jack's workspace. He'd connected Rosa's phone to his computer, bypassing the broken screen to access the memory.

"I recovered her messages," Jack said. "Last text she sent was Thursday at five forty-seven p.m." He pulled it up on his screen.

The message read: *Found something else in the chamber. Need to show you. Can you meet me there at 6?*

"Who did she send it to?" I asked.

"Unknown number. I traced it, but it's a burner phone, purchased with cash in Chattanooga three weeks ago. Activated the day it was purchased, used sporadically since then. No way to trace the buyer."

"Someone bought that burner before Augustus's murder," Corbin said.

"Did the recipient respond?" I asked.

"No. Rosa's text went unanswered," Jack replied.

"So either they saw the message and ignored it," I murmured, "or they saw it and went to meet her."

Jack pulled up another file. "There's more. Rosa took several photos Thursday evening, right before she sent that text. Look at this."

He displayed a photo on his screen. It showed the metal box we'd found in the hidden room, but Rosa had photographed something we'd missed; a small jewelry box. She'd photographed it open.

Inside the jewelry box was a document. It looked like an official certificate of some kind, old and yellowed. The photo was slightly blurred, taken quickly in dim light with one hand while holding a flashlight with the other.

"Can you enhance this?" I asked.

Jack worked on the image, adjusting contrast and sharpness. The document became clearer. I could make out "State of Tennessee" at the top and what looked like an official seal. The format was distinctive.

"That's a birth certificate," Corbin said.

"From the size and style, probably from the 1920s or 1930s," Jack added. "But the names are too blurred to read. Rosa's camera was focused on the jewelry box, not the document inside. I can see there's text, but I can't make out what it says."

"So Rosa found a birth certificate hidden in that jewelry box," I said. "A certificate important enough that Augustus kept it locked away with Augustus II's confession. And important enough that someone killed Rosa to get it back."

"Whose birth certificate was it, I wonder?" Corbin asked.

"That's the question," I said. "Emily died in 1925. If this is from the twenties or thirties, it could be related to her family, her siblings' children, or—" I paused, thinking. "Or it could prove someone's real identity. Someone who's connected to this case now."

"I guess the killer took it when they murdered Rosa," Jack said. "Whatever was on that certificate, they couldn't risk us finding it."

I stared at the blurry image, frustrated. A birth certificate proving someone's connection to Emily Caldwell or revealing a secret identity. It could be the key to this entire case, and we couldn't read it.

"We need to figure out whose certificate this was," I said. "Rosa saw it clearly enough to think it was important. She texted someone about it; someone she thought would care or need to know. That someone is our killer."

"So what's our next move?" Corbin asked.

"We need that fingerprint analysis from the brandy bottle. If it matches anyone we printed this morning, we make an arrest. And we need to identify who bought that burner phone. Do we know where it was purchased? There could be security footage."

My phone buzzed again with a text from Hawk: "Preliminary fingerprint results. Need to discuss. Can you come to the lab?"

"Let's go," I said to Corbin.

As we headed for the forensics lab, I thought about Rosa Martinez. She'd been smart, dedicated, observant. She'd found Augustus II's confession and reported it to us properly. Then she'd gone back, found something else, and made the fatal mistake of texting someone she trusted.

That trust had gotten her killed.

And now we had two bodies, a century-old secret, and a killer who'd murdered twice to keep the truth hidden.

But there were clues. We needed to find out what was in that jewelry box, and who Rosa had trusted enough to meet that Thursday evening.

In the corridor outside the lab, the vending machine hummed and the fluorescents flickered. Somewhere down the hall a printer started up; paper feeding, facts becoming ink. I touched the brandy-bottle case file under my arm. One print, one face, and the whole story might finally stop whispering and start talking.

11

Dead Ends and Secrets

HAWK WAS WAITING IN THE FORENSICS LAB WHEN CORBIN AND I arrived, surrounded by fingerprint analysis reports and comparison charts spread across two tables. His expression told me everything before he said a word.

"No match," he said.

I'd been hoping for better news. "The partial print from the brandy bottle doesn't match anyone we printed?"

"Correct. I ran it against all the elimination prints we took —family members, staff, everyone. No match." Hawk pulled up comparison images on his computer. "The partial is about forty percent of a thumbprint. That's enough to exclude people definitively, but not enough for a positive identification through CODIS."

"So either the print is too degraded to match," Corbin said, "or the killer is someone we haven't printed yet."

"Or the print isn't the killer's at all," I added. "It could belong to anyone who handled that bottle at any time. A guest, a delivery person, someone who touched it weeks ago."

"The bottle was in Augustus's private collection," Hawk said. "Limited access. But you're right; we can't prove the print belongs to the killer."

I stared at the enhanced image of the partial print. It was tantalizingly close to being useful but ultimately told us nothing.

The lab was quiet... no, it hummed: the fume hood, the refrigerator compressors, the whisper of the air system. Monitors washed our faces in cold light. On the wall clock, the second hand kept its steady climb, seemingly indifferent to our lack of answers.

"What about the jewelry box Rosa found?" I asked. "Any prints on that?"

"Multiple prints, all degraded by rain and mud. I pulled partials from at least three different people, but none match our database or the elimination prints. Without better samples, I can't identify who touched that box."

Another dead end. Rosa had found a birth certificate that could solve this case, and the killer had taken it. The empty jewelry box gave us nothing.

"Keep working on it," I said. "If you can enhance any of those partials, do it. We need something."

"I'll do what I can," Hawk said.

JACK HAD MADE some progress on the burner phone, but it wasn't helpful.

"The phone was purchased at the Walmart on Gunbarrel Road," Jack said, pulling up his research. "Three weeks ago, October second. Paid cash, no name required for burner phones. I pulled security footage from that day."

He played the video on his screen. The timestamp showed 2:47 PM on October 2. A figure approached the electronics counter, selected a burner phone from the display, and paid cash at the register. The figure wore a dark hoodie, the hood pulled up obscuring their face. Average height, average build, baggy clothes that hid body shape. It could've been male or female, young or old. The footage quality wasn't good enough to see details.

"Can you enhance it?" I asked.

"I've tried. The angle is wrong, the hood shadows the face, and the person kept their head down. They knew there were cameras and how to avoid them."

"So all of this was pre-planned," Corbin said. "Three weeks before Augustus's murder, someone bought a burner phone specifically to avoid being traced."

"Premeditation," I agreed. "No, this wasn't spontaneous. Someone with a motive planned Augustus's death weeks in advance."

"Or maybe they were planning something else and adapted the plan," Jack suggested. "We don't know the phone was purchased specifically for this murder. Could've been for any number of reasons."

"But Rosa texted that number Thursday evening," I said, "and shortly after, she was dead. So whoever bought that phone is connected to her murder, even if they didn't originally buy it for that purpose."

Jack pulled up phone records. "The burner was activated October second, same day it was purchased. Since then, it received eleven text messages and made seven calls. All to regular phones, nothing suspicious. Mostly brief exchanges: 'Running late,' 'See you at 6,' that kind of thing. Normal communication."

"Who were they texting and calling?"

"I'm still working on that. But here's what's interesting: the pattern of use suggests someone maintaining a normal relationship. Not criminal activity, not obviously hiding something. Just... regular communication with someone."

"Someone having an affair?" Corbin suggested.

"Possibly. Or someone who wanted a private line for legitimate reasons. The content of the messages doesn't suggest anything illegal. And don't forget, whoever it is didn't reply to Rosa's text. That's also significant. Maybe whoever it was didn't want to get involved in whatever it was Rosa was up to."

The words 'up to' lingered. In my head I heard Rosa's final text again: six o'clock, the hidden room, a promise of truth. And I pictured a thumb hesitating over a screen before deciding not to answer. I shook my head and took a deep breath as I thought about that timeline. Someone bought a burner phone three weeks ago for unknown reasons. They used it normally, maintaining some kind of relationship or contact that they wanted to keep private. Then Rosa found something in the hidden room, texted that number saying she needed to meet, and was murdered.

Either Rosa had texted the killer directly, I thought, *trusting them enough to arrange a meeting. Or Rosa had texted someone connected to the killer, and that person had alerted them... Or not! Geez!*

"Keep tracing those numbers," I said. "I want to know everyone that burner phone contacted. One of them might lead us to the killer."

"I'm on it," Jack said.

BY MONDAY AFTERNOON, we'd brought several people back in for follow-up interviews. Rosa's murder had changed the investigation. We now had two victims and a century-old secret that had apparently triggered both deaths.

The hallway to Interview Room Two smelled of old coffee. Through the one-way glass the room looked like a stage set: a table, three chairs, a pitcher of water nobody ever drank.

Marcus Webb sat across from me in Interview Room Two, looking exhausted. The estate manager hadn't slept well since Rosa's body was found, and it showed. His hands trembled slightly as he answered questions.

"Mr. Webb, tell me about Thursday evening," I said. "October seventeenth. Where were you between six and eight p.m.?"

"At the estate. I was in my office doing paperwork until about seven, then I went to my cottage."

"Anyone see you?"

"Claudia came by around six-thirty to ask about next week's schedule. We talked for maybe ten minutes."

"And after that?"

"I was alone. I worked until seven, then walked to my cottage. Made dinner, watched TV, went to bed around ten."

"Did you see Rosa Martinez that evening?"

Marcus hesitated. "No. I knew she'd called in sick Friday, but I didn't see her Thursday."

"You hesitated," Corbin noted. "Why?"

"Because I..." Marcus rubbed his face. "I did see her, actually. Earlier, around five-thirty. She was heading toward the old carriage house carrying something. I thought it was odd because she wasn't on duty, but I didn't think much of it at the time."

"You didn't mention this before," I said.

"I didn't remember until you asked. I've been stressed, with everything happening. My mind isn't processing things clearly."

"What was Rosa carrying?"

"I don't know. Something small, maybe a box or bag. I only saw her from a distance."

I studied Marcus carefully. He was nervous, hiding something. But was he hiding involvement in Rosa's murder, or something else?

"Mr. Webb, we know about the embezzlement," I said quietly.

His face went pale. "I've been paying it back. I have a plan—"

"Augustus discovered you'd stolen fifty thousand dollars. He gave you thirty days to repay or face criminal charges. That's a powerful motive for murder."

"I didn't kill him!" Marcus's voice cracked. "Yes, I embezzled money. Yes, I was desperate. But I didn't poison Augustus. I couldn't."

"You're former military," Corbin said. "Army Ranger. You have skills most people don't."

"Skills for combat, not murder. I made mistakes with the estate accounts, but I'm not a killer."

"Where were you Sunday night?" I asked. "The night Augustus died."

"In my cottage. Alone. I know that's not an alibi, but it's the truth. I was drinking, trying to figure out how to come up with fifty thousand dollars in a month. I passed out around midnight."

"Anyone see you?"

"No."

"So," I said, leaning back in my chair and folding my arms, "you have no alibi for Augustus's murder. No alibi for Rosa's murder. You have motive, military skills. It's not looking good for you, Mr. Webb."

He just sat there staring at me, his eyes watering. I almost felt sorry for him. Something about his fear felt genuine. He was terrified, desperate, clearly hiding something. But murder? I didn't know.

"Don't leave town," I said. "We'll have more questions."

AUGUSTUS IV WAS NEXT. He arrived with Allison, both of them dressed expensively but looking strained. The debt was crushing them, and it showed in their tense faces and clipped answers.

Allison's perfume hit first—sharp, citrusy—then the papery scratch of Augustus smoothing a cuff as if neatness could pass for control.

"This is harassment," Augustus IV said as he sat down. "You've already questioned us multiple times."

"Your father was murdered," I said. "His estate manager's daughter was murdered. I'll question you as many times as necessary."

"We had nothing to do with Rosa's death. We barely knew her."

"But you knew about the hidden room in the carriage house," Corbin said. "Rosa found evidence there. Evidence that got her killed."

"What evidence?" Allison asked.

"That's what we're trying to determine," Corbin said. "Did either of you go to the estate Thursday evening?"

"No," Augustus said. "We were home."

"Together?"

"Yes. We had dinner, watched a movie, went to bed."

"What movie?" I asked.

Augustus hesitated. "I don't remember the title. Some thriller on Netflix."

"You don't remember what you watched three days ago?"

"We watch a lot of movies. They blur together."

I made a note. His alibi was weak, depending entirely on Allison to corroborate. And given their financial situation, they both had motive to want Augustus III dead.

"Tell me about your father's will," I said.

"What about it?"

"He was planning to change it. Reduce Melissa's inheritance, maintain yours at forty percent. That's almost five million dollars you stood to inherit once he signed the new will."

"I didn't know about the will changes until after he died," he insisted.

"Really? Your father never mentioned he was meeting with his attorney, making changes to his estate planning?"

"He kept his financial matters private."

"But you knew you were in his will. You knew you'd inherit millions when he died."

"Of course I knew. But I didn't kill him for it," he snapped.

"You're four and a half million dollars in debt," Corbin said. "Some of that debt is to questionable creditors who don't take 'no' for an answer. Your father refused to help you. His death solves all your financial problems."

Augustus' jaw tightened. "I didn't kill my father."

"Where were you Sunday night between nine and midnight?"

"I already told you. Allison and I attended a charity function, then came home."

"What time did you leave the function?"

"Around eleven."

"Witnesses say you left earlier," I said, watching his reaction. "Around nine-thirty. You said you felt ill, went to the car. Allison stayed until after eleven."

Augustus glanced at Allison, panic flashing across his face. She looked away.

"I..." he stammered. "Yes, I remember now. I did leave early. I felt sick, went outside for air."

"But you didn't go home, did you?" I said. "Where did you go?"

"I drove around. I needed to clear my head. Then I went to a bar. I needed a drink"

What bar?" Corbin asked.

"I... The Big River Grille. I was stressed. The debt, my

father's attitude, everything. I had a drink. I don't know what time it was when I drove home."

"So you have no alibi for the time window when your father was poisoned," Corbin said.

"I didn't kill him!" Augustus stood abruptly. "Yes, I'm in debt. Yes, I lied about leaving the party early. But I didn't poison my father. I couldn't do that. I... loved him, believe it or not."

"Sit down, Mr. Aldridge," I said quietly.

He sat, shaking with anger or fear. Allison reached for his hand, but he pulled away.

I watched him for a moment, then inwardly shook my head. "We're done for now," I said. "But don't leave Chattanooga. We'll have more questions."

AFTER THEY LEFT, Corbin and I returned to my office. The whiteboard was filling with notes, connections, timelines. Two murders, multiple suspects, everyone hiding something.

A storm was stacking up in the west; through the window the light went pewter, and the buzz of the fluorescent light seemed to get louder.

"Marcus Webb has motive, no alibi and possibly opportunity," Corbin said. "Augustus has motive, a questionable alibi, and opportunity. Melissa stands to lose millions if the will changes. Graham Crawford was helpful but married into the family under circumstances we still don't fully understand. Even Victoria could've poisoned her husband; they slept in separate rooms, she had access to everything."

"Everyone's guilty of something," I said.

"Two murders," Corbin said, staring at the photos on the board. "Augustus and Rosa."

"Same killer?" I muttered.

"Has to be; doesn't it?" He replied, his eyes not leaving the board. "If Rosa found something that connected to Augustus's murder, the killer couldn't risk her revealing it, right?"

I stared at the crime scene photos. Augustus in his library, Rosa in the ravine. Different methods, different locations, but connected by Emily Caldwell's century-old secret, or were they? Maybe I was obsessing over the century-old murder. After all, nine times out ten, money is the motive for murder. I cleared my head.

"The birth certificate," I said. "That's the key. I'm sure of it. Rosa found a birth certificate in that box. Someone's birth certificate from the 1920s or 1930s. It proved something the killer couldn't allow to be exposed."

"And we've no idea whose it is," Corbin stated.

"Right. But someone connected to this case has a secret about their identity or their family history. A secret worth killing twice to protect."

I was about to get up when Chief Johnston called.

"Kate, how's the investigation progressing?"

"Slowly, Chief. We've got multiple suspects, all with motive, but nothing concrete yet."

"The media is asking questions about Rosa Martinez's murder. They're connecting it to Augustus Aldridge, speculating about a serial killer targeting the estate."

"It's not a serial killer," I replied, testily. "I think it's connected to the family's history."

"Can you prove that?" he asked.

"Not yet. But I will."

"Keep me updated. The mayor's office is pressing me."

"I understand."

After hanging up, I turned back to the whiteboard. Somewhere in this tangle of motives, alibis and hidden secrets was the truth. Someone had carefully planned Augustus's murder, bought a burner phone weeks in advance, administered digitalis in brandy, and walked away clean. Then, when Rosa threatened to expose them, they'd killed again, violently, spontaneously, desperately.

Two different methods, two different mindsets. The first murder was calculated and patient. The second was panicked and brutal. *Two different killers?* I wondered. It was possible, but I didn't think it likely.

"We needed to find out whose birth certificate it is," I said. "That's how we identify the killer."

"Tough to do without the actual certificate?" Corbin muttered.

"We figure out who it could've been," I said. "Who in our suspect pool has a secret about their birth or identity? Who might have a forged certificate, or an adoption record, or a family history they're desperate to hide?"

I thought about our suspects. Marcus Webb, former military, embezzler. Augustus IV, drowning in debt with a weak alibi. Melissa, facing reduced inheritance. Graham Crawford, surgeon who married into the family. Victoria, protecting family secrets. *Helen Park, the cook. We're forgetting about her.*

"Tomorrow we start digging into the background checks," I said. "Birth certificates, adoption records, family histories. Someone in this case isn't who they claim to be. And when we find out who, we find our killer."

Corbin nodded. "What about tonight?"

I looked at my watch. It was after seven. I'd been working for twelve hours straight, and exhaustion was starting to cloud my thinking.

"Tonight I go home, feed my dog, and try to remember what sleep feels like. This case will still be here tomorrow."

"Good plan," he replied with a grin.

On my way out, I killed the office lights. The whiteboards glowed for a moment—names, arrows, dates—then sank into darkness. Samson's nails clicked a steady rhythm down the hallway. The day was over, and I was glad of it.

12

Alibis Crumble

TRACY RAMIREZ KNOCKED ON MY OFFICE DOOR AT EIGHT-thirty the following morning, holding a notebook filled with interview notes. She looked tired but energized.

"I've got news on Augustus IV's alibi," she said.

A cool front had pushed through overnight; the window rattled once in its frame and the air smelled faintly of wet leaves from the firehouse lot. Samson thumped his tail without lifting his head.

I waved her in. Corbin was already there, working through the background check requests we'd filed the day before. Samson was on his bed under the window looking thoroughly bored. We needed to get out and about.

"What'd you find?" I asked.

Tracy flipped open her notebook. "I spoke with twelve attendees from the charity function Sunday night. Every single one confirms seeing Allison Aldridge there until well after eleven p.m. She was actively socializing, participating in the silent auction, very visible."

"And Augustus IV?"

"Ah, now that's the thing. Multiple witnesses confirm he was there early in the evening, but that he left around nine-thirty. He told Allison he felt ill, was going to the car to rest. He told her to stay, enjoy the event, and get a ride home with friends."

"So Allison covered for him in our initial interviews," Corbin said.

"She did. I pressed her on it yesterday. She admitted she was embarrassed by the social faux pas: her husband abandoning her at a charity function. So when we asked about their alibi, she said they were together all evening. Easier than explaining he left her there."

I thought about Augustus's nervous demeanor during our interview. He'd lied about leaving early, only admitting it when we confronted him with witness statements.

Lies have a particular aftertaste: tinny, like blood on a split lip. Once you've heard enough, you can pick them out of any crowd.

"What about his claim that he went to a bar after driving around?" I asked.

"I checked. He said he went to Big River Grille, had a drink and then drove home. The bar manager remembers someone matching Augustus's description—tall, well-dressed, clearly upset about something. Confirms he was there from approximately eleven p.m. until just after midnight."

"Which gives him an alibi from eleven to midnight," I said, "but leaves nine-thirty to eleven completely unaccounted for."

"Ninety minutes," Corbin said. "That's more than enough

time to drive to the estate, poison his father, and leave before Augustus died."

Tracy nodded. "There's more. I pulled his credit card receipts. He bought gas at the Pilot station on Shallowford Road at ten-fifteen Sunday night."

I looked at the map on my whiteboard. "That's near the estate. He could've been driving from there back toward downtown."

"Or he could've been fueling up before driving around aimlessly like he claimed," Tracy said. "But combined with the timeline gap, it's suspicious."

"Very suspicious," I agreed. "A man four and a half million dollars in debt, whose father refused to help him, who had ninety unaccounted for minutes during the window his father was poisoned. That's not just suspicious; that's probable cause."

We were interrupted when Jack North called with the DNA results.

"Captain, I've got results on the comparison you requested."

My pulse quickened. "Augustus IV?"

"Yes. I ran his DNA profile against the family samples we collected. The results are... not what we expected."

"Tell me."

"Augustus IV is not Augustus III's biological son. No genetic relationship whatsoever. I ran it three times to be sure."

I felt the case shift beneath me. "You're certain?"

"Absolutely. Augustus IV shares no DNA markers with Augustus III. They're not related."

"What about Victoria?"

"I don't have her DNA for comparison. She refused to provide a sample, citing medical privacy. But based on family genealogy and the samples I do have, if Augustus IV isn't related to Augustus three, he's likely not Victoria's biological child either."

"He's adopted," I said.

"Or switched at birth, or the product of an affair. Whatever the explanation, Augustus Aldridge IV is not the biological son of Augustus Aldridge III."

After hanging up, I looked at Corbin and Tracy. "We need to bring Augustus IV back in. And this time, we need Victoria too."

TWO HOURS LATER, Augustus IV sat in Interview Room One, looking pale and defensive. We'd asked him to come in alone; no Allison, no attorney yet. He'd agreed, probably thinking cooperation would help his case.

"Mr. Aldridge," I began carefully, "we've received DNA test results from the medical examiner's office."

His face went blank. "DNA results? Why would you test my DNA?"

"Routine in murder investigations involving family members. We need to establish biological relationships, rule out various scenarios."

"And?"

"The results show you're not Augustus Aldridge III's biological son."

The silence in the room was absolute. Augustus IV stared at me, mouth slightly open, not comprehending.

"That's... that's impossible," he said finally. "I'm their son. I have a birth certificate. Baby pictures. I grew up in that house."

"The DNA doesn't lie," Corbin said. "You share no genetic markers with Augustus III. You're not biologically related to him."

"Then the test is wrong. Run it again."

"We ran it three times. Same results."

Augustus IV's hands started shaking. "I don't understand. My mother, my father, they raised me. I'm their son."

"You're the son they raised," I said gently. "But you're not their biological child. Did you know you were adopted?"

"I wasn't adopted! I've seen my birth certificate. Victoria Aldridge gave birth to me at Erlanger Hospital on March 15, 1982. I've seen the hospital records, the photos from the day I was born. This doesn't make sense."

But it was starting to make sense to me. Victoria's fierce protection of family secrets. Augustus III's research into Emily Caldwell's descendants. The will change that would disinherit Augustus IV. It was all connected to a secret that had been hidden for forty-two years.

"We need to speak with your mother," I said. "Victoria needs to explain this."

VICTORIA ALDRIDGE ARRIVED an hour later with Dr. Nathaniel Ross at her side. She looked composed as always, but there was something fragile beneath the surface. She knew why we'd called her in.

Ross positioned himself a precise chair's width from her shoulder; the legal equivalent of a shield.

"Mrs. Aldridge," I said once we were seated in Interview Room Two, "we have DNA evidence showing Augustus IV is not your husband's biological son."

Ross started to object, but Victoria raised her hand, silencing him.

"I know," she said quietly.

Augustus IV, who'd been brought into the room to hear this, looked at his mother in shock. "You knew?"

"I've always known," Victoria said. "I'm sorry, Augustus. I'm so sorry."

"What are you talking about?" His voice cracked. "How could you know? You're my mother. You gave birth to me."

Victoria's composure finally broke. Tears formed in her eyes, though she didn't let them fall. "I didn't give birth to you, Augustus. I gave birth to a son, but he was stillborn. March 15, 1982. I held him for a few minutes, and then he was gone."

The room went silent except for Augustus IV's sharp intake of breath.

"Your father was away on business," Victoria continued. "I was alone, devastated, broken."

"Then who am I?" Augustus IV whispered.

"You're Sarah Caldwell's son. She was my best friend, had been for years. She was unmarried, pregnant, desperate. She came to see me at the hospital two days after I lost my baby. She'd just given birth to you at a different hospital, and she couldn't keep you. She was alone, no family support, no money. She begged me to help her."

"So you took her baby," I said. "You took Augustus... him, and raised him as your own."

"Yes. Sarah and I made an arrangement. I would raise you as my son, give you everything: family, wealth, security. Sarah would remain in your life as 'Aunt Sarah,' someone who visited regularly but never revealed the truth. Your father never knew. I told him you were born while he was away, showed him the birth certificate I'd had falsified. He believed you were his son."

"You... You... You," Augustus IV said, his voice breaking. "My entire life is a lie."

"I loved you," Victoria said fiercely. "From the moment Sarah placed you in my arms, I loved you as my own. You are my son in every way that matters."

"Except biologically," Corbin said. "Except legally. Except when it comes to inheriting the Aldridge estate."

Victoria's face hardened. "Augustus found out. Three weeks ago. He'd been researching Emily Caldwell's descendants, trying to trace her family line. He found records showing Sarah Caldwell had given birth to a son in 1982. He confronted me, demanded the truth. I told him everything."

"How did Sarah Caldwell connect to Emily?" I asked.

Victoria took a shaky breath. "Sarah was Emily's sister's granddaughter. Her older sister, Margaret Caldwell. In the early 1920s, Margaret had an affair with Brigadier General Augustus Aldridge. My husband's grandfather. The affair produced a daughter in 1924, kept secret to protect both families."

I felt the pieces clicking into place. "The General's illegitimate daughter."

"Yes. That daughter was raised quietly by the Caldwell family, never publicly acknowledged by the Aldridges. She married, had a daughter of her own: Sarah Caldwell. Sarah was Emily's great-niece by blood, but also the General's great-granddaughter. When she had Augustus in 1982, she was continuing both family lines."

"So Augustus IV is descended from both the Aldridges and the Caldwells," I said, my head spinning. "He's the General's great-grandson through the illegitimate line."

"Exactly. When my husband discovered this, he realized the legal implications were staggering. Augustus IV had Aldridge blood through the General's affair, but he wasn't Augustus III's son. The will needed to address this."

"He was going to disinherit Augustus IV," Corbin said.

"Not entirely," Victoria said. "Augustus wanted to establish a trust fund—generous, enough to live comfortably—but exclude him from the direct inheritance. The estate would go to Melissa, since she was his biological daughter. Augustus IV would receive compensation for being raised as an Aldridge, but no legal claim to the family assets."

This was all new information, and it contradicted what we thought we already knew about the changes to the will. Even Ross, all posture and polish, looked older by a decade.

Augustus IV was staring at his mother, tears streaming down his face. "He was going to throw me out. After forty-two years, he was going to declare me an imposter."

"He said it was about honesty," Victoria said bitterly. "About legal clarity. But it would have destroyed you, exposed our family's secrets, created a scandal that would overshadow everything."

"Did you kill him?" I asked quietly. "Did you poison your husband to protect Augustus IV's inheritance?"

Victoria looked at me directly. "No. I hated what Augustus was planning to do, but I didn't kill him. I argued with him, begged him to reconsider, threatened to expose other family secrets if he went through with it. But I didn't murder him."

"Where were you Sunday night between nine and midnight?"

"In my room. Alone. Reading. I've already told you this. It's not an alibi, but it's the truth."

I looked at Augustus IV. "Where were you during that time window?"

He wiped his face roughly. "I don't know anymore. I thought I knew who I was, where I came from. Now I don't know anything."

"Answer the question," Corbin said firmly.

"I drove around. I didn't know my father was planning to disinherit me, but I knew he was disgusted with my debt. I was thinking about my life, my failures. I parked somewhere —I don't remember where—and sat in my car for maybe an hour. Then I went to the Grille. That's all."

"Did you kill your father?"

"No! And he wasn't my father!" he shouted. "Apparently, he was never my father. My father is some nameless man who got Sarah Caldwell pregnant and abandoned her. My mother is dead. My entire identity is based on a lie. So no, I didn't kill Augustus Aldridge III. But I'm not sorry he's dead either."

That last sentence hit the table like a dropped wrench. In grief, truth and bravado wear the same coat.

After they left—Victoria composed again, Augustus IV shattered—Corbin and I sat in my office trying to process what we'd learned.

"The birth certificate Rosa found," Corbin said. "It must have been Sarah Caldwell's birth certificate from 1955, or her mother's from 1924. Something proving the connection between Emily's sister, the General, and Sarah."

"That's why Augustus III kept it hidden with his father's confession," I said. "It was proof of the General's affair, proof that Sarah Caldwell was related to both families, proof that Augustus IV had no legitimate claim to the Aldridge estate."

"And when Rosa found it, she realized the implications. She texted someone—maybe someone she trusted to help sort it out. And that person killed her to keep the secret."

"But who?" I asked. "Victoria claims she didn't kill Augustus, and I'm inclined to believe her. She had motive to protect her son, but her grief over losing her husband seems genuine."

"Augustus IV had opportunity for both murders. No alibi for the night his father died, and we can't confirm where he was Thursday evening when Rosa was killed."

"But he genuinely didn't know about the baby switch until today. His shock was real. How could he kill to protect a secret he didn't know about?"

"Maybe he did know," Corbin suggested. "Maybe Sarah told him before she died five years ago. Maybe he's been living with this knowledge, waiting for the truth to come out."

I thought about Augustus IV's desperate financial situation. Four and a half million in debt, creditors pressuring him, his father refusing to help. Then Augustus III discovers the truth about his identity and plans to disinherit him legally. That's millions of dollars in motive.

"We need to verify his movements Thursday evening," I said. "Where was he between six and eight p.m. when Rosa was killed? If he knew about the birth certificate, if he knew Rosa found it—"

"He would've killed her to protect his inheritance," Corbin finished.

A text from Jack arrived: "Traced more numbers from the burner phone. One belongs to Augustus IV's personal cell. They exchanged texts three times in the past two weeks."

I showed Corbin the message.

"Augustus IV was in contact with whoever bought that burner phone," he said. "That's not a coincidence."

"No," I agreed. "That's conspiracy. Or at minimum, connection to Rosa's murder."

Samson lifted his head and gave a single quiet woof. I scratched his ear. "Yeah, buddy. I hear it too."

We had Augustus IV's motive now: protecting an inheritance worth millions. We had his opportunity: gaps in his alibi for both murders. We had his connection to the burner phone that Rosa texted before she died.

What we didn't have yet was proof. But we were getting close.

"Bring him back in tomorrow," I said. "Augustus IV is hiding something, and I'm going to find out what."

"What about Victoria?"

"She's protecting her son, even now. But I don't think she's the killer. Her love for Augustus IV is genuine. She's made some terrible choices, but murder? I don't see it."

"So we focus on Augustus IV."

"Yes. He's a man whose entire identity was built on a lie. A man who stands to lose everything if the truth comes out. A man desperate enough, frightened enough, to kill twice to protect his inheritance."

I looked at the crime scene photos on my whiteboard. Augustus Aldridge III, poisoned in his library while researching family secrets. Rosa Martinez, bludgeoned in the woods after finding proof of those secrets.

Both victims killed to protect a lie about Augustus IV's true identity.

Tomorrow, we'd prove it. And Augustus Aldridge IV—or whoever he really was—would finally face justice for what he'd done.

13

_____

Hidden Connections

By now, I was convinced we had our killer. Augustus IV had motive, opportunity, and a connection to the burner phone. He stood to lose millions if his true identity was exposed. Everything pointed to him.

The boards in my office appeared to agree, the red lines and bullet points converging on his name like ants to sugar. Even Samson, chin on paws, watched that corner of the room as if it might move.

Then Cooper walked into my office with a file that changed everything.

"Captain, you need to see this," he said, dropping a thick folder on my desk. "Jack and I have been digging into Graham Crawford's background. There's something here you're not going to believe, and you're definitely not going to like it."

Corbin leaned forward as I opened the file. Birth certificates, genealogical records, hospital documentation. Cooper and Jack had been thorough.

"Graham Crawford," Cooper began, "born in Nashville, 1980. Raised by a single mother, Anne Caldwell Crawford, who died five years ago. No father listed on his birth certificate."

"Caldwell," I said, the name registering immediately. "As in Emily Caldwell?"

"Exactly. Anne Caldwell Crawford was Emily's great-niece, but not through Emily directly. Through Emily's older sister, Margaret Caldwell."

I felt the case shifting again beneath my feet. "Explain," I snapped.

Cooper pulled out a genealogical chart he'd constructed. "In 1924, Margaret Caldwell had an illegitimate child with Brigadier General Augustus Aldridge. That child, a daughter, was kept secret to protect both families. That daughter had two children of her own—Sarah Caldwell, born 1955, and Anne Caldwell, born 1952."

"Sarah Caldwell," Corbin said. "The woman who gave Augustus IV to Victoria."

"Right. Sarah and Anne were sisters. Sarah had Augustus IV in 1982 and gave him to Victoria. Anne had Graham Crawford in 1980 and raised him herself as a single mother."

I stared at the genealogy chart, seeing the connections. "So Graham Crawford and Augustus IV are cousins. Both descended from the General's illegitimate line. Both great-grandsons of Brigadier General Augustus Aldridge."

"Exactly. And here's where it gets really interesting. Graham discovered this connection eight years ago, shortly before he met and married Melissa Aldridge."

"How do you know when he discovered it?"

Jack North appeared in the doorway, holding a laptop.

"Because Graham submitted DNA to ancestry websites in 2016. I tracked his genealogical research through public records and DNA databases. He spent months building his family tree, tracing the Caldwell line back to Emily and her sister Margaret. He discovered the General's affair, the illegitimate children, and... his own connection to the Aldridge family."

"And then he married into that family," I said slowly. "Eight years ago. Right after discovering he was related to them."

"Seems like quite a coincidence," Corbin said, smiling.

"It's not funny," I snapped. "If Graham knew he was descended from the General's illegitimate line, knew Emily Caldwell was his great-aunt who was murdered by Augustus II, he might have married Melissa for revenge."

"Revenge for a murder that happened ninety-nine years ago?" Cooper asked.

"Revenge for generations of secrets, illegitimate children hidden away, family members denied their inheritance. Graham is the General's great-grandson, just like Augustus IV. But Augustus IV was raised as an Aldridge, given everything. Graham was raised by a single mother who struggled financially. That creates resentment."

Jack pulled up more research on his laptop. "Anne Caldwell Crawford worked as a nurse her entire life. Single mother, limited income, no family support. She died of cancer five years ago, and Graham paid for her treatment and funeral expenses. He went into significant debt for it."

"So Graham has financial problems too," Corbin said.

"And possibly felt the Aldridge family owed him something," I added. "His great-grandfather was the General. He has Aldridge blood. But he got nothing while Augustus IV got millions."

I thought about Graham's calm demeanor during our initial interviews. His helpful consultations about the autopsy. His medical knowledge about digitalis poisoning. He'd been right there from the beginning, offering assistance, seeming cooperative.

The most dangerous witness is the one who knows exactly when to stop talking.

Has he been playing us the entire time? I wondered.

"We need to interview him," I said. "Bring Graham Crawford in. And get Tracy to help. I want multiple perspectives on his reactions."

GRAHAM CRAWFORD ARRIVED at the police department two hours later, dressed in surgical scrubs under a jacket. He'd been at the hospital, he explained, and came directly from his shift.

The harsh fluorescent lights flattened his color; even so, he had that surgeon's steadiness: hands quiet, eyes clear, pulse running two beats slower than everyone else's.

"Dr. Crawford," I said as we sat in Interview Room One, "thank you for coming in."

"Of course. How can I help?" He looked genuinely puzzled, not defensive.

"We've been researching the family histories related to this case. Genealogical connections to Emily Caldwell and the Aldridge family."

"Okay, and how does that concern me?" Graham's expression didn't change.

"Your mother's maiden name was Caldwell. Anne Caldwell."

"That's right."

"Were you aware of your family's connection to Emily Caldwell?"

Graham hesitated, then nodded. "Yes. I discovered it several years ago when I was researching my family tree. My mother never talked much about her family, and after she died, I wanted to understand where I came from."

"And what did you discover?"

"That my grandmother—my mother's mother—was the illegitimate daughter of Brigadier General Augustus Aldridge and Margaret Caldwell, Emily's older sister. It was a family secret, kept hidden for generations."

"So you're the General's great-grandson," Corbin said.

"I am. Which makes me distantly related to the Aldridge family, though they never acknowledged the connection."

"Did you know this when you met Melissa Aldridge?" I asked.

Graham's eyes narrowed slightly. "Is that what this is about? You think I married Melissa because of some ancient family connection?"

"Did you?" Corbin asked.

"I married Melissa because I loved her. I still love her." He leaned back, folding his arms. "Yes, I knew about the family history when we met. I'd discovered it a few months earlier. But I didn't seek her out because of it. We met at a hospital fundraiser. We talked, connected, fell in love. The family history was... complicated, but it wasn't why I married her."

"Did you tell Melissa about your connection to her family?" Tracy asked.

"Eventually, yes. After we'd been dating for about six months, I told her everything. She was shocked at first, but ultimately she was sympathetic. She knew her family had secrets. This was just another one."

"How did she react to learning Emily Caldwell was your great-aunt?"

"She felt terrible about it. The murder, the cover-up, the way her family buried the truth. She agreed it was horrible, but it happened long before she was born. She couldn't change the past."

"What about Augustus III?" I asked. "Did he know about your connection to Emily?"

Graham paused. "Yes. I told him two years ago. I thought he deserved to know that his daughters husband was descended from the General's illegitimate line. He was... not pleased. We came to an understanding: I wouldn't make public claims to the Aldridge family, and he wouldn't make our connection public either."

"But recently, Augustus started researching Emily Caldwell's descendants," Corbin said. "He was looking into your family."

"I didn't know that. If he was, he never mentioned it to me."

I studied Graham carefully. He seemed calm, forthright, not particularly defensive. Either he was telling the truth, or he was an excellent liar. His gaze met mine and held. Most liars break at seven seconds; he didn't blink until ten. Inwardly, I shrugged. It wasn't proof, just a pebble in my shoe.

"Dr. Crawford, where were you Sunday night between nine p.m. and midnight?"

"At Erlanger Hospital. I was performing an emergency coronary bypass surgery. The patient came in around six-thirty with an acute myocardial infarction. We prepped and started surgery around seven. I was in the OR until just after midnight."

"Can anyone confirm this?"

"Of course, the entire surgical team. Two other surgeons, an anesthesiologist, three nurses, and various support staff. I can provide names if you need them."

"We'll need that list," I said.

Graham pulled out his phone and sent the information to my email. "Done. You'll find I was exactly where I said I was. I couldn't have poisoned Augustus Aldridge Sunday night. I was busy saving someone else's life."

It was a solid alibi. Too solid to be fabricated. We'd verify it, but I believed him. Graham had been in surgery during the critical window when Augustus was poisoned.

"What about Thursday evening?" Tracy asked. "October seventeenth, between six and eight p.m."

"I was also at the hospital. I had rounds until about seven, then attended a department meeting until eight-thirty. Again, multiple witnesses."

Another solid alibi. If Graham had killed Rosa Martinez, he'd done it with accomplices or not at all.

"Dr. Crawford," I said, "you're a cardiovascular surgeon. You work with cardiac medications regularly."

"Yes."

"Including digitalis?"

"Of course. Digitalis glycosides are standard treatments for certain heart conditions. I prescribe them, monitor patients on them, understand their pharmacology completely."

"Do you keep digitalis in your personal possession?"

Graham hesitated. "I have a medical bag in my car with various emergency medications, so yes. Standard practice for surgeons. If I encounter a medical emergency outside the hospital, I need to be prepared."

"Is digitalis in that bag?"

"It might be. I'd have to check."

"We'd like to check," I said.

Graham stood. "My car is in the parking garage. I'll show you."

Twenty minutes later, we stood in the police department parking garage examining Graham's medical bag. It was comprehensive: various medications, syringes, bandages, diagnostic equipment. And yes, a bottle of digitalis tablets.

"This is standard," Graham explained. "If I encounter someone with acute heart failure, I might need to administer digitalis as a bridge therapy until paramedics arrive."

"How much is in this bottle?" I asked.

Graham checked. "About forty tablets, I think. I refill it periodically."

"Would you notice if some were missing?"

"Probably not. I don't count them regularly."

So Graham had access to digitalis. He had knowledge of how to use it as a poison. He had motive—generations of family secrets, his mother's struggles while the Aldridges lived in wealth. He'd married into the family shortly after discovering his connection to them.

But he also had an airtight alibi for the night Augustus was poisoned.

"Dr. Crawford," I said carefully, "I need to ask you directly. Did you kill Augustus Aldridge III?"

"No, I did not."

"Did you have anything to do with his death?"

"No, I did not."

"What about Rosa Martinez? Did you kill her?"

"I didn't even know Rosa Martinez. Why would I kill her?"

"She found evidence connecting your family to the Aldridges. Evidence that might have exposed secrets you wanted to keep hidden."

Graham shook his head. "Captain, I understand why you're suspicious. My family connection to the Aldridges, my medical knowledge, my access to digitalis; it all looks bad. But I didn't kill anyone. I'm a surgeon. I save lives. I don't take them."

He sounded sincere. But then again, intelligent killers often did.

"Don't leave Chattanooga," I said. "We'll have more questions."

"I'm not going anywhere," Graham replied.

A little while later, Corbin, Tracy, and I stood in the parking garage talking together.

"He's hiding something," Tracy said. "His calm demeanor is too practiced. Like he's been preparing for this interview."

"Or he's genuinely innocent and answering honestly," Corbin countered.

"His alibis check out," I said. "We'll verify them thoroughly, but I believe he was in surgery Sunday night and at the hospital Thursday evening. Unless he hired someone to commit the murders, he didn't physically poison Augustus or kill Rosa."

"Could be a conspiracy," Tracy suggested. "Graham plans it, someone else executes it."

"Who?" I asked. "Who would help him commit murder?"

"Melissa," Tracy said. "She's his wife. She knew about his family connection. Maybe they planned it together, revenge for Emily's murder, securing the inheritance before Augustus could change his will."

It was possible. Melissa stood to lose millions if the will changes went through. Graham had the knowledge to plan a sophisticated poisoning. Together, they could have orchestrated Augustus's death.

But Melissa didn't have access to digitalis. She didn't have medical knowledge. And her grief over her father's death had seemed genuine.

"We need to look at Augustus IV again," I said. "He had opportunity, motive, and connection to the burner phone. And now we know he and Graham are cousins, both descended from the General's illegitimate line. What if they worked together?"

"Two cousins conspiring to kill Augustus III?" Corbin said. "That's elaborate."

"But it explains everything," I said. "Graham provides the poison and the medical knowledge. Augustus IV administers it Sunday night during his unaccounted for ninety minutes. They both benefit. Graham gets revenge for family secrets, Augustus IV protects his inheritance."

"What about Rosa?" Tracy asked.

"Same conspiracy. Rosa found the birth certificate proving the General's illegitimate line. She texted the burner phone, which we know communicated with Augustus IV. One of them—maybe both—met her Thursday evening and killed her to protect the secret."

It made sense. Two cousins, both with motives, both with connections to the case, working together to commit murder.

But we still couldn't prove it.

"Tomorrow we bring Augustus IV back in," I said. "We confront him with Graham's connection, the family relationship, the conspiracy theory. We see if he breaks."

"And if he doesn't?" Corbin asked.

"Then we keep digging. Because somewhere in this web of family secrets and illegitimate descendants and century-old murders is the truth. And I'm going to find it."

We headed back inside, leaving Graham's digitalis sitting in his medical bag in his car. Legal, explainable, but undeniably suspicious.

I thought about two cousins, both descended from a general's affair with a murdered woman's sister. Both raised in vastly different circumstances—one in wealth, one in poverty.

And both were now suspects in two murders.

On the board I drew a new red line—COUSINS—between their names. It looked thin, but it held.

Tomorrow would bring answers. Or at least, I hoped it would.

Because right now, I had two equally viable suspects, one with a solid alibi, the other not quite so solid, and both with motives that ran generations deep.

And one of them was a killer and would kill again if threatened.

I locked the office, clipped on Samson's leash, and stepped

into a dusk the color of old bruises. And somewhere, I knew there was a burner phone, and two bloodlines curled together around a lie.

14

The Conspiracy Theory

AFTER A RESTLESS NIGHT, I WOKE AT FIVE-THIRTY THURSDAY morning, unable to sleep. The case had been churning around in my mind all through the night; I dreamed about it: two cousins, both descended from the General's illegitimate line, both with powerful motives. Graham's calm denials. Augustus IV's desperate confusion. Something wasn't adding up.

Fragments of a dream clung like cobwebs: gloved hands, a library lamp burning low, a brandy bottle that kept refilling itself no matter how much I poured out. Every time I blinked, the label read a different name.

Samson sensed my restlessness and padded over to the bed, his tail wagging hopefully. He knew what early morning wakefulness meant.

"Yeah, I know. You want to go for a run, don't you, boy?" I said, swinging my legs out of bed. "Me, too, I think. Give me a minute and we'll go, okay?"

He gave me one of those looks.

Twenty minutes later, we were running along the Tennessee River greenway. The October air was crisp, almost cold, and fog hung over the mirrored water in wispy sheets. Chattanooga was still sleeping; just a few other early risers out with their dogs, a couple of dedicated joggers, the city was quiet before rush hour began.

A freight horn moaned from the far shore, the note stretching across the water like wire. I matched my breathing to it—four beats in, four out—trying to file suspects and time-lines into tidy drawers. Drawers that wouldn't close.

Samson loped along beside me, his energy boundless despite the early hour. Running with him always cleared my head, forced me to focus on breath and movement instead of endless details. But this morning, even the rhythm of my foot-falls on pavement couldn't quiet my thoughts.

Digitalis isn't magic; it's math. Dose, interval, absorption. If the bottle was seeded earlier, the timeline widens, the alibis harden, and intent—not opportunity—becomes the lever.

Graham Crawford had an ironclad alibi. Hours of surgery, multiple witnesses, security footage confirming his presence at the hospital. Unless he'd poisoned the brandy days in advance—risky and uncertain—he couldn't have killed Augustus III. *But somehow...* Somehow the brandy kept pointing back to someone who understood patience. Not rage. Patience.

Augustus IV had gaps in his timeline but no physical evidence linking him to either crime. The partial fingerprint didn't match him, or Crawford for that matter. The burner phone couldn't be traced to him. His motive was strong, but so was his apparent confusion about his own identity.

We reached the turnaround point at the pedestrian bridge and headed back. Samson paused to investigate something fascinating in the grass—probably a squirrel trail—then bounded after me when I called.

A cyclist flashed by, back light pulsing red. For a second it looked like the recording light on a camera. Evidence watches even when we don't.

If they were working together, though... it made sense. But if Graham and Augustus IV weren't working together, if neither had acted alone, then who? Melissa with her millions at stake? Victoria protecting her "son"? Someone else entirely? *Geez, what a frickin' mess.*

By the time we got back to my apartment, the sky was lightening to gray. I fed Samson, showered, dressed in jeans and a white sweater, made a pot of strong coffee, slipped a bagel into the toaster and then sat down at the kitchen table. Two minutes later, I buttered the toasted bagel and sat down again to eat it. My mind felt clearer, focused. *Today I'll confront both suspects with the conspiracy theory. Today someone will crack... Geez, I hope so.*

I wrote three questions on a sticky note—WHO KNEW, WHO COULD, WHO BENEFITS—and stuck it to my phone. If the answers triangulated on the same person, we'd be done. If not, back to the river.

It was a little before seven-thirty when Samson and I arrived at the office, ready to build the case that would finally break the investigation open.

"They have to be working together," I told Corbin as I sat down behind my desk. "It's the only explanation that makes sense. Separately, they have problems. Graham has an ironclad alibi, Augustus IV has a weak opportunity. But together? They could've planned the perfect murder."

"How?" Corbin asked, playing devil's advocate.

"Graham provides the medical knowledge and the poison. He's a cardiovascular surgeon, he understands digitalis pharmacology perfectly. He has access to the drug through his medical practice. He knows exactly how much would be lethal, and how long it would take to work."

"But he was in surgery Sunday night."

"Which is the perfect alibi. He couldn't have physically administered the poison, but he didn't need to. That's where Augustus IV comes in."

I stood and walked to the timeline board. "Augustus IV leaves the charity function at nine-thirty. He has ninety unaccounted for minutes before he shows up at the bar at eleven. That's more than enough time to drive to the estate, poison his father's brandy, and leave. By the time Augustus drinks it and dies, Augustus IV is visible at a bar with witnesses."

"And Graham's in surgery," Corbin said, following my logic. "They both have alibis for the actual time of death."

"Exactly. It's clever. They planned it weeks in advance—that's when the burner phone was purchased. They coordinated timing, method, everything. Graham provides expertise, Augustus IV provides execution."

"Okay, so what about this?" Corbin said. "Suppose they're not working together—"

"They have to be," I said, interrupting him. "If not…"

"We've been working on the theory that he was killed that night. But what if he wasn't?"

I furrowed my brow. *What the hell is he talking about?* Then

I got it. "You're saying the brandy could have been poisoned... any time—"

Corbin shrugged. "It was his own private stock. It wasn't likely he would share it with anyone else. Suppose the poison was added earlier, say between... oh, I don't know; five and six that evening, or even earlier."

"I think I already made that point," I muttered. "What about Rosa's murder?"

"Same pattern. Rosa finds the birth certificate proving their connection to the General's illegitimate line. She texts the burner phone; probably thinking she's contacting someone neutral, someone who can help sort out the family complications. Instead, she's texting one of the killers."

"Which one?" I asked.

"Could be either. The phone can't be traced. But whoever received that text—Graham or Augustus IV—met Rosa Thursday evening and killed her to protect the secret."

Corbin studied the boards. "It fits. But we have no proof. No physical evidence linking them to a conspiracy, no communications between them that suggest they were planning a murder."

"Then we find the proof," I said. "We'll bring them both in. Question them together, and see how they interact. If they're conspiring, they'll slip up. They'll coordinate stories too well, or contradict each other in ways that reveal planning."

"When?" he asked.

"Now. I want them here this afternoon."

I texted Hawk to warm up the observation room and told Tracy to pull every camera angle from the lobby to the interview hall. If either man glanced at the other a beat too long, I wanted it on video.

By two p.m., we had both suspects in separate interview rooms. Graham Crawford in Room One, Augustus IV in Room Two. The plan was to question them individually first, then bring them together and watch their dynamic.

I started with Augustus IV. He looked terrible: red-eyed, unshaven, like he hadn't slept since our last interview. Learning his entire identity was a lie had broken something in him.

"Mr. Aldridge," I began, "we need to talk about your relationship with Graham Crawford."

He blinked, confused. "What about it?"

"You're cousins. Both of you are descended from Brigadier General Augustus Aldridge through his illegitimate children. You know this?"

"I just found out I'm not really an Aldridge at all. So no, I didn't know Graham and I were related until you just told me."

"Have you been in contact with Graham recently? Phone calls, meetings, text messages?"

"We see each other at family events. Melissa's my sister, Graham's her husband. We're polite but not close."

"Phone records show you've exchanged calls and texts with Graham's number several times in the past three months."

Augustus IV shrugged. "Probably about family stuff. Coordinating dinners, that kind of thing. I don't remember specifically."

"A burner phone was purchased three weeks before your father died. That phone was in contact with your personal cell phone. Three text exchanges over two weeks." Augustus IV looked genuinely surprised. "A burner phone? I don't know anything about that. If someone texted me from an unknown number, I probably assumed it was spam."

I pulled up the text records Jack had provided. "These texts say things like 'Tuesday at 6' and 'Same place as before.' Those sound like coordination, not spam."

"I don't... I don't remember getting those texts. Can I see my phone?"

We provided his phone, which we'd retained as evidence. Augustus IV scrolled through his messages, frowning.

"I don't see any of these texts in my history," he said.

"They were deleted," I said. "But phone company records show they were received."

"Then someone else deleted them. Or I deleted them thinking they were spam. I get a lot of random texts."

It was plausible, but convenient.

I switched tactics.

"Let's talk about your access to the estate. When's the last time you were in your father's library before Sunday night?"

Augustus IV thought for a moment. "Maybe a week before? Ten days? I stopped by the estate to ask my father for money. He refused, we argued in the library. That was probably Wednesday, October ninth or tenth."

"Did you go near his brandy collection?"

"No. I mean, I saw it. The cabinet was right there. But I didn't touch anything. I was too angry to drink with him."

"What about other visits? In the weeks before his death, did you have opportunities to access the library alone?"

"I suppose. I've been to the estate dozens of times over the years. Sometimes I'd wait in the library if my father was busy. But I never touched his brandy. Why would I?"

"Because digitalis could have been added to that bottle

days or even weeks before Sunday night. Your movements Sunday evening might be irrelevant if you poisoned the brandy on October ninth."

Augustus IV's face went pale. "I didn't poison anything. Not Sunday night, not any other time."

"Can anyone verify your visit on October ninth or tenth?"

"My father could, but he's dead. Maybe Victoria saw me arrive. I don't know."

"Let's talk about Graham's medical knowledge," I said. "Did he ever discuss digitalis with you? Cardiac medications, how they work, their toxicity?"

"No. Graham doesn't talk about work much at family gatherings. We're not that close."

"But you know he's a cardiovascular surgeon. You know he has access to cardiac medications."

"Everyone knows that. It's not a secret."

"Did Graham ever suggest your father's death might benefit you? That his will changes would hurt you?"

"What? No! Graham barely talked to my father. They were polite but distant."

"Yet Graham told us he informed your father two years ago about his connection to Emily Caldwell. They had conversations about family history."

Augustus IV looked lost. "I didn't know that. Nobody tells me anything, apparently. My whole life is built on lies."

I switched tactics. "Where were you Thursday evening, October seventeenth, between six and eight p.m.?"

"I already told you. Home with Allison."

"Can she confirm that?"

"She was there. Ask her."

"We will. What were you doing at home?"

"I don't know. Watching TV? Drinking? I've been in a fog since my father died and my finances collapsed. The days blur together."

"Rosa Martinez was killed Thursday evening. She found evidence connecting you to the General's illegitimate line. Evidence that could destroy your claim to the Aldridge inheritance."

"I didn't kill Rosa! I barely knew her. Why would I kill someone over an inheritance I've now learned I have no right to anyway?"

He had a point. Augustus IV had been shattered by learning his true identity. Would he kill to protect an inheritance he now knew wasn't rightfully his?

Unless he'd known the truth before we told him. Unless Sarah Caldwell had told him years ago, and he'd been living with that secret, waiting for it to be exposed.

"Did your mother Sarah ever tell you the truth about your parentage?" I asked.

"No. I never knew Sarah was my biological mother. I thought she was Aunt Sarah, my mother's friend. I thought Victoria gave birth to me."

"Sarah died five years ago. Did she try to contact you before she died? Tell you anything about your past?"

"She sent me a letter." Augustus IV's voice was barely a whisper. "Right before she died. She said there were things I needed to know about my family. She said she was sorry for the secrets. But she died before I could visit her, before she could explain. I thought she was just rambling, dying and confused. I didn't pursue it."

"Do you still have that letter?"

"I threw it away. It didn't make any sense at the time."

Convenient again. Or tragic. I couldn't tell which.

GRAHAM CRAWFORD WAS CALMER when I interviewed him thirty minutes later. He sat relaxed, hands folded, meeting my eyes directly.

"Dr. Crawford, let's talk about your relationship with Augustus IV."

"We're family. Sort of. I'm married to his sister."

"You're also cousins. Both descended from the General's illegitimate children."

"So you've discovered," he replied. "I didn't know that until recently either."

"When did you find out?"

"Eight years ago. I'd been researching my family tree, and I found the connection. I was surprised, but it made sense of some family dynamics."

"Did you tell Augustus IV?"

"No. We're not close. I saw no reason to tell him."

"But you told Augustus III two years ago about your connection to Emily Caldwell."

"That was different. He was Melissa's father, my father-in-law. I felt he deserved to know his daughter's husband had Caldwell blood. It was a courtesy."

"How did he react?"

"He was uncomfortable but civil. We agreed not to make it public. It would've complicated things unnecessarily."

"Did Augustus III ever discuss his research into Emily Caldwell's descendants with you?"

"No. If he was researching my family, he never mentioned it."

I pulled out the phone records. "You've been in contact with Augustus IV several times in the past three months. Calls and texts."

"Coordinating family events, mostly. Melissa likes us to do family dinners. I call Augustus IV to check schedules."

"Did you purchase a burner phone on October second?"

"No."

"Do you own any phone besides your personal cell and work phone?"

"No."

"Phone records show a burner phone was in contact with Augustus IV's personal cell. That same burner phone received a text from Rosa Martinez before she died."

Graham's expression didn't change. "I don't know anything about a burner phone. If you think I bought one, check security footage from wherever it was purchased. You won't find me."

We had checked. The hooded figure in the Walmart footage could've been anyone.

"Let's talk about digitalis," I said. "You're an expert on cardiac medications."

"It's part of my specialty, yes."

"You could easily calculate a lethal dose of digitalis."

"I could. So could any physician, pharmacist, or medical student with access to a textbook."

"You have digitalis in your medical bag."

"Standard equipment for a cardiovascular surgeon. If someone has acute heart failure and I'm first on scene, I need to be able to provide bridge therapy."

"Could someone have taken digitalis from your medical bag without you noticing?"

Graham paused. "Possibly. As I told you before, I don't inventory it daily. If someone took a few tablets, I might not realize until I needed to refill."

"Who has access to your medical bag?"

"It's usually in my car. Sometimes at home. Melissa could access it. So could anyone who broke into my car, though it's usually locked."

"Where were you Thursday evening between six and eight p.m.?"

"At Erlanger Hospital. I had rounds until seven, then a department meeting. I've already provided you with names of people who can confirm this."

"We're checking. But meetings have gaps. You could've left for thirty minutes, met Rosa, killed her, returned."

"Except I didn't. I was visible at the hospital the entire time. Check security footage if you don't believe me."

We would. But I suspected it would confirm his alibi.

"Let's talk about your access to the estate," I said. "How often do you visit?"

"Once or twice a month, usually. Family dinners, holidays, that sort of thing."

"When's the last time you were there before Augustus died?"

Graham pulled out his phone and checked his calendar. "That would be Sunday, October thirteenth. Melissa and I had dinner with her parents. We left around eight-thirty."

"Did you go into Augustus's library that evening?"

"Briefly. Augustus asked me to look at a medical journal

article he'd found about cardiac health. We spent maybe ten minutes in there discussing it."

"Were you ever alone in the library?"

Graham hesitated. "For a minute or two, perhaps. Augustus stepped out to take a phone call. I waited in the library."

"Near his brandy collection?"

"The brandy cabinet is in that room, yes. But I didn't touch it."

"You realize the digitalis could have been added to that bottle on October thirteenth, not Sunday the twentieth? In which case, your surgical alibi for Sunday night becomes irrelevant if you poisoned the brandy a week earlier."

"Except I didn't poison anything. And I wasn't alone in that library long enough to tamper with bottles, calculate dosages, and cover my tracks."

"How long were you alone?"

"Two minutes. Three at most."

"That's ample time to add pre-measured digitalis to a bottle."

"Which I didn't do."

AT FOUR P.M., I brought both men into Interview Room One together. Graham and Augustus IV sat on opposite sides of the table, not looking at each other.

"Gentlemen," I said, "you're both suspects in two murders. You're also cousins, both descended from the General's illegitimate line, both with motives to want Augustus III dead. It's all too much of a coincidence."

They glanced at each other, both looking confused.

"I didn't know we were related," Augustus IV said to Graham. "Did you know?"

"I found out about eight years ago," Graham admitted. "I didn't tell you because... well, you know."

"Why didn't you tell me?" Augustus IV's voice rose. "If you knew I was descended from the General too, if you knew about the illegitimate line—"

"It wasn't my place to reveal family secrets. I assumed you knew your own history."

"I didn't know anything! My whole life has been a lie!"

I let them argue, watching their dynamic. They seemed genuinely surprised to be confronting each other. If this was acting, it was good.

"Here's what I think happened," I said, interrupting their argument. "I think you two planned Augustus III's murder together. Graham, you provided the medical knowledge and access to digitalis. Augustus IV, you administered the poison Sunday night during your ninety unaccounted for minutes, or even earlier in the day. You coordinated using a burner phone to avoid detection. Then Rosa found evidence of your connection, and one or both of you killed her to protect the secret."

Both men stared at me.

"That's insane," Graham said finally.

"I didn't kill anyone," Augustus IV said. "Least of all with Graham's help. We barely talk to one another!"

"Phone records show otherwise. You've been in contact multiple times."

"About family dinners!" Augustus IV shouted. "About

whether Melissa wants to do Thanksgiving at our house or theirs! Not about murdering my father!"

"Then explain the burner phone texts," I demanded.

"I can't! I don't know about any burner phone!"

I looked at Graham. "What about you? Explain your connection to that phone."

"I don't have a connection. You're creating a conspiracy where none exists."

They weren't breaking. Either they were innocent, or they were better liars than I'd anticipated.

"We're done for now," I said. "But don't leave Chattanooga. Both of you remain suspects."

AFTER THEY LEFT, Corbin and I sat in my office, frustrated.

"They didn't seem like conspirators," Corbin said.

"No. They seemed genuinely confused by each other."

"So maybe they're not working together."

"Or they're smart enough to fake confusion."

I stared at the evidence boards. Two cousins, both with motives, both with connections to the case. But neither quite fitting the profile of a calculated killer.

"We're missing something," I said. "Something that explains how all this fits together."

"What if they really aren't working together?" Corbin suggested. "What if one of them did it alone, and we're so focused on conspiracy we're missing the simpler explanation?"

"Then which one?"

"I don't know. But we need to figure it out before the trail goes completely cold."

For the first time in a long time, I felt beaten. This thing seemed to be going nowhere. It was a tangled mess that was hiding a killer. I was sure it was one or both of them, but how to dig it out of them, I had no idea. But I would, even if it meant tearing this entire investigation apart and starting over.

I uncapped my marker, drew a small empty circle on the board between their names, and wrote one word inside it: TRIGGER. Find that, I told myself, and the rest collapses. Samson thumped his tail once, as if he agreed.

15

Pressure and Alibis

I SPENT FRIDAY MORNING DOING WHAT I SHOULD'VE DONE DAYS ago—meticulously reconstructing every movement of my two prime suspects. If Graham and Augustus IV weren't conspiring together, then one of them was guilty alone. And I figured the key to proving it was finding the crack in their alibis.

I dragged a fresh pad onto the table and sketched a big block—"FRICTION MAP"—where times rubbed against times, stories scraped against video, words grated on physics. Murder investigations break not on headlines but on seams. Find the snag; pull.

"Let's start with Augustus IV," I said to Tracy and Corbin. "We know he left the charity function at nine-thirty Sunday night. He claims he drove around, then showed up at Big River Grille at eleven. That's ninety minutes unaccounted for."

Tracy pulled up her interview notes. "The bar manager

confirms someone matching his description arrived around eleven and stayed until midnight"

"So between nine-thirty and eleven, he could've driven to the estate, poisoned the brandy, and driven back downtown," Corbin said.

"Could've," I agreed. "But did he? Let's trace his route." I pulled up a map on my computer. "The charity function was at the Hunter Museum. Big River Grille is what, ten blocks away?"

"About that," Tracy confirmed.

"So if he drove directly from the museum to the bar, it's a five-minute drive. But he didn't arrive until ninety minutes later. Where did he go?"

"He said he drove around to clear his head," Corbin said.

"Then we should be able to track him. Have Jack check the security cameras, credit card purchases. Let's build his route."

I circled intersections like moulage around a wound: Market, Broad, 4th, Aquarium Way. If he drifted east toward the ridge, he wanted privacy; west toward the river, he wanted cover. Neither choice smelled like grief. Both smelled like planning.

We spent the next two hours reconstructing Augustus IV's movements that night. Credit card records showed he bought gas at the Pilot station on Shallowford Road at ten-fifteen, near the estate, as Tracy had discovered earlier. But that was the only documentation of his whereabouts. None of the city's security cameras captured his license plate. If he drove to the estate and back, he did it without leaving a digital trail.

"What about his phone?" I asked. "GPS data?"

"His phone was off or in airplane mode from nine-thirty

until eleven-fifteen Sunday night. No GPS data, no cell tower pings, nothing."

"Okay. That's suspicious," I said. "Who turns off their phone during a crisis unless they're hiding something? Get a warrant for his vehicle, Tracy. I doubt they'll find anything, but it will give him a fright, maybe enough to get him to break."

Tracy nodded and picked up her phone.

Corbin rolled a stress ball from hand to hand. "If he turned it off to avoid pings," he said, "he learned that somewhere." I wrote TRAINED HABIT? and underlined it twice. Augustus didn't strike me as the Boy Scout-prepared type. Somebody coached him.

GRAHAM CRAWFORD'S alibi was more complicated. He claimed to be in surgery from seven p.m. to midnight Sunday, with multiple witnesses. I needed to verify every minute of that timeline.

"Get me the surgical schedule from Erlanger Hospital," I told Jack. "I want the OR logs, staff assignments, everything."

"You're going to need a warrant," he replied.

"So, get on with it. You know the routine."

By noon, I had the documentation. Graham had indeed been scheduled for an emergency coronary bypass surgery starting at seven-fifteen p.m. The patient had arrived just before six with an acute myocardial infarction—heart attack. The surgery had lasted until twelve-oh-five a.m.

OR boards don't lie: badge swipes, narc counts, instrument trays signed like chain-of-custody. The rhythm of surgery leaves paperwork music behind. Graham's name was on every measure.

I called the hospital and requested interviews with the surgical team. By three p.m., I'd spoken with the assisting surgeon, the anesthesiologist, and two of the scrub nurses.

Everyone confirmed the same story: Graham had been in the OR the entire time, performing a complex five-hour surgery. There were no gaps, no unexplained absences, no opportunities for him to leave the hospital.

"He was focused and professional throughout," Dr. Patricia Chen, the assisting surgeon, told me. "That surgery required absolute concentration. If Graham had been distracted or stressed about something else, I would've noticed. He was completely present."

"Did he make any phone calls during the surgery?" I asked.

"Impossible. We're scrubbed in, sterile. We can't touch anything non-sterile, including phones. Graham didn't leave the OR once from seven-fifteen until after midnight."

So Graham's alibi was solid. Unless he'd somehow poisoned the brandy before Sunday night, he couldn't have murdered Augustus III.

But present in one room doesn't mean innocent of another room, I reminded myself, *but a clean timeline is a hard door to kick in.*

But what about Rosa's murder on Thursday evening?

Graham claimed he'd been at the hospital from six to eight-thirty Thursday, doing rounds and attending a department meeting. I needed to verify that too.

The hospital's security footage showed Graham entering the building at five-forty p.m. Thursday. He was visible on various cameras throughout the evening—walking to patient rooms, sitting in a conference room during the department meeting, talking to colleagues in the hallway.

The footage showed him leaving the building at eight-thirty-five p.m. Thursday night. Rosa had been killed between six and eight p.m. Graham had been at the hospital, visible on security cameras, for that entire window.

Another solid alibi.

"He couldn't have killed Rosa," I told Corbin, frustration creeping into my voice. "He was at the hospital. Multiple cameras confirm it."

"So if Graham didn't kill either victim, what's his connection to the case?"

"Maybe he's exactly what he claims to be—someone who discovered his family history, married into the Aldridge family legitimately, and is now a suspect only because of unfortunate coincidence."

"Do you believe that?"

I thought about Graham's calm demeanor, his practiced answers, his convenient explanations for everything. "No. He's hiding something. I just can't prove what."

"And then there's this," I said. "I've been thinking about the interviews yesterday," I said to Corbin as we reviewed the timeline boards. "Both Augustus IV and Graham admitted to being in that library within two weeks of the murder."

"Augustus IV on October ninth or tenth, Graham on the thirteenth," Corbin confirmed. "And Graham admitted to being alone in the library for two or three minutes while Augustus took a phone call. That's enough time to add pre-measured digitalis to a bottle."

"Augustus IV said he never went near the brandy cabinet during his visit. But he was angry, arguing with his father about money. Who's going to notice him walking past a cabinet in the heat of an argument?"

"Exactly. And both visits were recent enough that Augustus might not have drunk from that particular bottle yet. The poisoner just had to wait."

"So what do we do with this information?"

"We verify both visits. Talk to Victoria about whether she remembers seeing Augustus IV on the ninth or tenth. Check if any staff saw Graham alone in the library on the thirteenth. And we look at whether there were any other visits we don't know about yet."

"That expands our timeline considerably."

"It does. But it also means we can't dismiss either suspect based on Sunday night alibis. The murder could have been set in motion days before Augustus actually died."

I wrote a single word over the calendar: PRIMING. Whoever did this primed the scene, then walked away and let time do the work. That's not passion, it's engineering.

By late afternoon, I'd expanded the investigation to include Melissa and Allison. If Graham and Augustus IV had alibis, maybe their wives were involved.

Melissa Aldridge sat across from me in Interview Room Two, elegant as always, though strain showed around her eyes.

"Mrs. Crawford," I began, "I need to ask you about your husband's medical bag."

"What about it?"

"It contains digitalis. Did you know that?"

"I assume Graham carries various medications for emergencies. I don't inventory his medical supplies."

"Have you ever accessed his medical bag?"

"No. I have no reason to. If I need medication, I go to a pharmacy."

"Where does Graham keep the bag?"

"Usually in his car. Sometimes he brings it inside if he's been called to an emergency."

"Was it inside your house Sunday night?"

Melissa frowned, thought for a moment, then said, "I don't remember specifically. Graham had been on call that weekend. It might have been inside, or it might have been in his car. I didn't pay any attention."

"Could someone have taken digitalis from the bag without Graham noticing?"

"I suppose. But why would I know that?"

"Because you stood to lose two point four million dollars if your father's will change went through. That's a powerful motive for murder."

Melissa's composed expression cracked. "I didn't kill my father. Yes, I was upset about the will changes. Yes, I argued with him about it. But I didn't poison him."

"Where were you Sunday night between nine and midnight?"

"We've already gone over this. We had an early dinner, then Graham got the emergency call around six-thirty and left for the hospital. I spent the rest of the evening alone. "

"Can anyone besides Graham confirm you were home?"

"No. I was alone."

"What about Thursday evening? Where were you between six and eight p.m.?"

"Home. Graham was at the hospital. I was alone, reading."

"No one can confirm that either?"

"I live a quiet life, Captain. I don't require witnesses for every hour of my day."

I studied Melissa carefully. She had motive and opportunity for both murders. She could've taken digitalis from Graham's medical bag. She had access to the estate, knew her father's routines. And she had no solid alibi for either murder.

But she also seemed genuinely grieving. Her relationship with her father had been strained, but there was real sadness beneath her composed exterior.

"Did Graham ever discuss your father's research into Emily Caldwell?" I asked.

"No. Graham doesn't talk much about family history. It's a painful topic for him."

"Because he's descended from the General's illegitimate line?"

"Yes. He grew up knowing his family had been shut out, denied their heritage. It's created some bitterness."

"Bitterness enough to kill?"

"No. Graham saves lives. He doesn't take them."

"What about you? Bitterness enough to kill? When was the last time you were in the library?"

Melissa's eyes hardened. "I loved my father, despite our disagreements. I didn't kill him. And I certainly didn't kill Rosa Martinez, who never did anything to hurt me. As to when I was last in the library; it would have been at least a week before he died. I rarely go in there. It was his private domain."

When she left, the chair clung to the ghost of her perfume

—citrus and something sharper. It faded fast, unlike the certainty that she was lying.

ALLISON ALDRIDGE WAS MORE defensive when I questioned her an hour later.

"This is harassment," she said immediately. "You've questioned us multiple times. You have no evidence. You're just fishing."

"I'm investigating two murders, Mrs. Aldridge. If you're innocent, cooperation helps establish that."

"Fine. What do you want to know?"

"Where were you Sunday night between nine-thirty and midnight?"

"You know where I was. I was at the charity function until after eleven. Then I got a ride home with the Morgans, friends of ours. I arrived home around eleven-thirty. Augustus came home around twelve-thirty, drunk."

"Multiple witnesses confirm you were at the function until after eleven. But what about Augustus? You told us initially you were together all evening."

Allison's face reddened. "And I've already explained that as well. I told you I was embarrassed. My husband abandoned me at a charity event, left me to explain his absence. I didn't want to admit that in our initial interview."

"You lied to police in a murder investigation."

"I omitted a detail. There's a difference."

"What about Thursday evening? Where were you?"

"Home. Alone. Augustus was... I don't know where he was.

We've been living separate lives since the financial troubles started."

"So neither of you have an alibi for Thursday evening?"

"I didn't realize I needed one. I didn't kill anyone."

"But your husband might have?"

Allison hesitated. "I don't think Augustus is capable of murder. He's weak, not violent. He crumbles under pressure rather than fighting back."

"Poisoning isn't violent. It's passive. It's something a weak person might do when they feel cornered."

"Augustus loved his father, despite everything. He wouldn't kill him."

"Not even for millions of dollars in inheritance?"

"Not even for that."

She sounded sincere. But she'd also lied to us before. How could I trust anything she said?

"When was the last time you were in the library?" I asked.

She looked taken aback. "When was I… Hell, I don't know. Augustus didn't like visitors when he was in there. It wasn't long before he died, perhaps four, maybe five days. He was there, that much I do remember."

Her timeline slid across Melissa's like wet cards—close, unhelpful, annoyingly plausible.

BY SIX P.M., I'd hit another wall. Augustus IV had gaps in his alibi and suspicious behavior, but no physical evidence linking him to either crime. Graham had solid alibis but suspicious connections and knowledge. Their wives had opportunity but questionable motives.

"We need physical evidence," I told Corbin as we sat in my office, staring at the evidence boards. "Something that definitively links one of these people to the murders."

"The partial fingerprint on the brandy bottle doesn't match any of them," Corbin said.

"And the burner phone can't be traced to any of them," I muttered.

"Rosa's phone shows she texted that burner phone," Corbin said, "but we don't know who received the message."

"And we still don't know whose birth certificate Rosa found," I said.

I thought about that birth certificate. It was a key piece of evidence that had gotten Rosa killed. It proved someone's connection to the General's illegitimate line. But whose?

"We've been assuming the birth certificate belonged to Sarah Caldwell or her mother," I said slowly. "Proving the connection between the General and Augustus IV or Graham. But what if it wasn't?"

"What do you mean?" Corbin asked.

"What if the birth certificate proved someone else's connection? Someone we haven't considered?"

"Like who?"

"I don't know. But Rosa found that certificate and immediately texted someone she thought could help. Who would she trust with that information?"

"Family?" Corbin suggested. "Miguel?"

"Miguel's mind is too fragile. Rosa wouldn't burden him with something like that."

"A friend? Another staff member?"

"Maybe," I said. "Or maybe she texted someone she thought was neutral but turned out to be the killer."

We sat in silence, processing what we knew, and more to the point, what we didn't know. Somewhere in this investigation was a piece we'd overlooked. A connection we'd missed. A person we'd dismissed as irrelevant.

"Starting Monday," I said finally, "we start over, go back to basics. We go back through every interview, every piece of evidence, every assumption we've made. Because we're missing something fundamental. I want everybody in on it."

"What if we're not?" Corbin asked. "What if one of our prime suspects really did it, and we just can't prove it?"

"Then we keep digging until we can prove it. Because two people are dead, and someone is walking around thinking they got away with murder. Have a nice weekend, Corbin. I'm taking it off. I need time to think."

On my way out, I stopped at the whiteboards and added a new column: TRUST. Under it, I wrote two names: Rosa's, Miguel's, and one blank line. Whoever fills that line is either the witness we've missed... or the hand that pushed her into the ravine. I nodded to myself, then turned and looked at Samson who was waiting at the door. It was time to go for a run: time to think. "Come on then," I said. "Home first to change, then the Riverwalk."

16

_____

The Cousins Turn on Each Other

THE WEEKEND HAD GIVEN NOT ONLY ME TIME TO THINK, TO worry, to let pressure build, but everyone else too, especially the suspects, and I was counting on that pressure to crack someone open.

Pressure is a tool if you meter it right; too little and people coast, too much and they lock up. This morning I wanted the sweet spot: the moment a story stops feeling safe in the teller's mouth. Samson thumped his tail against my desk as if to say, "go get 'em, girl."

First thing Monday morning, I brought both Graham and Augustus IV back in. Separately first, then together again. The theory of conspiracy was dying, but I wanted to see what happened when desperate people turned on each other.

Augustus IV looked worse than before. He'd aged years in the days since learning his true identity. His expensive clothes hung loosely on him, as if he'd lost weight from stress.

"Mr. Aldridge," I began, "let's talk about Graham Crawford."

"What about him?"

"He's your cousin. Both of you descended from the General's illegitimate children. Both of you have Aldridge blood. But you were raised in wealth while Graham grew up with a struggling single mother. That creates resentment, doesn't it?"

"I didn't know we were cousins until you told me."

"But Graham knew. He discovered it eight years ago, but he didn't tell you, did he? He researched his family history, found the connection, then married into your family. Doesn't that seem calculated to you?"

Augustus IV frowned. "I never thought about it like that."

"Maybe you should. Graham married Melissa eight years ago, shortly after discovering he was related to the Aldridges. He positioned himself inside the family, waiting for an opportunity."

"An opportunity for what?"

"Revenge. To claim what he thought should've been his. He had the medical knowledge to plan a sophisticated poisoning. He knew digitalis pharmacology, had access to the drug. All he needed was someone on the inside to administer it."

Augustus IV's eyes widened. "You think Graham got me to poison my father?"

"Did he?"

"No! Hell no! I barely talk to Graham. We're not close enough for him to convince me to commit murder, especially my father."

"But you communicated with a burner phone that Graham could've been using. You had ninety unaccounted for minutes the night your father died. You bought gas near the estate.

And you admit to being in the library three or four days before the murder. It all points to you being on scene. That, sir, is opportunity, and you needed the money. That's motive. Graham provides the poison. That's the weapon. That's the holy trinity of a murder investigation."

"I didn't kill my father, and you can't prove that I did," Augustus IV said, but his voice lacked conviction. He sounded tired, beaten down by weeks of accusation.

"Then help me understand Graham's role," I pressed. "Because from where I'm sitting, he's the mastermind and you're the patsy. He used you to get access, to execute his plan, and now you're taking the fall while he walks away clean."

"That's not what happened."

"Then what did happen?"

Augustus IV was silent for a long moment. When he spoke, his voice was bitter. "Maybe Graham did kill my father. He had more reason than I did. His mother died in poverty while we lived in luxury. His family was denied everything while we got everything. If anyone had motive for revenge, it was Graham."

"You're saying Graham acted alone?"

"I don't know what I'm saying anymore. I don't know what to believe. But I know I didn't poison my father, and if someone did, Graham makes more sense than me."

He was starting to break, starting to point fingers. Good. Desperate people made mistakes.

As he spoke, his right heel tapped the chair rung in a quick, arrhythmic tattoo. Not anger, anticipation. He wanted me to go arrest Graham and be done with it. Innocent people want clarity; guilty ones want a trade. I logged it and moved on.

AN HOUR LATER, I sat across from Graham Crawford. He was calmer than Augustus IV, more controlled, but I could see strain around his eyes.

"Dr. Crawford, your cousin Augustus is starting to talk."

"About what?"

"About your relationship. About how you might have manipulated him into helping you murder his father."

Graham's expression didn't change. "That's absurd, and you know it."

"Is it? Eight years ago you discovered that you were related to the Aldridge's. You married Melissa shortly after. You positioned yourself inside the family, learned their routines, gained their trust. You're a cardiovascular surgeon with expert knowledge of digitalis. You had means, motive, and opportunity."

"I had an alibi. I was in surgery when Augustus died."

"You were in surgery when he actually died, yes. But the poison could've been administered hours earlier, even days earlier. You could've poisoned the brandy any time in the days or weeks before Sunday night."

"I could've, but I didn't."

"Your cousin says you might have done it alone. He says you had more motive than he did."

For the first time, Graham showed emotion; a flash of anger. "Augustus is deflecting. He's desperate to save himself, so he's throwing blame at me. But I wasn't the one who left a charity function early. I wasn't the one who bought gas near the estate. I wasn't the one drowning in debt and desperate for inheritance."

"So you're saying Augustus did it alone?"

"I'm saying I don't know who killed his father, but it wasn't me. Maybe it was Augustus. Maybe it was someone else entirely. But pinning it on me because I'm a convenient suspect solves nothing."

"Tell me about Rosa Martinez," I said, switching topics. "Did you know her?"

"I'd met her a few times at family gatherings. She seemed nice."

"She found a birth certificate in the hidden room. A certificate proving someone's connection to the General's illegitimate line. We think that's why she was killed."

"I didn't kill Rosa either."

"You were at the hospital Thursday evening. We've confirmed that. But what about earlier in the day? You could have met Rosa before your shift, learned what she'd found, and realized it threatened you?"

"I didn't meet Rosa. I didn't know what she'd found. I had nothing to do with her death. And the old man knew all about my lineage."

"Whose birth certificate did she find, Dr. Crawford?"

"I don't know."

"It wasn't Sarah Caldwell's. We've already traced that lineage. It must have been someone else's."

Graham looked genuinely puzzled. "I don't know whose certificate it was. If it proved someone's connection to the General, it could've been anyone in the illegitimate line. There might be more descendants we don't know about."

Now that was an interesting thought. What if there were more descendants beyond Graham and Augustus IV? Other grandchildren or great-grandchildren of the General's various indiscretions? *I mean, the general was obviously a lady's man. Who knows? It might be worth taking a look.*

"Let me ask you again," I said. "Did Augustus help you kill his father?"

"No. Because I didn't kill anyone."

"Did you help Augustus IV kill his father?"

"No."

"Are you protecting someone else?"

Graham hesitated. "No."

Ah hah! That hesitation was telling. He was hiding something, even if it wasn't direct involvement in murder.

I watched his eyes drift, not to the door, not to the table, but to the one-way glass where Melissa had once stood during another interview. Not guilt. Concern. Whoever he was shielding, he cared about them. I wrote one word: PROTECTING.

AT NOON, I brought both men into Interview Room One together again. This time, the atmosphere was charged. They'd both started pointing fingers at each other. Now I wanted to see them do it face to face.

"Gentlemen," I said, "you're both accusing each other of murder. Let's settle this."

Graham and Augustus glared at each other across the table.

"Augustus," I said, "you told me Graham had more motive than you did. Explain that."

"Graham's mother died in poverty," Augustus said, looking at Graham. "She struggled her whole life while my family lived in luxury. Graham discovered we were related and then married into the family. That's calculated. That's revenge."

"I married Melissa because I loved her," Graham shot back. "Not because of some ancient family grudge."

"Then why didn't you tell anyone you were related to us?" Augustus yelped. "Why keep it secret?"

"I told your father more than two years ago! I didn't keep it secret from everyone."

"But you didn't tell me. You didn't tell Melissa until after you were dating. You hid it until you'd already wormed your way into the family."

"I didn't worm my way anywhere. We met by chance, fell in love, got married. My family history wasn't relevant."

"Wasn't relevant?" Augustus's voice rose. "You're the General's great-grandson, just like me! That's extremely relevant!"

"Only if you think bloodline determines identity," Graham said coldly. "Which apparently you do, since you're so desperate to cling to an Aldridge inheritance you have no legal right to."

Augustus stood abruptly. "The will is legal. The changes haven't been signed. And at least I didn't marry into the family for revenge!"

"Sit down," I said firmly. "Both of you."

They sat, still glaring at each other.

"Augustus," I said, "where were you Sunday night between nine-thirty and eleven p.m.?"

"Hell's bells," he shouted. "That again? I already told you. Driving around."

"Graham, where were you?"

"In surgery. With witnesses."

"Augustus, you bought gas near the estate at ten-fifteen. That's suspicious."

"I was driving around! I needed gas!"

"Graham, you have digitalis in your medical bag. That's suspicious."

"It's standard medical equipment!"

I let them argue, watching their dynamic. They were genuinely angry at each other, genuinely defensive. This didn't feel like conspiracy. This felt like two scared men trying to deflect blame.

"Here's what I think," I said finally. "I think you're both hiding something. Maybe not murder, but something. And until you tell me the truth, you're both going to remain suspects."

"I've told you everything," Graham said.

"So have I," Augustus added.

"Then explain the burner phone. Explain whose birth certificate Rosa found. Explain why you both look guilty as hell but I can't prove either of you did it."

Neither man answered.

"You're both free to go," I said. "For now. But this isn't over."

AFTER THEY LEFT, Corbin and I sat in exhausted silence.

"They're either both innocent," Corbin said, "or one of them is a much better liar than the other."

"Or they're covering for someone else," I suggested.

"Like who?"

"I don't know. But there's something missing. Something we haven't seen yet."

I thought about the birth certificate Rosa had found. The one piece of physical evidence that could solve this case, and it was gone. Taken by her killer? Had to be, and if it wasn't one of the cousins, who the hell was it?

"We need to figure out whose birth certificate it was," I said. "That's the key. It wasn't Sarah Caldwell's. It wasn't Anne Caldwell Crawford's. So whose was it?"

"Maybe it was the General's illegitimate daughter's," Corbin suggested. "The one born in 1924. Proving she existed, proving the affair with Margaret Caldwell."

"Possible. But why would that get Rosa killed? We already know about that affair. It's not a secret anymore."

"Then maybe the certificate proved something else. Some other connection we haven't discovered."

I pulled up the genealogy research Cooper and Jack had compiled. The General's family tree, the Caldwell family tree, all the illegitimate children and hidden connections.

Somewhere in this tangle of names was another secret. Another descendant. Another person with motive to kill.

I drew a fresh branch on the board labeled UNKNOWN and, underneath, three question marks. "If Rosa texted someone she trusted," I said, "it wasn't either of them."

Corbin looked at the board, then at me. "So who does Rosa trust? Someone who straddles both worlds; family and staff?" The marker squeaked in my hand. A name nudged the back of my mind and slipped away like a frisky fish. Tomorrow I'd land it.

And tomorrow, by heaven, I was going to find out who it

was. Even if it meant tearing apart every assumption I'd made about this case.

17

The Evidence Doesn't Fit

IT WAS ONE OF THOSE COLD, RAINY MORNINGS I SO HATED. I rose early, but was unable to take Samson for our usual run, and I could tell the big dog was missing it. By seven I was totally bored and ready to go, so I did, arriving at the police department at just after seven-thirty to find Corbin already there.

"You feeling it, too?" I asked.

"Feeling what?" he replied.

"The weather," I replied. "It's awful; dreary, miserable, depressing."

Corbin shrugged. "It is what it is. You want coffee? I took the liberty and made a pot. It's not bad."

Now that was the best bit of news I'd had so far.

I poured myself a mug full and went to my office, sat down at my desk and stared at the whiteboards. I'd been staring at them for almost an hour, my coffee going cold on my desk,

Samson sleeping at my feet, and I could still see nothing: no pattern, nothing that jumped out at me. But deep down I knew something was wrong. The pieces didn't fit together the way they should.

When a puzzle won't click, it isn't because you're dumb; it's because some of the cardboard doesn't belong to the box. That's what this case felt like: stray pieces from someone else's picture.

At just after eight-thirty, Corbin knocked on the door and stepped inside. "Take a seat," I said. "Maybe you'll see something I've missed. I didn't get a wink of sleep last night. I couldn't stop thinking about it. Nothing adds up, Corbin. We're missing something fundamental."

"Walk me through it."

I stood and approached the main board. "Augustus III was poisoned with digitalis administered through his brandy. The method isn't sophisticated. Anyone with a little knowledge or access to Google could figure it out: gather a little foxglove from the garden, squeeze out a little digitalis, and you have your weapon. Motive? There's more than enough to go round, but the cousins are the prime suspects. Opportunity. Anyone during a period of a few days could have gained access to the library and added the digitalis to the old man's brandy bottle. Proof? We don't have any. Not even a frickin' smidgin."

"If you ask me, it's Graham," Corbin said.

"Of course," I replied. "Graham's a cardiovascular surgeon. He understands digitalis completely. But Graham has an iron-clad alibi for that Monday evening. He doesn't have an alibi for the days and weeks before though. But, again, it's all circumstantial and no prosecutor worth his salt would take it on."

"So he couldn't have done it."

"Yes, he could have done it. They all could have done it. Every member of the family and staff could have done it."

"But Graham is still the most likely. He poisoned the brandy earlier. Days or weeks before, leaving it to be discovered whenever Augustus drank from that bottle. It was after all his own private stock."

"But that's risky," I said, "and it's circumstantial. What if someone else drank from that bottle? What if Augustus didn't drink from it at all?"

"Unlikely," Corbin said. "The old man was a drinker. We know that. Sooner or later, he was going to take a 'little taste.'" I still think the surgeon did it."

I heaved a sigh and moved to the second board. "Rosa Martinez was killed Thursday evening between six and eight p.m. She was hit with a blunt object—a rock, a heavy object—then her body was dragged to a ravine. It's violent, spontaneous, desperate."

"Different from the calculated poisoning," Corbin observed.

"Very different. The poisoning was patient, planned. Rosa's murder was brutal and immediate. These don't feel like the same killer."

"You think we're looking for two killers?"

"No. One killer, two different situations. The poisoning was premeditated, planned for weeks or months. Rosa's murder was reactive; she found something that threatened the killer, and they acted immediately."

"Okay, so one killer with two different methods," Corbin asked. "What does that tell us?"

I returned to my desk, pulling up the evidence files on my

computer. "The partial fingerprint on the brandy bottle doesn't match Graham or Augustus IV. It doesn't match anyone in our database."

"Could be degraded, unusable."

"Hawk said it's forty percent of a thumbprint. That's enough to exclude people definitively. It excludes our prime suspects."

"So the person who handled the brandy bottle isn't one of our suspects?"

"Or it's an old print from weeks or months ago, unrelated to the poisoning," I replied.

I pulled up the burner phone records. "The burner phone was purchased on September 23rd, three weeks before the murder. It was used normally: brief texts, short calls, maintaining some kind of relationship. Then Rosa texted it Thursday, saying she'd found something, asking to meet. That means she knew who owned the burner."

"And she was killed shortly after," Corbin stated.

"Right. But here's what bothers me: Augustus IV's phone shows he received texts from that same burner number, but he doesn't remember them. He says he might have deleted them thinking they were spam."

"Or he's lying."

"Or someone else had access to his phone and deleted the texts to frame him."

Corbin frowned. "That's elaborate."

"This whole case is elaborate. Someone bought a burner phone weeks in advance, communicated with multiple people, poisoned Augustus III with medical precision, then killed Rosa Martinez to cover their tracks. That's not amateur work."

I jotted the burner's pattern on the glass: NORMAL → LURE → SILENCE. Whoever used it had discipline. Most killers get chatty; this one tightened their radius.

I stood again, pacing. "And then there's the birth certificate. Rosa found it, photographed it, texted someone about it. That certificate proved someone's connection to the General's illegitimate line. But whose?"

"We've assumed it was Sarah Caldwell's or her mother's."

"But what if it wasn't? What if it proved someone else's connection? Someone we haven't considered?"

Corbin leaned back in his chair. "You're saying we've been focused on the wrong suspects."

"I'm saying the evidence doesn't fit Graham or Augustus IV as neatly as I thought. Graham has solid alibis for both murders. Augustus IV has gaps in his alibis, but no physical evidence linking him to either crime. The fingerprint isn't his. The burner phone can't be traced to him. His motive is strong, but so is his confusion about his own identity."

"So if it's not Graham or Augustus IV, who is it?"

That was the question. I looked at the other names on the board: family members, staff, people we'd interviewed but not seriously suspected.

"Melissa had opportunity and motive," I said. "She stood to lose millions if the will changes went through."

"But she has no medical knowledge. How would she know how to poison someone with digitalis?"

"She's married to a cardiovascular surgeon. She could've learned from Graham, taken digitalis from his medical bag."

"Would Graham let his wife murder her own father?"

"Not if he knew about it. But what if he didn't? What if

Melissa acted alone, using knowledge she'd gained from Graham's work?"

Corbin considered this. "Her alibis are weak. She was home alone both nights. But Melissa doesn't seem like the type to commit violent murder. She's controlled, sophisticated."

"The poisoning fits her personality. The violence of Rosa's death doesn't."

"Unless Rosa threatened to expose her."

I thought about Melissa's composed demeanor during interviews. Her lack of obvious grief. Her careful answers that never quite revealed what she was thinking. She was a cold one.

"We should bring her in again," I said. "Press harder."

"What about Victoria?" Corbin suggested. "She had motive to protect Augustus IV. If Augustus III was going to disinherit him, expose the baby switch, Victoria might've killed to prevent that."

"Victoria's grief seemed genuine," I said. "And she had nothing to gain financially. She's independently wealthy."

"But she had everything to lose emotionally. Augustus is her son, even if not biologically. She raised him, loved him. Would she kill to protect him?"

"Maybe," I said. "But then we come back to the digitalis. I think that would be one hell of a stretch, Google or not."

"You've said it yourself," Corbin replied. "The estate has foxglove in the gardens. Anyone who knows about plants could extract digitalis from foxglove leaves."

I stopped pacing. "Foxglove. We noted that early in the investigation but didn't pursue it. If someone extracted digitalis from plants on the estate, they wouldn't need medical connections or Graham's medication bag."

"Who on the estate would have that kind of botanical knowledge?" I muttered. "A staff member!"

We both looked at the board, at the names of staff members we'd barely questioned.

"The gardener," Corbin said. "Rosa Martinez. But she's the victim, not the killer."

"What about the cook?" I asked. "Helen Park. She's been at the estate for thirty years. A cook would know about herbs, plants, extractions."

"Do we have anything suggesting Helen Park is connected to this case?"

"No. She was barely mentioned in initial interviews. We focused entirely on family."

I sat down, pulling up Helen Park's initial statement. It was brief. She'd been in her cottage Sunday evening, heard nothing unusual, found out about Augustus's death Monday morning when Victoria told the staff. Nothing suspicious.

I scanned payroll and deliveries. A line item jumped out: bulk glycerin and cheesecloth ordered for the kitchen garden preserves workshop. Perfectly innocent for jellies. Also perfect for plant extractions. I didn't circle it; I boxed it in red.

"We need to interview her again," I said. "Properly this time. We've been so focused on family and their financial motives that we overlooked the staff completely."

"Marcus Webb was investigated for embezzlement."

"Right, because he had obvious motive. But what about the others? What about Claudia Rivera, who manages the household? We treated them as witnesses, not suspects."

Corbin nodded slowly. "You're right. We assumed family

members killed Augustus for money. But what if someone on the staff has a completely different motive?"

"What motive would staff have?" I said.

"I don't know. But we won't find out unless we ask."

I looked at the evidence boards again, seeing them differently now. We'd constructed elaborate theories about conspiracy between cousins, about calculated revenge for family secrets. But what if the answer was simpler? What if someone with daily access to the house, to the brandy, to Augustus's routines, had killed him for reasons we hadn't even considered?

"So, tomorrow we interview all the staff again. Not as witnesses but as potential suspects. We look at their backgrounds, their connections, their access to the estate. We've been looking up at the family. It's time to look down at the people who served them."

"What about Graham and Augustus IV?"

"We don't rule them out. But we expand our focus. Because right now, the evidence doesn't point clearly at either of them. And in my experience, when the evidence doesn't fit, it's because you're looking at the wrong suspect."

Corbin stood. "I'll call Cooper and Jack. Have them start background checks on all estate staff."

"Thorough ones. I want complete histories: where they came from, why they took jobs at the estate, any connections to the family beyond employment."

After Corbin left, I sat alone in my office, staring at those enigmatic boards. In the meantime, I had other cases I was responsible for. It was almost the end of the month, and I needed to catch up in my paperwork. The chief does not like it when I'm late with my reports.

Samson huffed, rolled onto his side, and thumped a paw against the baseboard; his version of a nudge. I uncapped my marker and wrote one last line under the STAFF header: "People who pour the drinks don't need invitations to the club." In the silence, the rain found the windows and kept time. Tomorrow we'd stop asking who hated Augustus and start asking who knew his habits well enough to wait him out.

18

Overlooked and Invisible

COOPER AND JACK HAD WORKED THROUGH THE NIGHT, compiling comprehensive background checks on all the Aldridge estate staff. By Wednesday morning, I had files on my desk for Marcus Webb, Claudia Rivera, and Helen Park.

"Start with Marcus Webb," I told Corbin as we reviewed the files. "We know about his embezzlement, but what else?"

Corbin flipped through Webb's file. "Former Army Ranger, served eight years, honorable discharge. Worked security jobs before being hired as estate manager eight years ago. References were solid. No criminal history before the embezzlement."

"Family?"

"Divorced, no kids. Parents deceased. One sister in Florida he's estranged from. He's isolated, which probably contributed to the gambling problem."

"Motive for murder?"

"The embezzlement gives him strong motive," Corbin

replied. "Augustus threatened to fire him and press charges. That's career-ending, possibly prison time. But I don't see him as the type to plan sophisticated poisoning."

"What about Rosa's murder?" I asked.

"More his style, if he did it. Blunt force trauma fits someone with military combat training. But what motive would Marcus have to kill Rosa?"

"If she found evidence of his embezzlement. Or if she threatened to expose something else about him. But you're right. I don't like him for it either."

We moved to the next file.

"Claudia Rivera," I said. "Household manager. She's been at the estate for twenty five years."

"Single, never married," Corbin read. "She came from Atlanta, where she worked for another wealthy family. Her references are impeccable. She has no criminal history, and no apparent financial problems."

"Why would she kill Augustus?" I asked.

"She has no obvious motive. She had steady employment, a good salary, and seemed content with her position."

"And Rosa's murder?"

"Again, no motive. Claudia and Rosa worked together well, according to the other staff. No conflicts, no tension."

That left Helen Park.

"Head cook, age seventy-one," I read from her file. "Been at the estate for thirty-two years. That's longer than anyone else."

"Thirty-two years," Corbin repeated, shaking his head. "That's dedication."

I nodded as I flipped through Helen's background information. "Born Helen Park in Nashville, 1953. Never married, no children. Started working as a cook for wealthy families in her twenties. Came to the Aldridge estate in 1992, hired by Victoria to manage the kitchen."

"Any criminal history?"

"None. No financial problems, no apparent issues. She's lived in staff housing on the estate the entire time, seems to have devoted her life to the job."

"Why?" Corbin asked. "That's unusual, isn't it? Thirty-two years in the same position, never marrying, no other life outside the estate?"

"Maybe she loved her work. Maybe she's one of those people who finds purpose in service."

"Or maybe she had another reason for staying."

I looked at Corbin and frowned. "What do you mean?"

"Think about it. We've been focused on family members with financial motives. But what about someone with a personal motive? Someone who's been close to this family for decades, watching them, knowing their secrets?"

"You think Helen Park had a personal reason to kill Augustus?" Corbin said. "I mean, she was being terminated after more than thirty years.

"I think it's worth investigating. She's been there longer than anyone. She prepared the family's food for three decades. She had access to everything—the library, the brandy collection, knowledge of family routines."

He was right. Helen Park had more access and opportunity than anyone except family members. And she'd been overlooked completely because we assumed domestic staff had no motive.

"What's in her personnel file?" I asked.

Corbin found the documents. "Annual performance

reviews, all excellent. Salary increases over the years. No complaints, no disciplinary issues. She was apparently the perfect employee."

"Too perfect maybe?"

"Maybe," he replied. "Let's see what else Cooper found."

I called Cooper.

"Captain," he answered. "I'm still digging into Helen Park's background."

"What have you got?"

"That's the thing; not much. Her early life is vague. Her birth certificate shows Helen Park, born Nashville 1953, mother's name is Margaret Park. Father listed as unknown."

"Unknown father. That's interesting."

"Margaret Park died in 1978, according to death records. I can find no other family. Helen seems to have no living relatives, which is unusual, to say the least."

"What about before she came to the Aldridge estate? Employment history?"

"She worked for two other wealthy families in Nashville from 1975 to 1992. Then she came to the Aldridges. Her references from those families were excellent, but I haven't been able to reach anyone to verify. The families have either moved or the people who employed her have died."

"So we're taking her employment history on faith," I said.

"Basically, yes. From 1992 onward, everything's documented at the Aldridge estate. Before that, it's sketchy."

"Keep digging, Tony. I want to know everything about Helen Park's early life. Where she grew up, who her mother was, why her father wasn't listed on her birth certificate."

"On it," he replied.

After hanging up, I turned to Corbin. "Helen Park's past is

vague. Unknown father, deceased mother, no verifiable references from her early employment."

"That's suspicious for someone applying to work for a prominent family. The Aldridges should've required thorough background checks."

"Maybe they did, thirty-two years ago. Or maybe Victoria trusted her because she came recommended by someone."

"We need to interview Helen Park again," Corbin said. "Thoroughly this time."

"Agreed. But let's be careful. If she's been overlooked for three decades, we don't want to spook her by coming on too strong."

"How do you want to approach it?" he asked.

"Routine follow-up questions about Rosa. Helen and Rosa worked together for years. We can ask about Rosa's state of mind, whether she mentioned finding anything unusual, who she might have contacted. See if Helen's reactions tell us anything."

"And if she seems suspicious?"

"Then we push harder."

WE DROVE to the Aldridge estate at noon, finding Helen Park in the kitchen preparing lunch. She was a small woman, thin and wiry, with her gray hair pulled back in a neat bun. She wore a simple dress and apron, her hands moving efficiently as she chopped vegetables.

"Ms. Park," I said, entering the kitchen. "We have a few questions. Can we talk?"

She looked up, showing no surprise. "Of course, Captain. Would you like to sit in here, or somewhere else?"

"Here is fine," I replied.

Helen wiped her hands on her apron and gestured to the kitchen table. "Can I offer you coffee? I just made a fresh pot."

"That would be nice, thank you," I said.

She poured three cups of coffee, then sat down at the table across from us. Her movements were calm, controlled. If she was nervous about police questioning, she didn't show it.

"We're following up on Rosa Martinez's death," I began. "I know you've already given a statement, but we'd like to ask a few more questions."

"Of course. Poor Rosa. Such a tragedy."

"You worked with Rosa for how long?" I asked.

"She started as assistant gardener about twelve years ago, then took over as head gardener five years ago when her father's dementia got worse. I've known her the entire time."

"Were you close?" Corbin asked.

"As close as staff can be. We were friendly, cordial. Rosa was a good woman, dedicated to her work."

"Did she seem troubled in the days before her death? Worried about anything?"

Helen thought carefully. "She seemed excited, actually. Wednesday evening—the day before she died—she mentioned finding something interesting while working outside."

"Did she say what she found?" Corbin asked.

"No. Just that she'd found something historically related to the estate. She was always curious about family history. Especially about the general."

"Did Rosa ever discuss the family with you? Their secrets, their past?"

"Sometimes. Staff do talk, you know. But Rosa was discreet. She respected the family."

"What about you, Ms. Park? You've been here thirty-two years. You must know the family's secrets better than most."

Helen smiled slightly. "I know a great deal, yes. But I keep confidences. That's part of being in service."

"Tell me about Sunday night, October twentieth," I said, casually leaning back in my chair. "Where were you between nine and midnight?"

"In my cottage. I'd finished cleaning the kitchen after dinner, went to my cottage around eight-thirty. Read for a while, and went to bed around ten."

"Did you see or hear anything unusual?"

"No. My cottage is on the far side of the property from the main house. I wouldn't have heard anything from the library."

"What about Thursday evening, October seventeenth? Where were you between six and eight that evening?"

"In the kitchen, preparing dinner. I made a roasted chicken with vegetables. The family ate around seven."

"Anyone see you during that time?"

"Claudia came through around six-thirty. Otherwise, I was alone. The kitchen is my domain."

Her answers were calm and consistent. Nothing in her demeanor suggested guilt or nervousness. She was simply a longtime employee answering police questions.

But something bothered me about her extreme calm. Most people showed some emotion when discussing murder: fear, sadness, anxiety. Helen showed nothing.

I let the silence stretch. The kitchen clock ticked with the slow, patient rhythm of a metronome. Somewhere behind us, a kettle began to whistle and Helen rose to kill the flame without looking; muscle memory honed by decades. Unflappable. Or rehearsed.

"Ms. Park, how well did you know Augustus Aldridge?"

"Very well. I cooked for him for thirty-two years. I knew his preferences, his routines, and his habits."

"Did you like him?" Corbin asked.

Helen paused, considering. "Mr. Augustus was demanding. Very particular about things. But he was a fair employer. I respected him."

"That's not the same as liking him," Corbin said.

"No," she replied. "But in service, respect is more important than affection."

"What about the rest of the family? Did you like them?"

"Mrs. Victoria is kind. Mr. Augustus IV is troubled but not unkind. Miss Melissa is... complicated. Dr. Crawford is polite. Mrs. Allison is distant. They're all people I've served for years. I get along with all of them."

"You've watched them grow up, in some cases," I said. "You watched their lives unfold."

"Yes. That's true."

"That must create strong feelings," I said. "Loyalty, perhaps. Or resentment if they took you for granted."

"I have no resentments, Captain. I chose this life."

"Thirty-two years is a long time to stay in one position. Most people move on, change jobs, pursue other opportunities. Why did you stay?"

For the first time, Helen's composure flickered slightly. "I found my purpose here. This is my home."

"You have no family of your own?" I observed. "No desire for marriage, children?"

"Some of us aren't meant for that kind of life," she replied.

"What about your past? Before you came here?"

"I worked for other families. This was the best position, so I stayed."

"Your father wasn't listed on your birth certificate. Why not?"

Helen's eyes narrowed. "That's a very personal question. Why d'you ask?"

"It's relevant to our investigation," I replied, easily.

"How?" she asked, frowning.

I sat up straight and leaned forward. "I'll ask the questions, Mr. Park. Why wasn't your father listed?"

"Because my mother didn't name him. It's not uncommon for that era."

"Do you know who your father was?" I asked.

Helen stood abruptly. "I think this interview is over. You came to ask about Rosa, not interrogate me about my parentage."

"Sit down, Ms. Park."

"Am I under arrest?"

"No. But you're a person of interest in a double murder investigation. I can question you here voluntarily, or we can continue this at the police department. Your choice."

Helen sat slowly, her calm restored but with an edge beneath it. "I had nothing to do with those murders."

"Then help me understand your background. Who was your father?"

"I don't know. My mother never told me."

"What was your mother's name before she married?"

"She didn't marry. Her name was always Margaret Park."

"Where did she work?"

"Various places. Domestic positions."

"Did she ever work at the Aldridge estate?"

Helen's jaw tightened. "Briefly, yes. In the 1920s, before I was born."

And there it was. The connection I'd been searching for.

"Your mother worked here," I said softly. "For how long?"

"I don't know exactly. She didn't talk about it."

"Why did she leave?"

"I don't know."

"Yes, you do." I snapped. "Why did your mother leave the Aldridge estate?"

Helen stood again. "That's it. I'm done answering questions. If you want to know more, get a warrant."

She walked out of the kitchen, leaving Corbin and me sitting at the table with cold coffee.

"Her mother worked here," Corbin said quietly. "That's not a coincidence."

"No. And her reaction when I asked about it tells us she knows exactly why her mother left."

I glanced at the pantry on our way out. Neat rows of jars: preserves, cordials, herbal syrups labeled in Helen's tidy hand. One shelf held folded cheesecloth and brown bottles of glycerin. Perfectly innocent for jams. Perfectly useful for plant extractions. I photographed the labels.

I pulled out my phone and called Cooper. "I need everything you can find on Margaret Park. She worked at the Aldridge estate in the 1920s. I want to know when, and why she left, and who Helen Park's father was."

"On it," Cooper said.

As Corbin and I left the estate, I looked back at the main house. Helen Park stood at a kitchen window, watching us leave. Her expression was unreadable, but her posture was tense.

She knew something. I was sure of it. Something about her mother, her past, her connection to this family. And I wanted to know what it was.

If the rich wrote the history, the servants stored the footnotes in cellars, on recipe cards and in ledgers no one bothered to read. Tomorrow, we'd start reading. And this time, we'd start in the kitchen.

19

Her Story

Cooper called me early the following morning and he
sounded excited despite the early hour.

"This had better be good, Tony," I said, throwing back the
covers and swinging my legs out of bed.

"Oh, it's good, Captain, I found it. I found the connection."

"What connection?"

"Helen Park's grandmother, Margaret Park. She worked at
the Aldridge estate from 1922 to 1925. She was a household
servant—cleaning, cooking, whatever was needed." I was wide
awake now.

"Her grandmother. Go on."

"Margaret Park was dismissed in March 1925. I found a
notation in old estate records that Tracy dug up from the
county archives. She was let go for 'moral turpitude.' That was
code for pregnancy out of wedlock."

I felt the pieces clicking into place. "She was pregnant?"

"Right. Margaret left the estate in disgrace and had a baby

in December 1925—a daughter named Ruth Park. No father listed on the birth certificate."

"So Ruth Park is Helen's mother."

"Exactly. Ruth Park had Helen in 1953. So Helen's grandmother Margaret worked at this estate, got pregnant, and was forced to leave in shame. That daughter Ruth grew up in poverty, then had Helen. Helen is Margaret's granddaughter."

"Who was the father?" I asked, though I suspected I knew.

"There's no name on Ruth's birth certificate. But given the time period, given that Margaret was dismissed in disgrace rather than helped, given that she had no husband—"

"Brigadier General Augustus Aldridge's son Augustus II raped or coerced Margaret Park," I finished for him.

"That's my read on it," Tony replied. "And Helen Park has been working in this house—the house where her grandmother was raped—for thirty-two years."

I couldn't help but shiver a little. Not because of the revelation itself, but because I could suddenly see Helen's entire life reframed, a quiet, gray existence that was never about service or loyalty, but about silent endurance. How many years had she stood in that same kitchen, watching generations of Aldridges dine in luxury, smiling politely while nursing the ghosts of her bloodline?

The revenge motive was suddenly crystal clear. Helen was a descendant of the General, denied her heritage, working in the house where her family's trauma began.

"Get me everything," I said. "Complete timeline, all the documents, anything connecting Helen to this family."

"Already compiling it."

Outside, dawn was breaking. The sky was the color of tarnished pewter. Rain fell softly, steady and cold. It was the kind of morning that seemed to seep under your skin. As I dressed, I couldn't shake the image of a young woman in 1925, frightened, shamed, cast out while the man who violated her sat at a mahogany desk writing letters of command. History had a cruel way of echoing itself.

After hanging up, I lay back on my pillow, staring at the ceiling as the pieces fell into place. Helen Park was Augustus II's through the rape of a servant. Her grandmother Margaret had been forced out in disgrace in 1925, and her descendants —Ruth, then Helen—had lived in poverty while the Aldridges lived in wealth and luxury.

Helen had worked in that house for thirty-two years, cooking their meals, serving their family, invisible and over-looked. All the while planning her revenge.

Maybe it hadn't started as revenge. Maybe it began as curiosity, then grew into bitterness, then hardened into some-thing else—something that took root like a weed and refused to die.

I got off the bed and headed for the shower. Samson lifted his head, hoping for an early morning run, but I shook my head. "Not today, buddy. We've got a killer to catch." By seven-thirty, I was at the office. Corbin arrived shortly after, holding two cups of coffee.

"You look like you didn't sleep," he said, handing me one.

"Cooper called at an ungodly hour. Helen Park is Augustus II's granddaughter. He raped her grandmother Margaret and she was forced out in disgrace. Her descen-dants have lived in poverty while the Aldridges lived in wealth."

"That's powerful motive for revenge," Corbin said.

"Thirty-two years of planning," I replied. "She got herself

hired here, positioned herself perfectly, and waited for the right opportunity."

"But why kill Augustus III now?" he asked. "Why not years ago?"

"Because something triggered her. Maybe Augustus's research into Emily Caldwell's descendants threatened to expose Helen's connection. Maybe the birth certificate Rosa found proved Helen's lineage. Or maybe Helen just finally decided the time was right."

"We need to bring her in, then," he replied.

"Yes. But carefully. Helen's been patient for decades. She's smart, controlled. We need evidence, not just theory. Ideally, we need a confession."

Corbin smiled. "Good luck with that. She's not going to be easy to break."

He was right. Helen Park wasn't a criminal in panic; she was a woman who'd already outwaited time itself. Breaking her would mean finding the one place she still felt pain—and I wasn't sure such a place existed anymore.

I nodded, but didn't reply. I was thinking about what I wanted to do next.

"We have her family connection," Corbin said, reading my mind.

"Which isn't illegal," I replied. "We need to connect her to the actual murders. The digitalis, the brandy bottle, Rosa's death."

The word "digitalis" echoed in my head. It was the kind of poison that required patience—extracted, refined, measured with surgical precision. Just like Helen: methodical, meticulous, deliberate. The parallel wasn't lost on me.

I thought about Helen's botanical knowledge as a cook.

About the foxglove growing on the estate grounds. About how someone who'd worked in that kitchen for thirty-two years would know every inch of the property, every routine, every opportunity.

"The foxglove," I said. "Helen would know about medicinal plants and herbs. She could extract digitalis from foxglove leaves."

"But can we prove she did?" he asked.

"Maybe. If we search her cottage, we might find some equipment for making such extractions. Dried foxglove leaves, maybe. Something connecting her to the poison."

"We need a warrant," he replied thoughtfully.

"Then let's get one."

BY THE TIME we reached the estate, the air was heavy with the smell of rain-soaked earth. The manor loomed ahead, its windows dark and glistening. Somewhere inside, the cook was going about her work as if nothing had happened, as if she weren't the ghost of the very injustice that built those walls.

By noon, we had a search warrant for Helen Park's cottage. She wasn't there when we arrived—she was in the main house kitchen, preparing lunch as usual. And I'd stationed officers there to keep her occupied while we searched.

Helen's cottage was small but comfortable. One-bedroom, a tiny kitchen, sitting room with a fireplace. Everything was neat, organized, and impersonal. No photographs, no personal mementos, nothing that revealed who Helen Park really was.

That absence of identity chilled me more than any evidence could have. It was as if she'd erased herself long ago, leaving behind only the role she played for the Aldridges.

Hawk and Mike Willis went through the cottage systematically. In the bedroom closet, they found something interesting—a locked wooden box hidden under blankets on the top shelf.

"Captain," Hawk called. "You want to come and see this?"

I entered the bedroom as Hawk picked the simple lock. Inside the box were papers—old documents, carefully preserved.

A birth certificate for Margaret Park's daughter, born December 1925. Father listed as "unknown." A death certificate for that daughter, dated 1978. And handwritten letters—dozens of them—from Margaret Park to her daughter, spanning decades.

The papers smelled faintly of cedar and age, a ghostly scent of memory. The handwriting was elegant but unsteady, ink faded to brown. These weren't just relics; they were confessions from the grave. Each letter seemed to breathe with the grief of a woman long dead but not forgotten.

I read one dated 1950:

My dearest Ruth, I must tell you the truth about your father, though it shames me to write these words. He was a powerful man, a general's son, someone I could not refuse when he demanded what he wanted. He took what wasn't freely given, then cast me out when the consequences became visible. You are not illegitimate because of sin —you are illegitimate because of his violence and my powerlessness. Never forget what the Aldridge family took from us.

Ruth. Helen's mother was named Ruth, not Margaret. And Ruth had been born from rape.

Another letter, dated 1960:

Ruth, I know you want to confront them, to demand acknowledgment, but it would destroy you. They are powerful. We are nothing. Keep your dignity, raise your daughter well, and let God judge them in the end.

So Ruth had wanted revenge, but Margaret had counseled restraint. Helen had grown up hearing these stories, knowing her grandmother's trauma, understanding her family had been victimized by the Aldridges.

A legacy like that doesn't fade, it festers. Generation after generation of silence hardens into something sharp, something that cuts. Helen's revenge wasn't born in a moment of rage; it had been nurtured like a seed passed down through blood.

"Keep searching," I told Hawk. "I want anything else in this cottage that connects Helen to the murders."

In the kitchen, Mike found what we needed—a small notebook tucked behind cleaning supplies under the sink. The notebook contained handwritten notes about plants, their properties, extraction methods.

One page was titled "Digitalis purpurea—Foxglove." Below it, detailed notes about where foxglove grew on the estate grounds, how to harvest the leaves, methods for extracting cardiac glycosides, and the proper drying techniques.

Another page showed calculations—dosages, lethal amounts, timing of symptoms.

"She was planning this," Willis said, holding the notebook carefully. "This is premeditation."

"It's circumstantial," I replied. "All that shows is that she could have done it, not that she did. We need more."

Still, I could feel the weight of inevitability pressing in.

The pieces weren't just fitting, they were locking into place, cold and final. The line between evidence and understanding was blurring; I could almost see Helen's steady hands measuring powder, her quiet satisfaction as she sealed the brandy bottle.

And we found it. In a drawer, we found dried plant material in small cloth bags. Mike Willis photographed everything, then sealed the bags as evidence.

"Get it to the lab," I told him. "I want confirmation it's foxglove, and I want it tested against the digitalis found in Augustus's system."

OUTSIDE, the rain had stopped, but the air hung thick and heavy, the kind of stillness that comes before a reckoning. I had no doubt now; we were about to confront a woman who'd carried an entire family's sin for nearly a century and finally decided to make them pay.

By four that afternoon, we had Helen Park in Interview Room One. She sat calmly, hands folded, showing no concern despite being brought in for formal questioning.

Her eyes, sharp and dark, held no fear, only fatigue, maybe even relief. I'd seen that look before in killers who believed they'd already served their sentence long before they were caught.

"Ms. Park," I began, "we've searched your cottage."

"I'm aware," she replied. "Your officers made quite a mess."

"We found some interesting things. Letters from your grandmother Margaret Park to your mother Ruth. Letters about the Aldridge family."

Helen's expression didn't change.

"Your grandmother worked at this estate in the 1920s," I continued. "She was raped by Augustus II. She became pregnant, was dismissed in disgrace, and spent the rest of her life in poverty. Your mother Ruth was the issue of that rape. You, Helen, grew up hearing these stories."

"My family history is none of your business," she snapped.

"It's very much my business when it provides motive for murder," I replied. "You're Augustus II's granddaughter, Helen. You have Aldridge blood. But you were denied everything while legitimate descendants lived in wealth. How do you feel about that?"

A long silence hung between us, taut as piano wire. The hum of the fluorescent lights seemed louder than breathing. When Helen finally spoke, her voice carried decades of buried pain. She shrugged slightly, looked away to her left, then looked me in the eye and said, "How d'you think I feel about it?"

"I think you spent thirty-two years working in the house where your grandmother was raped, cooking for the family that destroyed your grandmother's life, waiting for the right moment to take revenge."

"That's an interesting theory, but it means nothing."

"Oh, I think it does," I replied. "It's not theory. We found your notebook. The one with notes about foxglove, digitalis extraction, lethal dosages. We found dried plant material in your cottage. We're testing it now, but I'm confident it'll match the digitalis that killed Augustus Aldridge."

For the first time, Helen's composure cracked slightly. "Where did you find that?"

"In your kitchen drawer. It wasn't very well hidden, Helen. Almost like you wanted us to find it."

"Hah! I keep notes on all kinds of medicinal plants. It's a hobby."

"No. It's evidence of premeditated murder. You extracted digitalis from foxglove growing on the estate grounds. You poisoned Augustus's brandy, knowing he drank alone in his library on Sunday evenings. You killed him to avenge your grandmother's rape and your family's suffering."

Helen was quiet for a long moment. When she spoke, her voice was cold. "Augustus Aldridge III was a descendant of a rapist. He was an evil man, just like his grandfather. He lived in luxury built on my grandmother's shame. Why should I feel guilty about anything, especially ending his life?"

"So you admit it, then?" I asked, surprised, and leaned back in my chair.

"I'm not admitting anything legally actionable. I'm simply stating facts. The Aldridge family owed my family everything. They gave us nothing."

"What about Rosa Martinez?" I asked. "What did Rosa do to deserve death?"

Helen's jaw tightened. "Rosa found something she shouldn't have. She was always poking her nose where she shouldn't."

"It was the birth certificate, wasn't it? She found your mother Ruth's birth certificate proving Augustus II's rape of your grandmother."

"Rosa was going to expose everything. She texted me Thursday evening, said she'd found proof of my family connections, and wanted to show me. She thought I'd want to know there were other descendants from the General's line.

She didn't understand what it would mean if that certificate became public."

"So it was your burner phone and you killed her," Corbin said.

"I protected my revenge. I'd waited thirty-two years. I wasn't going to let some nosey gardener ruin everything."

"So you met her at the carriage house Thursday evening," I said. "You hit her with something, then dragged her body to the ravine, and you took the birth certificate."

"Rosa should've minded her own business," she retorted.

The confession was spilling out now, Helen's control finally breaking.

"Tell me how you poisoned Augustus," I said. "Walk me through it."

Helen leaned back, folded her arms, almost relaxed, and sighed. "I extracted digitalis from foxglove leaves. It took weeks to accumulate enough, to refine it properly. I calculated the dosage carefully—enough to kill but not so much it would be immediately obvious as poisoning. I wanted it to look like natural heart failure."

Her voice softened as she spoke, almost tender, like a teacher explaining a recipe. There was pride in her precision, but not joy. It was the voice of someone who believed she'd done what history demanded of her.

"When did you poison the brandy?"

"On Sunday afternoon. While the family was at the charity function. I went to the library, added digitalis to the brandy bottle. I knew Augustus would drink from it that evening. He always had brandy in the library Sunday nights."

"Weren't you worried someone else would drink it?"

"No one else drank that particular brandy. It was Augustus's private stock. I'd watched his habits for thirty-two years. I knew exactly what he'd do."

"And Rosa Martinez?" I asked. "Walk me through what happened."

HELEN'S JAW TIGHTENED. "Rosa should've minded her own business. When she showed me Ruth's certificate—my mother's birth certificate—I knew I had to act. I picked up a rock and hit her on the back of her head. Then I dragged her into the woods."

"And you took the birth certificate."

"I burned it. Now there's no evidence."

"Except we have Rosa's photograph of it. She documented everything before meeting you."

Helen's expression darkened. "I didn't know about the photograph."

"It shows your mother Ruth's birth certificate, proving she was born in 1925, daughter of Margaret Park. Father unknown. That certificate, combined with your family letters, proves you're Augustus II's granddaughter."

"So what? Being related to them doesn't make me a murderer."

"No. But the foxglove notebook, the dried plant material, your confession just now—that makes you a murderer."

Helen smiled slightly. "You've been recording this?"

"Of course."

"Good. I want it on record. I want everyone to know what the Aldridge family did to my grandmother. I want the truth to be told after a century of lies."

And there it was; the truth, raw and terrible. She hadn't

killed for silence; she'd killed for remembrance. For the world to finally see the blood beneath the Aldridge name.

"The truth will be told. In a murder trial, with you as the defendant. You'll go to prison, Helen, probably for the rest of your life."

"I don't care. I got my revenge. I killed Augustus Aldridge, just like his grandfather killed my grandmother's. Justice, Captain. Finally, after ninety-nine years, there's justice for what they did to her."

"Justice would've been exposing them, suing them, demanding recognition. Murder is never the answer to anything."

"You don't understand. My grandmother begged for help. She told people what happened. No one believed her. The General was powerful, respected. She was nothing—a servant who'd been 'ruined.' She died poor and broken, her daughter Ruth raised in shame. I grew up hearing those stories, seeing the Aldridge mansion from a distance, knowing their blood ran in my veins but I'd never be acknowledged."

"So you spent three decades planning revenge," Corbin said.

"I spent three decades earning the right to justice. I watched them, learned from them, became invisible to them. I was just another servant, unimportant, overlooked. And then, when the time was right, I took what they owed us."

"Two lives," I said.

"Two lives to balance a century of suffering," she snapped.

Helen's eyes were bright now, almost fevered. She'd been holding it all inside for so long, and now that it was out, she seemed relieved.

"Helen Park," I said formally, "I'm arresting you for the

murders of Augustus Aldridge III and Rosa Martinez. You have the right to remain silent—"

"I don't want to remain silent," Helen interrupted. "I want everyone to know what I did and why. I want the world to understand that the Aldridges aren't the noble family they pretend to be. They're built on violence and lies, and I made them pay for it; I *will* make them pay for it."

As officers took her away, Helen looked back at me.

"Tell them," she said. "Tell everyone about Margaret Park. Tell them what the great General did to her. That's all I ever wanted; for the truth to come out."

The door closed behind her, leaving Corbin and me alone in the interview room.

"So, we got what we needed," Corbin said, "a confession."

"She wanted to confess," I muttered. "This was never about getting away with it. It was about revenge and making sure people knew why."

"Do you think she's right? About justice?"

I thought about Margaret Park, raped and discarded. About Ruth, born in shame. About Helen, growing up in the shadow of the Aldridge wealth, knowing she was their blood but would never be acknowledged.

"What happened to her grandmother was terrible," I said finally. "Augustus II should've been held accountable. Margaret should've been supported, not dismissed. But murder isn't justice. It's just more violence on top of old violence."

"Helen got what she wanted though," Corbin said. "Now everyone will know about Augustus II's rape of Margaret Park. The secret's out. I wonder if she'll write a book."

I smiled at that. "Yes. Along with the secret that Helen Park is a double murderer who spent thirty-two years planning revenge. I'm not sure that's the legacy she was hoping for. As to writing a book, if she doesn't, I'm sure someone will."

We left the interview room and walked back to my office. Outside, Halloween decorations adorned the police department—fake cobwebs, plastic skeletons, orange and black bunting. It seemed absurd given what we'd just uncovered.

A century of secrets. Rape, murder, cover-ups, denial. All of it exploding into the present with two more deaths. And at the center of it all, an invisible woman who'd served the family that destroyed hers, waiting decades for her moment of revenge.

When the door shut behind us, the silence that followed was almost reverent. I'd expected triumph; instead, all I felt was sorrow. Justice had been claimed, but it was hollow, bitter —another ghost added to the long, haunted ledger of the Aldridge name.

And for the first time, I understood the symbolism. Every family hides its ghosts; the Aldridges just happened to have one that finally decided to strike back.

Helen Park would spend the rest of her life in prison. But in her mind, she'd already won.

20

Resolution

THE NEWS BROKE FAST. BY FRIDAY MORNING, EVERY MEDIA outlet in Tennessee was running the story: longtime Aldridge estate cook arrested for poisoning prominent Chattanooga businessman Augustus Aldridge III. By afternoon, reporters had dug deeper and found the connection: Helen Park was the General's great-granddaughter through rape by his son, Augustus Aldridge II.

The Aldridge family's century of secrets was now public knowledge.

The headlines came like gunfire; blunt, merciless, and everywhere. Every news anchor wore the same somber mask, speaking in tones meant to sound respectful but hungry for scandal. The words "rape," "murder," and "revenge" scrolled beneath polished smiles. No one cared about nuance; they wanted blood and legacy in equal measure.

I spent Friday morning at the county prosecutor's office, ensuring the case against Helen Park was airtight. We had her confession, the foxglove notebook, the dried plant material, Rosa's photograph of Ruth's birth certificate, and testimony from everyone involved.

"This is solid," Assistant District Attorney Rebecca Morrison said, reviewing the evidence. "Premeditation, confession, physical evidence. She'll be convicted."

"She wants to be convicted," I said. "I think she'll plead guilty. This was never about getting away with it."

"That'll make the trial interesting. A defendant who actively wants the world to hear about her victim's crimes."

"Augustus II's crimes, not Augustus III's. Augustus III didn't rape anyone. He just had the misfortune of being born into a family with terrible secrets."

"Helen Park won't see it that way. To her, all the Aldridges are guilty."

Rebecca leaned back in her chair, tapping her pen thoughtfully. "You ever think about what justice even looks like in a case like this?" she asked. I didn't answer. Because I wasn't sure I knew anymore.

After the meeting, I drove to the Aldridge estate. I'd requested a meeting with the family; I figured I owed them an explanation, even though most of it would be painful.

Victoria, Augustus IV, Melissa, and Graham sat in the library: the same room where Augustus III had died two weeks earlier. The irony wasn't lost on anyone.

The air in the library was thick with grief and old dust. Sunlight filtered through heavy drapes, striking the same decanter that had once held poison. I could almost feel the weight of ghosts pressing against the walls.

"You arrested Helen," Victoria said. Her voice was steady, but she looked older, worn down by revelations.

"Yes. She confessed to both murders. The evidence is over-whelming."

"Why?" Melissa asked. "Why did she kill my father?"

Her voice cracked on the word "father." No amount of privilege or polish could disguise the tremor of disbelief beneath it.

"Because your great-grandfather's son raped Helen's grandmother, Margaret Park, in the 1920s. Margaret was a servant here. She became pregnant, was dismissed in disgrace, and spent the rest of her life in poverty. Her daughter Ruth—Helen's mother—grew up knowing what the General had done and how her mother had suffered."

"So Helen killed my father for something that happened a century ago?" Melissa's voice rose. "That's insane."

"To you, it's ancient history. To Helen, it's family trauma that shaped her entire life. She grew up hearing about her grandmother's rape, her mother's shame, the Aldridge wealth built on violence and lies. She got herself hired here thirty-two years ago specifically to plan revenge."

Melissa's hand trembled as she reached for her husband's. No one spoke. The ticking of the mantel clock filled the silence like a heartbeat counting down the end of an empire.

"Thirty-two years," Victoria whispered. "She's been planning this for three decades?"

"Yes. She waited patiently, learned your routines, became invisible as a servant. Then, when Augustus started researching family connections and Emily Caldwell's descendants, Helen saw an opportunity. She was afraid his research might expose her connection to the family."

"Did it?" Graham asked.

"Not directly. But Augustus was getting close. And when

Rosa found Ruth's birth certificate—proving Ruth was born in 1925, daughter of a servant, fathered by the General's son—Helen panicked. She killed Rosa to protect her secret and her revenge."

Victoria closed her eyes, her lips trembling in silent prayer. "Dear God," she whispered. "So much pain. So much arrogance."

"Rosa died because she found a birth certificate?" Augustus IV sounded broken. "An old piece of paper cost her life?"

"She died because she threatened to expose a secret Helen had guarded for decades. Helen couldn't let that happen, not before she'd completed her revenge against your family."

The room was silent. I let them process, understanding this would take time.

Finally, Victoria spoke. "I knew about Margaret Park."

Everyone turned to look at her.

"You knew?" Melissa said.

"When I married Augustus, his mother—your grandmother—told me some of the family's darker history. She mentioned that the General's son had... relations with servants. She said Margaret Park had been one of them. I didn't know it was rape. I thought—" Victoria's voice broke. "I thought it was an affair, consensual. I didn't realize the General's son had forced himself on her."

Her admission fell into the room like a stone into deep water: silent at first, then rippling outward. The others stared at her, and I could see the dawning horror on their faces as generations of silence turned into complicity.

"Did Augustus know?" I asked.

"I told him years ago. He said it was ancient history,

nothing to be done about it now. He didn't want to dwell on family shame."

"So Helen's grandmother's rape was known within the family, but never acknowledged publicly," Graham said quietly. "Never addressed, never apologized for. Just buried and forgotten. No wonder she wanted revenge."

I'd seen many families destroyed by greed, but never by guilt this deep. The Aldridges weren't monsters—they were heirs to unatoned sins, prisoners of their own silence.

"We didn't forget," Victoria insisted. "But what could we do? The General died in 1941, August II in 1956. Margaret Park died decades ago. There was no one left to apologize to, no way to make amends."

"Except there was," I said. "Helen Park was here, working in your kitchen, a living descendant of Augustus II's violence. She was right under your roof for thirty-two years, and none of you acknowledged her connection or tried to help her family."

"We didn't know she was Margaret's descendant!" Victoria said. "If we'd known—"

"Would it have made a difference? Would you have acknowledged her as family? Given her a share of the estate? Or would you have dismissed her too, to avoid scandal?"

Victoria had no answer.

For a long moment, only the sound of wind against the old windows filled the room. Outside, autumn leaves scraped the cobblestone drive like dry whispers of judgment.

Augustus IV spoke, his voice hollow. "We're all connected, aren't we? Graham and I are cousins through the General's affair with Emily's sister. Helen is our cousin through

Augustus II's rape of Margaret Park. We're all descendants of the General's violence and secrets."

"Yes," I said simply.

It was the first truly honest moment I'd ever seen from that family. No pretense. No wealth. Just weary humanity.

"Does Helen have a legal claim to the estate?" Graham asked. "As Augustus II's granddaughter?"

"That's for lawyers to determine," I replied. "But typically, descendants of rape victims don't have inheritance rights, especially for crimes committed a century ago. Helen won't benefit financially from her connection."

"So she killed my father for nothing," Melissa said bitterly.

"She killed him for revenge and recognition," I corrected her. "She wanted the world to know what the general's son did to Margaret Park. Now everyone knows. In that sense, she got what she wanted."

And in that instant, I realized: the truth can destroy more thoroughly than any bullet.

"At the cost of two lives," Victoria said. "Augustus and Rosa, both dead because of something the General's son did in the 1920s. How is that justice?"

"It's not," I replied. "It's tragedy on top of tragedy. But Helen doesn't see it that way. To her, she balanced the scales."

Victoria turned away, her reflection caught in the glass cabinet beside her. For the first time, she looked like someone who truly saw the ghost behind her own face.

I paused, then continued. "There are practical matters to address. Augustus's will—"

"The will stands as written," Victoria said. "Our attorney confirmed that this morning. Because Augustus died before he could execute the changes, his previous will remains in effect. Melissa inherits forty percent of the estate as his biological daughter. Augustus also receives forty percent."

Augustus IV's head snapped up. "What? But I'm not his biological son."

"The will doesn't say 'biological son,'" Victoria said quietly. "It says 'my son Augustus Aldridge IV.' We raised you as our son. Augustus's will recognized that, even if the changes he planned didn't."

"So I get money after all," Augustus IV said bitterly. "Money built on lies and violence."

"It's money that can help you rebuild your life," Victoria said. "What you do with it is up to you."

I cleared my throat. "What about the estate itself? The property?"

"We're selling it," Melissa said. "None of us can live here anymore. The memories, the publicity, the knowledge of what happened here—it's too much. We've already contacted a realtor."

"And the staff? Claudia Rivera, the groundskeepers?"

"Claudia will stay on until the sale is complete, then she has a generous severance package," Victoria said. "She's already received job offers from other families. She'll be fine."

"What about Marcus Webb?"

Victoria's expression hardened. "Marcus was terminated for embezzlement. He won't face criminal charges—I didn't want more scandal—but he'll never work in estate management again. I made sure of that."

"And the rest of you?" I asked. "Where will you go?"

"I'm moving to Asheville," Victoria said. "I have a sister there. Somewhere no one knows the Aldridge name."

"Allison and I are moving to Atlanta," Augustus IV said. "Fresh start. New city. Allison's family is there."

"Graham and I are staying in Chattanooga," Melissa said, her hand finding her husband's. "This is our home. We won't let the past drive us away. But we won't live at the estate. We've bought a house in North Shore."

I stood to leave. "The prosecutor will be in touch about the trial. You'll likely be called as witnesses about family history. I'm sorry this has been so difficult."

"Captain," Graham said as I reached the door. "What happens to Helen now?"

"She'll be tried for double murder. Given her confession and the evidence, she'll be convicted. She'll spend the rest of her life in prison."

"And our family's reputation?"

"Is destroyed. Augustus II's crimes are public knowledge now. Emily Caldwell's murder, Margaret Park's rape, all the secrets you've kept for generations—it's all out there. How you rebuild from this is up to you."

I left them sitting in the library, surrounded by the ghosts of their family's past. Outside, the November air was cold and crisp. The estate grounds were beautiful—well-maintained gardens, ancient trees, the mansion standing proud against the sky.

But it was all built on violence. The family's wealth, the family's status, everything they'd inherited came from a man who raped servants and covered up murders.

And Helen Park had spent thirty-two years making them pay for it.

THAT EVENING, I was seated in my office writing my final report on the case, Samson dozing at my feet, exhausted from a long day.

The case was solved. Helen Park would be convicted. Justice—such as it was—would be served.

But I couldn't shake the feeling that everyone had lost.

Augustus III was dead—not because of anything he'd personally done, but because he carried the weight of his grandfather's sins.

Rosa Martinez was dead—collateral damage in a revenge plot that had nothing to do with her.

Helen Park would die in prison, achieving her revenge but destroying her own life in the process.

And the Aldridge family would live with public shame, their name forever connected to rape, murder, and cover-ups spanning a century.

Emily Caldwell's story was finally told. Margaret Park's trauma was finally acknowledged. But the cost was devastating.

"Is it ever worth it?" I asked Samson, who opened one eye to look at me. "All these secrets, all this pain. Is revenge ever really justice?"

Samson had no answer. He closed his eye and went back to sleep.

I finished my report, filed it with the prosecutor's office, and locked up my desk. Tomorrow I'd testify before the grand jury. Next week, Helen Park would be formally indicted. In a few months, there'd be a trial.

But tonight, I was going home. I'd feed my dog, pour myself a glass of wine, try to remember what life looked like outside of murder and secrets and century-old sins coming home to roost.

As I drove through Chattanooga's streets, I couldn't help but think about the invisible people: servants, staff, people overlooked and underestimated. Helen Park had been invisible for thirty-two years. She'd cooked thousands of meals, served hundreds of gatherings. And the entire time, she'd been planning how to destroy the family that had destroyed hers.

That kind of patience, that depth of rage, that willingness to wait decades for revenge; it was chilling. It was also, in its own twisted way, impressive.

Helen Park had proven that invisible people see everything. They remember everything. And sometimes, when they've been hurt deeply enough, they act on that knowledge.

The Aldridge family would never forget that lesson.

And neither would I.

21

Aftermath

THE GRAND JURY INDICTED HELEN PARK ON TWO COUNTS OF first-degree murder. Her arraignment was scheduled for the following week, and she'd waived her right to bail. She wanted to tell her story publicly, and she'd get that chance at trial.

The courthouse lawn was already filling with reporters that morning: microphones, cameras, and vans with satellite dishes crowding the curb. Chattanooga hadn't seen this much attention since the Caldwell murders resurfaced in the papers. Justice, it seemed, was now a public spectacle.

I spent Monday morning at the medical examiner's office with Doc Sheddon, finalizing autopsy reports and evidence documentation. Everything needed to be perfect for trial.

"It's an interesting case," Doc said as we reviewed Augustus III's toxicology reports. "Professionally speaking, I mean. The digitalis extraction from foxglove was quite sophisticated. Helen knew exactly what she was doing."

"She'd been planning it for decades. She had time to get it right."

"The dosage was calculated perfectly—lethal but not immediately obvious. If Augustus had received medical attention within the first hour, he might have survived. But by the time symptoms became severe, it was too late."

"She knew he'd be alone in the library that night. She knew no one would find him until it was too late."

"Premeditation at its finest." Doc sealed the evidence reports. "What about Rosa Martinez? That was messier."

"That was panic. Rosa threatened Helen's plan, so Helen acted impulsively. Different mindset entirely from the calculated poisoning."

"Two very different murders from the same killer. That'll be interesting at trial."

Doc took off his glasses and rubbed his eyes. "You ever wonder," he said quietly, "if justice and revenge just share different costumes?"

I didn't answer. There wasn't a right answer to that kind of question.

By afternoon, I was meeting with Chief Johnston in his office. He wanted a complete briefing on the case before it hit trial.

"Walk me through the whole thing," he said. "Start to finish."

I laid out the timeline, from Augustus III's research into Emily Caldwell's descendants, his discovery of various illegitimate children from Augustus II's crimes, Helen Park's family connection through her grandmother Margaret's rape, to the poisoning itself.

"And Helen confessed to everything?" Johnston asked.

"She wanted to confess. The whole point was exposing the Aldridge family's crimes. She didn't care about going to prison if it meant the truth came out."

"Well, the truth is certainly out. The media's having a field day with this. A general's son rapes a servant and gets her pregnant, and the family covers it up for a century, and the victim's descendant murders for revenge. It's every headline writer's dream."

"It's a nightmare for the Aldridges," I said.

"They'll survive," he replied. "Old money always does. But their reputation is destroyed."

"Good," I said, surprising myself with the vehemence. "They should be destroyed. They knew about Margaret Park's rape. Victoria admitted she knew. They never tried to help her family, never acknowledged the trauma, just buried it and moved on."

Johnston gave me a sharp look. "You're sympathizing with the killer."

"I'm sympathizing with the victim. Margaret Park was raped by a powerful man who faced no consequences. Her daughter was born in shame, her granddaughter grew up knowing her family had been violated and denied. That's worth a little sympathy."

"But not worth murdering for," he said, dryly.

"No. Helen crossed a line when she killed Augustus and Rosa. Whatever sympathy I have for her family's history doesn't excuse double murder."

"Good. Because you'll need to testify at trial, and I can't have my lead detective expressing sympathy for the defendant."

"I'll testify professionally. Helen Park is guilty. She

confessed, the evidence is overwhelming, she'll be convicted. But I can acknowledge that the Aldridge family created the conditions for this tragedy."

Johnston nodded. "Fair enough. What's next?"

"Trial preparation. Making sure every piece of evidence is documented, every witness is prepared, every legal argument is anticipated. Rebecca Morrison is good; she'll get the conviction. But Helen will use the trial as a platform to tell her story."

"Let her. The jury will hear about century-old crimes, but they'll also hear about Helen murdering two people. History doesn't excuse murder."

That evening, I drove to the Martinez cottage on the estate grounds. Miguel was being cared for by Claudia Rivera now, but he'd asked to speak with me.

The old man sat in his small living room, looking diminished by grief and confusion. His daughter's death had broken something in him that would never heal.

"Captain," he said when I entered. "Thank you for coming."

"Of course, Mr. Martinez. How are you holding up?"

"I don't understand most of what's happened. They tell me Helen killed Rosa, but I don't remember Helen being a bad person. Was she always bad?"

"Helen wasn't bad, exactly. She was hurt. Very hurt, for a very long time. And that hurt turned into something dangerous."

"My Rosa found something, they said. A paper about families."

"Yes. Rosa found a birth certificate proving Helen's family connection to the Aldridges. Helen was afraid that certificate would ruin her plans, so she killed Rosa to keep the secret. I'm sorry."

Miguel's eyes filled with tears. "Rosa was just being curious. She liked history, liked knowing about families. She didn't mean any harm."

"I know. Rosa was innocent in all of this. She was a victim of someone else's decades-old pain."

"Will Helen go to prison?"

"Yes. For the rest of her life."

"Good. She took my Rosa. She should pay for that."

His words were simple, but they carried the weight of centuries, the cry of every father who'd lost a child to someone else's sins. It was hard to meet his eyes for a moment.

We sat in silence for a while. Miguel's memory was fragile, drifting in and out of present awareness. But his grief was sharp and immediate.

"Mr. Martinez," I said gently, "is there anything I can do for you? Anything you need?"

"Tell me Rosa didn't suffer. Tell me it was quick."

I thought about Doc's report—the blunt force trauma, the defensive wounds on Rosa's hands. She'd seen it coming and tried to protect herself.

"It was quick," I lied. "She didn't suffer."

Miguel nodded, accepting the kindness. "Thank you, Captain. Thank you for finding who did it."

"There's something else you should know," I said. "The Aldridge family has set up a fund in Rosa's name. It'll provide for your care for the rest of your life, and any money left over will go to a scholarship fund for children of immigrant families. Rosa's legacy will help others."

Miguel's eyes welled up again. "Rosa would have liked that. She always wanted to help people."

When I left, I paused on the porch, watching the lights of the great house flicker through the trees. The wind carried the faint smell of foxglove and rain. Justice, grief, revenge: they all blurred together in the cold air.

As I left the cottage, I felt the weight of the case pressing down on me. Two murders solved, killer confessed and arrested. But the victims—Augustus and Rosa—were still dead. Their families were still grieving. And nothing I'd done brought them back.

Justice was cold comfort sometimes.

Back at the office, I found Corbin, Hawk, Tracy, Jack, and Cooper gathered in the conference room. They'd ordered pizza and were reviewing case notes one final time before handing everything to the prosecutor.

"Captain," Tracy said as I entered. "We're just making sure we haven't missed anything."

I grabbed a slice of pizza and sat down. "Find any gaps?"

"None. The case is solid. Helen's confession, the physical evidence, the motive—it all supports conviction."

"What about Helen's defense?" I asked. "What argument could her attorney make?"

"Temporary insanity?" Cooper suggested. "Generations of family trauma leading to a psychological break?"

"Won't work. She planned this for thirty-two years. That's the opposite of temporary insanity."

"Diminished capacity due to lifelong emotional abuse?" Jack offered.

"She's not claiming abuse. She's claiming justice. Her

whole argument is that she knew exactly what she was doing and did it deliberately."

"Then her defense attorney has nothing," Corbin said. "Helen will be convicted, sentenced to life in prison, and that'll be the end of it."

"Except it won't," I said. "This story will haunt the Aldridge family for generations. Every time someone googles their name, they'll find articles about Augustus II's raping Margaret Park. About Emily Caldwell's murder. About a century of secrets and cover-ups."

"That's their problem," Tracy said. "They made those choices."

"The current generation didn't make those choices. Augustus III didn't rape anyone. Melissa and Augustus IV didn't cover up any murders. They're paying for sins committed by ancestors they never knew."

"That's how generational trauma works," Hawk said quietly. "The sins of the fathers visited on the children. It's biblical."

"It's tragic," I corrected.

The room went still for a moment, the kind of silence that settles when everyone's too tired to argue. The pizza boxes sat open, the air smelled of cold cheese and coffee. Outside, sirens echoed faintly, another case beginning somewhere else.

We finished reviewing the evidence, signed off on final reports, and called it a night. As everyone left, I stayed in the conference room, looking at the murder boards one last time.

Augustus Aldridge III's photo. Rosa Martinez's photo. Two victims of a revenge plot that stretched back a century.

Emily Caldwell's photo from 1925. Margaret Park's

servant records. Ruth's birth certificate. All the pieces that had led to this moment.

And Helen Park's booking photo from last week. An elderly woman with cold eyes and no regrets. She'd achieved her goal. The truth was public. The Aldridge family was exposed.

And she'd murdered two people to make it happen.

I turned off the desk lamp, leaving only the glow of the hallway light spilling across the boards. For a moment, it looked like the faces on them were watching me—silent, waiting. Maybe for forgiveness. Maybe for nothing at all.

Tomorrow I'd start preparing for trial testimony. Next week, Helen Park would be arraigned. In a few months, there'd be a verdict.

But tonight, I was done. The case was solved. The killer was in custody. My job was finished.

Samson and I went home, leaving the ghosts of the Aldridge estate behind us.

At least, I tried to leave them behind.

Some cases stayed with you long after they were solved.

This was going to be one of them.

22

Epilogue

Six Months Later

SPRING HAD COME TO CHATTANOOGA. THE DOGWOODS WERE blooming, the Tennessee River sparkled in the sunshine, and life had moved on from the Aldridge murders.

The city had a way of forgetting quickly. New scandals replaced old ones, and yesterday's outrage became tomorrow's trivia. Still, sometimes when I drove downtown and saw the headlines framed behind café counters—*"THE Aldridge Legacy"*, *"The Cook's Revenge"*—I felt the echo of it.

Helen Park's trial had lasted three weeks. She pleaded not guilty and testified in her own defense, spending hours on the stand describing her grandmother Margaret's rape, her mother Ruth's suffering, her own lifelong awareness of being Augustus II's granddaughter but being denied any acknowledgment or support.

The jury had listened sympathetically. But the prosecutor had shown them the evidence—the premeditation, the calculated poisoning, the brutal murder of Rosa Martinez. The foxglove notebook. The confession.

The jury deliberated for four hours before returning guilty verdicts on both counts of first-degree murder. Helen was sentenced to life in prison without the possibility of parole.

She'd smiled when the sentence was read. She'd gotten what she wanted: the truth was out, and she'd spend the rest of her life as a martyr for historical justice.

When the verdict came down, the courtroom was silent: no gasps, no outbursts. Just the sound of Helen whispering something I couldn't quite catch. Later, I learned she'd said, "Now they'll remember her." She didn't mean herself. She meant Margaret.

The media coverage had been extensive. Documentaries were already in production. True crime podcasts dissected every detail. The Aldridge family had become synonymous with murder and century-old cover-ups.

I testified at the trial, laying out the evidence professionally. I'd avoided editorial comments about the Aldridge family's culpability in creating the conditions for Helen's revenge. That wasn't my job.

But privately, I still felt the family bore responsibility for their own tragedy.

Sometimes, in the quiet hours after court adjourned, I'd look over at the defense table. Helen sat upright, composed, her gray hair pulled back neatly. She reminded me more of a schoolteacher than a killer. And yet, when her eyes met mine, I could still see the furnace behind them: the rage born of generations.

ON A WARM SATURDAY IN MAY, I visited the Aldridge estate one final time. The property had been sold the previous month to a tech entrepreneur from California who planned to convert it into a boutique hotel. The irony wasn't lost on me: a house built on wealth and violence becoming a symbol of new money and reinvention.

The "For Sale" sign was gone now, replaced by a sleek developer's board announcing "The Aldridge House Hotel — Opening 2026." Workers were clearing debris from the fountain, pressure-washing the marble lions until they shone again. The ghosts didn't seem to mind.

Victoria had moved to Asheville as planned. I'd heard through the grapevine that she'd become active in local charities, quietly trying to rebuild the Aldridge name through good works. It would take generations to undo the damage, if it could be undone at all.

Augustus IV and Allison had settled in Atlanta. According to my sources, Augustus had used part of his inheritance to pay off his debts—he'd managed to get most of them restructured—and invest in a small business. He was seeing a therapist, working through the trauma of discovering his entire identity was built on lies. Allison had stood by him through it all. Maybe their marriage would survive. Maybe not. Time would tell.

Melissa and Graham had bought a house in North Shore, a trendy neighborhood across the river from downtown. Melissa had taken a position on the board of a women's shelter, using her inheritance to fund programs for victims of domestic violence. Graham continued his work as a cardiovascular surgeon, his reputation untarnished by the family scandal.

They seemed to be building something good from the ashes of their family's shame. I hoped it would last.

For the first time, I thought maybe some good could come from so much ruin, that perhaps, in a strange way, Helen had forced them to confront what they'd never dared to face. Maybe awareness was its own kind of justice.

The mansion stood empty, waiting for renovations to begin. I walked through the grounds where Rosa had worked, where she'd found the hidden room and the birth certificate that had cost her life.

Miguel had died in March, his mind finally giving out under the weight of grief. He was buried next to Rosa in a small cemetery on the edge of town. The Rosa Martinez Scholarship Fund had already awarded its first grants—five children of immigrant families would attend college on Rosa's legacy.

I'd attended the small memorial. No press, no cameras—just quiet music, a handful of mourners, and a spring breeze carrying the scent of lilac. Rosa's name carved into granite beside her father's. Justice had many forms, I realized; sometimes it was a scholarship instead of a sentence.

In the library where Augustus had died, I stood looking at the empty shelves. The family had sold most of the contents, scattering generations of accumulated history to estate sales and auction houses.

The secret drawer in Augustus's desk was still there, now empty. The genealogy book was in police evidence storage, along with Emily Caldwell's diary and the letters proving Augustus II's guilt.

Emily's murder had finally been solved, ninety-nine years after her death. The truth was known. Augustus Aldridge II had strangled her in this library because she threatened to expose their affair and force him to marry her.

The General had covered it up, protecting his son, burying Emily's pregnancy along with her body.

And Margaret Park had been raped by the same Augustus Aldridge II a year earlier, creating the bloodline that would eventually produce Helen Park.

Century of secrets, all emerging in the space of a few violent weeks.

I ran my hand along the mantel, tracing the grooves carved by craftsmen long dead. The wood was smooth, almost warm, like it remembered. Maybe it did. Houses keep stories even when people forget.

I WALKED DOWN to the old carriage house where Rosa had found the metal box with Augustus II's confession and the jewelry box with Ruth's birth certificate. The hidden room had been sealed now, its secrets removed to evidence storage.

But the history remained. So did the ghosts of Emily and Margaret and Ruth and Rosa: all women who'd suffered because of Aldridge men's violence and pride.

The air was thick with the scent of honeysuckle and silence. Somewhere a crow cawed, sharp and distant. I wondered if Helen, in her cell, still thought about this place, or if she finally felt peace knowing the truth had outlived her rage.

Helen Park was in prison at the Tennessee Prison for

Women in Nashville. I'd heard she spent her days in the prison library, reading and writing letters. She'd become something of a folk hero among certain circles, a symbol of resistance against generational injustice, despite being a double murderer.

Her story had accomplished what she'd wanted. No one could say the name "Aldridge" in Chattanooga without thinking of rape and murder and cover-ups.

The family's reputation was destroyed forever.

Marcus Webb, the former estate manager, had moved to Florida. Last I heard, he was working as a security guard at a shopping mall, his career in high-end estate management finished. The embezzlement that had seemed so important at the start of the investigation had turned out to be a red herring—a crime, yes, but unrelated to the murders.

Claudia Rivera had taken a position with another wealthy family in Nashville, complete with glowing references from Victoria Aldridge. She'd been a consummate professional through all the chaos, and her career had survived intact.

Sometimes, the survivors carried the heaviest burdens; not the guilt of crime, but the memory of it.

BACK AT THE police department that Monday morning, I had a new case on my desk. A domestic homicide in East Chattanooga, straightforward and tragic. A husband killed his wife during an argument, called 911 himself, confessed immediately.

Not every case was as complicated as the Aldridge murders. Most weren't.

But those complicated cases—the ones with layers of history and secrets and pain stretching back generations—those stayed with you.

Corbin brought me coffee and sat down. "You still thinking about the Aldridge case?"

"Sometimes. It's hard not to."

"Helen Park got what she wanted. The truth is out there," he said.

"But at the cost of two lives," I said. "Was it worth it?"

"That's not for us to decide," he replied. "We just solve the murders and let the courts determine justice."

"But what is justice in a case like that? Helen was right that her grandmother was raped, her family was destroyed. The Aldridges never faced consequences for that. So she created her own consequences."

"By murdering innocent people."

"Augustus wasn't innocent. He knew about Margaret Park's rape and did nothing. He was complicit in the cover-up."

"He didn't deserve to die for that."

"No," I agreed. "But cause and effect, Corbin. Actions have consequences, even if those consequences don't come for a hundred years."

"That's pretty philosophical for a Monday morning," he said, smiling.

I smiled back at him. "Blame it on the Aldridge case. It makes you think about history, about how violence in the past creates violence in the present."

"And whether revenge is ever justified."

"Is it?" I asked.

Corbin thought for a moment. "No. But I understand why

Helen thought it was. That doesn't excuse murder, though, but I understand the impulse."

"Me too." I said.

We sat in companionable silence, drinking coffee and thinking about complicated morality and simple law. Murder was murder, regardless of motive. That's what the law said, and that's what we enforced.

But understanding why someone murdered, understanding the history and pain that led to violence, that was important too.

In that silence, I realized this was the part of the job no one ever told you about—the aftermath, the thinking, the wondering if any of it made a difference.

Helen Park would die in prison. The Aldridge family would live with shame but slowly rebuild. Emily Caldwell and Margaret Park and Rosa Martinez would remain dead, their stories finally told but their lives still stolen.

There were no winners in this case. Just different degrees of loss.

THAT EVENING, I took Samson for a long walk along the Tennessee River. The sun was setting, painting the sky orange and pink. People were out enjoying the spring weather: families, couples, joggers, cyclists. Normal life, continuing despite all the darkness I dealt with daily.

And I knew that somewhere in Chattanooga, someone was planning a crime. Someone was keeping a secret. Someone was carrying generational trauma that might explode into violence someday.

That was the nature of the job. Crime never stopped. Secrets never stopped accumulating. And I'd be here, investigating and unraveling and seeking truth, for as long as I could do the work.

I paused on the pedestrian bridge, watching the river slide past, black and silver in the twilight. It looked peaceful, but underneath it moved with relentless force, like time, like guilt, like history itself.

The Aldridge case had taught me important lessons about patience, about looking at overlooked people, about understanding that sometimes the key to present crimes lies in past traumas.

Helen Park had been invisible for thirty-two years. I wouldn't make that mistake again—assuming staff and servants had no motive, no agency, no capacity for violence.

Everyone had capacity for violence under the right circumstances. Everyone had secrets. Everyone had pain that, if deep enough and old enough, could transform into something dangerous.

My job was to see that potential before it manifested in murder.

And when I failed—when someone died despite my efforts—my job was to find the truth and ensure justice was served.

However imperfect that justice might be.

Samson barked at a squirrel, pulling me back to the present moment. I laughed and rubbed his ears, grateful for his simplicity. Dogs didn't carry generational trauma. They lived in the present, found joy in simple things, offered unconditional love.

"Come on, buddy," I said. "Let's go home."

We walked back to my car as the sun set over the river.

Tomorrow would bring new cases, new challenges, new opportunities to seek the truth.

But tonight, I'd rest. I'd earned it.

The Aldridge case was closed. Helen Park was in prison. The dead had been accounted for. Justice—such as it was—had been served.

And I was still here, still working, still fighting for truth in a world full of lies.

That would have to be enough.

The ghosts of Emily Caldwell and Margaret Park and Rosa Martinez could rest now. Their stories were told. Their truths were known.

Until the next case came along, I'd take the time to breathe, to live, to remember why I did this work.

Because in this job, that's all you ever got—the knowledge that you'd done your best for the dead, even when the living made it complicated.

I drove home through the Chattanooga evening, Samson beside me, ready for whatever came next.

Oh, and about that book… You're reading it now!

The Next Book in the series is underway.
Keep a look out for, **The Murder of Orson Crane: Case 24**

A locked room. A dead judge. An impossible crime. Judge Orson Crane ruled his courtroom with an iron fist and his family with an even harder one. Now he's dead, shot in his locked study with a gun at his side and his key on the desk. **Suicide. Case closed.** *But Captain Kate Gazzara isn't buying it. Something about that locked room isn't adding up. As Kate digs deeper into the Crane family's secrets, she uncovers gambling debts, affairs, missing weapons, festering resentment, and a patriarch whose cruelty touched everyone around him. Two sons, each with a motive. A wife with secrets. Grandchildren who lived under his tyranny. Someone in that house wanted Orson Crane dead. Someone who committed an impossible crime.* **In her final case, Kate faces a killer who thought of everything. Well, almost everything.**

TURN the page for a list of books by Blair Howard . . .

Short Stories and Novellas

Buried Secrets(Harry Starke)

The Painted Lady(Kate Gazzara)

Stand Alone

Hunter's Moon(Kate & Harry)

Series

The Harry Starke Genesis Series

9 Books in Series as of 2026

The Harry Starke Series

26 Books in Series as of 2026

The Lt. Kate Gazzara Murder Files

24 Books in Series as of 2026

Randall And Carver Mysteries

4 Books in Series as of 2026

The Peacemaker Series

3 Books in Series as of 2026

The O'Sullivan Chronicles: Civil War Series

5 Books in Series as of 2026

Science Fiction From Blair C. Howard

The Sovereign Star Series

7 Books in Series as of 2026

also available in German

The Predecessors Series

The Last Station-Book One

The Infinity War-Book Two

Andromeda Rising-Book Three

Blair Howard is the international best-selling author of more than seventy novels that span the worlds of gritty detective fiction, espionage thrillers, sweeping historicals, and hard-science military space opera. A Royal Air Force veteran and former journalist, he draws upon a rich background of service and  storytelling to breathe life into unforgettable characters such as ex-cop turned private eye Harry Starke, and the fiercely determined homicide detective Lt. Kate Gazzara, who breaks her own trail as the head of a serious-crimes unit.

Under his sci-fi pen name Blair C. Howard, he expands his reach into the cosmos with the Sovereign Stars saga—an epic journey born from his lifelong love of the heavens, and the Predecessors hard science fiction trilogy. Whether unraveling a brutal crime scene or commanding starships in interstellar conflict, his stories are propelled by relentless pacing, vivid realism, and a watchful eye for justice.

Visit www.blairhowardbooks.com.
Email: BlairHoward@BlairHowardBooks.com

You can also find Blair Howard on Social Media

* 9 7 9 8 9 9 8 8 0 2 4 8 5 *